HOLIDAY TEMPTATION

This Large Print Book carries the
Seal of Approval of N.A.V.H.

HOLIDAY TEMPTATION

DONNA HILL
FARRAH ROCHON
K. M. JACKSON

THORNDIKE PRESS

A part of Gale, Cengage Learning

GALE
CENGAGE Learning·

Farmington Hills, Mich • San Francisco • New York • Waterville, Maine
Meriden, Conn • Mason, Ohio • Chicago

GALE
CENGAGE Learning·

LIBRARY OF CONGRESS CATALOGING-IN-PUBLICATION DATA

Names: Hill, Donna (Donna O.). A gift of love. | Rochon, Farrah. Holiday spice. | Jackson, K. M. From here to serenity.
Title: Holiday temptation / by Donna Hill, Farrah Rochon, and K. M. Jackson.
Description: Large Print edition. | Waterville, Maine : Thorndike Press Large Print, 2016. | Series: Thorndike Press large print African-American
Identifiers: LCCN 2016036057| ISBN 9781410493200 (hardback) | ISBN 1410493202 (hardcover)
Subjects: LCSH: Romance fiction, American. | African Americans—Fiction. | Large type books. | BISAC: FICTION / Romance / Contemporary. | FICTION / Romance / General.
Classification: LCC PS648.L6 H656 2016 | DDC 813/.08508—dc23
LC record available at https://lccn.loc.gov/2016036057

Printed in Mexico
1 2 3 4 5 6 7 20 19 18 17 16

CONTENTS

A Gift of Love

DONNA HILL

CHAPTER ONE

Funny the way dreams can get detoured. If anyone asked Traci Long eight years ago would she be a part-time theater instructor at the Artist Institute, she would have said "no way." *She* was an aspiring playwright. It had been her dream since she was a teen and saw her very first play, *A Raisin in the Sun* by Lorraine Hansberry. From that moment she was hooked. Yet, here she was, three years in, an instructor at a private college. Teaching aspiring thespians about the history of theater was her passion, only surpassed by her desire to stage her own play.

She'd been reworking *Beginnings* for the past year, with the goal of having it produced. It was a dream that continued to remain out of reach. Between the minimal teacher's salary and student loan debt, and the skyrocketing Brooklyn rents and daily living expenses, the dream continued to be deferred.

Traci stepped outside to the dimming afternoon. October was in full effect. The leaves had turned vibrant shades of burnt orange, red, and gold, while many trees had already begun to undress and in a matter of weeks would be bare in anticipation of its winter white coat.

She walked to the Borough Hall train station, caught the A train to the Broadway Junction hub, and transferred to the L line, which would take her into her neighborhood of Williamsburg. Her one-bedroom apartment was a third-floor walk-up in the trendy community. She'd lucked out and snapped up the space five years earlier — before the big boom. But with the escalating gentrification — as a result of the rising costs of rentals in Manhattan that pushed renters into Brooklyn — what was once affordable was fast becoming out of reach.

In the meantime, however, her cozy apartment was her haven, where she dreamed and wrote and aspired. But when she needed a change of atmosphere and some inspiration, she visited her favorite coffee shop — The CoffeeMate.

The vibe of the CoffeeMate was eclectic. It drew an array of the artsy type — poets, artists, painters, writers, and actors from the surrounding neighborhood. The coffee was to die for and the simple menu and baked goods were edible and economical. There was free Wi-Fi and one of the managers, Noah — according to his nametag — was tantalizing enough to keep her there for hours just so that she could steal periodic glances at him. To say that she secretly lusted after the sexy barista would be an understatement. He was the main reason why she came to the CoffeMate so often. Sometimes just seeing him move, smile, and interact with others gave her all kinds of crazy ideas of "what he would be like." She imagined tasting his lips, which were full, and she knew would be pillow soft. And those soulful eyes — they were dark, shaded even darker by thick lashes. She wanted to run her fingers through those locs of his. She pushed out a soft sigh.

They'd never actually had a conversation other than basic pleasantries, but he knew her order by heart and always brought it to her table. There was one time when he'd asked her what she was working on. When she told him a play, he seemed genuinely impressed. That was the extent of their relationship. In her head it was much more. However, she knew how easily what you want to believe had nothing to do with reality. Her ex-husband, Jason Logan, was proof positive of that. For all she knew, fine, sexy Noah, with his shoulder-length dreads, sweet Hershey chocolate skin, eyes like midnight, and a swagger to rival any bad boy, could be a nightmare waiting to happen.

The heavenly aroma of fresh brewed coffee and warm pastries shook up Traci's empty stomach, which growled for attention. She gave her tummy a reassuring pat as she joined the line to place her order rather than wait for table service.

Automatically, she looked along the counter to see if Noah was working. *There he is — at the end working the cappuccino machine.* A little tingle ignited in her center. She unbuttoned her coat and fanned her face with a menu that she'd taken from the rack.

While she inched down the order line, Traci worked very hard at studying the menu, which she pretty much knew by heart. In the background something smooth and bluesy was drifting through the speakers. The counter seating was almost full and there were still a few tables left. Her favorite spot in the back by the window was available.

Noah greeted her with his camera-ready

smile. He pointed a long, slender finger at her. "Mocha latte, extra whip."

Traci grinned. "One of these days I'm going to surprise you."

Noah's honey-toned eyes darkened. "Always up for a challenge." He turned away and prepared her latte.

Traci warned herself not to even go there behind his "challenge" response.

"Here you go." Noah handed her latte to her across the counter. "Enjoy."

"Thanks." She paid the cashier and took her latte in the direction of her favorite table, only to find that while she'd waited on line, her table was now occupied. She took a quick look around and found an empty spot on the other side.

Once she was settled, she took out her laptop and notebook and got down to work. Her play *Beginnings* had been her graduate thesis project when she attended New York University. Although her college years were well behind her, she'd never seen her play the way it should have been — on stage and attended by paying theatergoers, not only her graduating class.

She knew the play had flaws. Her professor had said as much. It was missing its heart. The story was only on the surface. Digging deeper had been her problem, trying to find the soul of the play to bring it to life — not just a bunch of lines and bodies walking across a stage.

By the time Traci looked up, it had grown dark outside and the makeup of clientele had shifted from the afterschool college crowd to the afterwork commuter.

Traci rotated her stiff neck and flexed her fingers. Time to head home. She glanced out the window and her stomach knotted. Her pulse raced. She blinked rapidly, bringing the image into focus. Gradually her pulse slowed. It wasn't him. She released the breath she'd held.

"How's the play coming?"

Her head jerked up. Noah was standing over her with that drop-dead smile and wicked gleam in his eyes. He collected her empty cup, napkins, and paper plate.

Traci's face heated. Could he see the fear in her eyes? She lowered her head, swallowed, and felt an irrational twinge of guilt that he was cleaning up after her, even though it was his job. "Umm, yep. Still at it."

He dropped the used items into a white plastic bag and wiped around her laptop and notes with a damp white cloth.

"Can I get you anything else?"

"No. Thanks. I'm getting ready to leave."

Her hands shook ever so slightly.

"Have a good evening. See you soon."

Man, that sounds like an invitation. "Thanks, you too." She watched him from beneath her lashes while he cleared tables and made small talk with the customers. If she'd fantasized for a minute that he was in the least bit interested in her, she was clearly mistaken. Noah was simply very skilled in customer service. Charm was the quality that they fooled you with, like she'd been fooled.

Traci loaded her tote with her computer and notebook, shrugged into her coat, and walked out.

CHAPTER TWO

Noah hoisted his sax case over his shoulder and pushed through the double doors of the Open End Bar and Lounge. It was located on South Fourth Street in the heart of Williamsburg. The Open End had blossomed from a hole-in-the-wall dive two years earlier to "the place" to be to hear great local musicians, toss back some of the best drinks in the area, and order from a menu to rival its neighborhood competitors. Its success was due to the vision and hard work of Anthony Fields, Noah's frat brother and best friend.

Noah and Anthony had crossed the line together at Howard University and came out on the other side as Omega Psi Phi men. The two buddies lived the ideals and principles of Omega men: integrity, loyalty, hard work, service, and brotherhood.

While he made his way to the back room to find Anthony, Noah nodded to one of the waitresses that he recognized. He felt like playing tonight and hoped to be able to sit in on the last set.

He exited the lounge area and walked down the short hall, which led to the kitchen and back offices. Anthony's door was open.

"Hey, bro," Anthony greeted when he looked up to see Noah in the doorway. "Come on in a sec. I was just finishing up the schedule for next week."

Noah strolled into the compact space and took a seat in the one chair and stretched out his long legs in front of him. He must have jabbed Anthony in the ribs about a hundred times to get a reliable manager to handle all of the day-to-day stuff so that he could concentrate on building and growing his business. His response was always the same. "I know you're right, but you handle stuff your way, I'll do it mine. I prefer more hands-on. You should talk," he would add, referring to Noah's own situation.

Noah had grown tired of the same conversation, so he'd stopped bringing it up, that's what made Anthony's announcement such a surprise.

Anthony finished entering the information into the computer. "Yo, I started interviewing for a manager."

Noah tossed his head back and chuckled.

"Say what? You, 'Mr. I Can Do It All Myself.' "

"All right, all right, don't rub it in," he said, holding up his hand to stave off any "I told you so" commentary.

"Cool." Noah leaned forward "Why now?"

Anthony relaxed in his chair and linked his fingers behind his head. "I think it's time that I follow your model. Open End is solid, in the black, and has developed a reputation that I feel can withstand the expansion."

Noah nodded in agreement as he listened. "What can I do to help?"

"Scout out some locations with me. You have an eye for that kind of thing. Ideally, I'd like to stay in Brooklyn, but with the rent of commercial space skyrocketing, I don't know if that's feasible."

"Unless we can find a good deal. Maybe something that needs rehab instead of ready to go."

"That's what I was thinking."

"Great minds," Noah quipped.

"Yeah," he co-signed, doing the two-fingered move from his eyes to Noah's. "So that's my story. What's up with you?"

"Thought I'd sit in on a set tonight."

"No problem. You're always welcome."

"Cool."

"You see that writer again?"

Noah half-smiled. "She was in the shop today."

"And . . . ?"

"And nothing. Usual 'hey, how you doing' — that's about it."

Anthony made a face. "Man, by the time you step past that, the both of you will be too old to give a damn."

Noah sputtered a laugh. "Yeah, yeah, whatever."

"I ain't never known you to be this hesitant with a woman. You usually make your move by now. What's up with that?"

Noah frowned in thought. "I don't really know," he said, his answer surprising him. "Whenever I see her, I lose my swag." He grinned.

"Umm, she must be something."

Noah looked off into the distance. *Yes, she is.*

"You decide what you want to do for the holidays? The offer is still open," Anthony said, switching topics. "The fam would love to see you."

"Still thinking on it, man."

Anthony's family was the family Noah didn't have. He was a product of the foster care system. Five families in total after he was removed at the age of ten from his drug-addicted mother. His father wasn't even a name on his birth certificate. The ambivalent relationship with his mother, the missing father, and multiple families had left their scars. Nothing anyone could see, but rather buried in his psyche, which made it hard for Noah to put his trust in relationships. He had to admit though, his last family, the Hunters — when he entered high school — put him on track for both academic and personal success. With their love and guidance he morphed from a mediocre student to the top of his classes. He graduated valedictorian with a full-ride scholarship to Xavier, Columbia, Temple, and Howard. He chose Howard University, which was where he met Anthony.

During his freshman year Noah lost both Mr. and Mrs. Hunter, six months apart; she from a heart attack and he from a stroke. That year was when Anthony's family became his family. Refusing to leave him alone on campus during the holidays, Anthony took Noah home with him to Atlanta. It had been a standing tradition ever since. But there was still the little boy in him who expected it all to disappear. Anthony was the exception, the only one who knew his demons. So Noah was always on guard, and rarely committed himself to anyone and steered clear of allowing women — in particular — to get under his skin and really know him. "Hit and run" was his motto.

"Plus I think Mia has someone she wants you to meet," Anthony said, cutting into Noah's trip down memory lane.

Noah chuckled. "Your sister always has someone for me to meet. It's tradition."

Anthony shrugged helplessly. He'd been a victim of his sister's matchmaking schemes for the better part of his adult life. He simply let it roll off his back to humor her.

"Whatever you decide, let me know sooner rather than later. Christmas will be here in a minute and tickets will be sky high."

"True. I'll let you know."

"Cool. Anyway, let me get with Ed and let him know you'll be sitting in on the last set."

"Thanks, man."

Playing the sax always relaxed him and cleared his head. By the time he turned the key in the door to his loft, at nearly 2 a.m., he was in a Zen state of mind, and had decided that the next time he saw Traci, he would say something of substance.

CHAPTER THREE

"I know we'd planned to go see that film tonight," Cara Harper was saying. "But, girl, I'm beyond beat. It's been a crazy week. Can I take a rain check?"

Cara and Traci had been friends for longer than either of them could remember. Over lunches, dinners, and girls' nights out, they'd often tried to recall how and when they'd first met. Each had a different version of their first meeting at a conference at NYU nearly a decade earlier.

"No problem. But we're still on for Pilates tomorrow, right?" Traci said. "Is everything okay?"

"Yes and yes. My caseload was pretty brutal this week. I had to remove two kids from a house right out of a horror show, but the kids didn't want to leave. Can you imagine?" She sighed heavily into the phone. "A movie and a drink would probably work wonders, but I don't have the energy."

"I'm so sorry, Cara. I swear I don't know how you do it."

"Most of the time more good is done by my work than harm, but it can be overwhelming. Anyway, I'm going to take a hot bath and dive into bed."

"I hear ya. If you need anything, you call me."

"Will do."

Traci disconnected the call and flopped back against the cushion of her armchair. So much for an evening out. She picked up the remote and aimed it at the TV. After ten minutes of scrolling it was clear that there was nothing worth watching on the more than three hundred channels. She tossed the remote onto the couch. She glanced at the time on her cell. The movie started in an hour.

She'd never gone to a movie alone, but she didn't feel like staying in, and going to a bar or a club alone was definitely out of the question.

What the hell. She hopped up and changed from her work clothes to a pair of faded jeans, oversized black cotton sweater, and ankle boots. She checked herself in the mirror, ran her fingers through her twist outs, and added a splash of lip gloss.

Traci drew in a breath of fortitude, grabbed her purse and coat, and headed out. *First time for everything.*

It was about a twenty-minute walk over to Metropolitan Avenue to the Nitehawk Cinema. The Nitehawk specialized in off-beat, independent, and foreign films. But its real claim to fame in the neighborhood was the reclined theater seating and meal service brought to your seat by a waitress.

Traci paid for her ticket, went upstairs, and found a seat in the sixth row. Shortly after, a waitress came to take her order. She opted for nachos grande and iced tea, then settled back to watch the noir film *The Train to There* — the untold story of the slave trade in New York City from the late 1600s to the 1800s, centered right on Wall Street. The irony didn't escape Traci.

The film was heartbreaking, enlightening, and inspiring. Traci left the theater, feeling awakened about the ugly past of this city she loved, and was more determined than ever to push forward with her own vision.

She stepped outside to the shock of the drop in temperature. She buttoned her coat, adjusted the strap of her purse on her shoulder, and was about to make the walk home, when she was pleasantly stopped.

"Hi."

Traci's heart did a complete tumble in her chest. For a moment she couldn't get her thoughts to line up. What was he doing here? *Same as you, silly.* She was alone on a Friday night. How dismal was that.

"It's . . . Noah from CoffeeMate," he said in response to her startled expression. He pointed a finger at her. "Mocha latte, extra whip." He grinned.

Traci blinked. "Of course. Hi. How are you?" She stealthily looked for his date to show up.

"I'm good. Which film did you see?"

"The Train To There."

His beautiful eyes widened. "So did I. How did you like it?"

"Loved it. Just political enough, without being preachy, and the history . . ." She sighed in awe.

Noah's smile lit his eyes. "I know exactly what you mean. Well worth the price. And what about that Wall Street scene? If people really understood the history . . ." He shook his head sadly, then looked into her eyes. His brows drew together for a moment. "We've never been formally introduced and here I am keeping you out in the cold." He stuck out his hand. "Noah Jefferson."

Traci allowed her hand to be enveloped in his. "Traci Long."

25

"Good to finally meet you, Traci." He paused a moment. "You waiting for someone?"

"Um, no."

"Me either. You in a hurry?"

Her lips parted, but nothing came out. She sort of shook her head no.

"Wanna grab something to eat, talk about the movie?"

"Well . . ."

"Ever eat at the Lo-Res?"

"The theater restaurant?"

"Yeah."

"No. I haven't."

"Food's good," he coaxed.

The appeal of those eyes and that smile could do serious damage. Should she trust him? Better yet, should she trust herself? Her instincts were telling her to take a chance.

Finally she gave a slight shrug, as if hanging out with Noah after a movie was no big deal. "Sure, why not."

"Great."

They did an about-face and returned inside, and Traci concentrated on putting one booted foot in front of the other and not the feel of Noah's gentle hand at the small of her back.

Once inside, Noah led the way. Lo-Res

26

was on the ground floor of the theater. They offered specialty drinks and a versatile menu, but it was the ambience that made it special.

Traci looked around in admiration. The retro restaurant and bar boasted a collection of long-forgotten videos that had been digitally preserved and were projected on a screen to the delight of the diners and drinkers. On any given night customers could be treated to one of the great classics, cult films, or something totally campy and anything in between. The lighting and red-and-black leather booths, jukebox, and fountain-like counter gave the space a feeling of being in a throwback diner.

"There's a spot in back," Noah said with a lift of his chin. He maneuvered Traci in front of him and guided her around the tables to the back.

Noah helped Traci out of her coat and draped it along the back of her seat. He slid in on the other side.

"This is nice. I had no idea," Traci said, looking around.

Casablanca, with Humphrey Bogart, was playing on the big screen.

"Sometimes I come here just for the atmosphere and a free movie," he added with a grin. "Hungry?" He flipped open his menu.

Traci did as well. She was starving, but she wasn't sure if she'd be able to eat a thing while sitting across from him. "Um, maybe something light."

"I'm going for my favorite, the Wolfpack."

Traci giggled. "What is that?"

Noah pointed to it on the menu. It was lasagna with Italian sausage, ground beef seasoned with oregano, homemade sauce, ricotta cheese, and a side salad. Traci's stomach rumbled.

"Hits the spot."

"Hmm, sounds good, but I think I will go with the quesadillas and a kale salad."

On cue a waitress sidled up to their table. "What can I get you tonight? Would you like to start with something from the bar?"

Noah gave Traci a quick look. "Sure. I'll have the Brooklyn Blast."

"Bottle or from the tap?"

"Tap."

"And you, ma'am?"

"White wine."

"Are you ready to order now or should I come back?"

"We're ready," Noah said.

They gave their orders, then settled back to wait for the drinks to arrive.

"I can't believe I've never been in here before," Traci said.

"Yeah, it's a pretty cool place. The owners who came up with this are really onto something. I've watched it grow and mature. I come here for inspiration."

Traci tilted her head to the right. "Inspiration? For what, if you don't mind my asking?"

"Hmm, what I'd like to do someday."

"What is that?"

He leaned forward. An eager gleam lit his eyes. "I would take the concept of Coffee-Mate and blend it with music, art, and theater. Basically, it would be a cultural sanctuary *with* food and drink." He weighed her expression for signs of dismissal or disbelief.

"Wow. I love the idea. I haven't been everywhere, but I've never run across anything quite like that."

The knot in his gut loosened. "I know. The closest that I've seen is the Knitting Factory in the Village. But even that club is pretty specific."

"True." She nodded her head thoughtfully. "So . . . how are you moving toward your dream?"

He offered up a half smile. "One step at a time." He linked his fingers together on top

29

of the table. "And you . . . always busy writing. How is that going?"

Traci blew out a breath. "Slow," she admitted. "It's a play. I've been working and reworking it for longer than I care to admit," she said with a self-deprecating laugh. "Ultimately I want to see it staged. I know it will happen . . . I just hope in my lifetime."

Noah laughed. "I'm sure it won't be that long."

The waitress returned with their drinks. "Your food'll be out shortly."

"Thanks," Noah said. He turned to Traci and raised his glass of beer. "To dreaming and fulfilling."

Traci tapped her glass against his.

The topic shifted back to the film and from that the state of black life in America. Noah had strong views on pretty much everything. He was focused and knowledgeable, well read and articulate, and funny. He had her cracking up with his take on some of the customers who came into CoffeeMate. She told him about her students and her love of theater, her years at NYU and her best friend, Cara. Before she realized it, they'd been in Lo-Res for nearly two hours. Their plates were long gone and their glasses were empty. The crowd had thinned, and when Traci looked around, it was clear that it was closing time.

Noah checked the time on his cell. "Wow. One-thirty. They close up shop in a half hour." He signaled for the waitress and handed over his credit card to pay the bill.

"I can pay my half," Traci insisted, and reached for her purse to get her wallet.

Noah covered her hand to halt her search. "Next time."

She stopped breathing for a second. *Next time.*

"Can I get you a cab?" Noah said once they were outside.

"No. I'm not that far. I can walk."

"Me too. Lead the way."

It was almost a date.

The twenty-minute walk was as equally entertaining as the earlier part of the evening. So much so that Traci was able to push aside her apprehensions, stop looking over her shoulder, and simply enjoy. Noah was full of anecdotes about the neighborhood, the effects of gentrification, and its ramifications on the community that was being pushed out.

"Did you grow up here?" Traci asked.

His expression tightened. He shoved his hands into his pockets. "No."

For the first time that night Traci felt that

31

she'd dipped her toe into murky waters and his answer didn't leave space for discussion. She let it drop.

"This is me," she said, stopping in front of her building.

He gazed up at the three-story brownstone, noted the number 40 on the front step. *Forty South Second Street.*

"We're practically neighbors."

"Oh." She shifted her weight from one foot to the other.

"I'd better let you get inside."

"Yeah," she said on a breath. Her eyes darted down the street, then returned to him. "Thanks for turning me on to Lo-Res."

"Glad you decided to join me. Maybe we can do it again sometime."

Traci hesitated.

"So I guess I'll see you for your next latte."

"Definitely."

"Good night."

"Night." She turned and walked up the steps to the double door at the top of the stoop. She took a glance over her shoulder and Noah was standing there waiting for her to go in. She fished her keys out of her purse, unlocked the door, and waved the all clear. Noah waved back and then headed down the street.

CHAPTER FOUR

"Remind me again why we decided to take Pilates classes?" Cara groaned as they made their way to the showers at the YWCA.

Traci laughed and ignored the faux whining. Even after six months it was still Cara's mantra every time they finished their Saturday class. But as much as she griped, she couldn't deny the results. Both of them had trimmed and tightened their core, strengthened their legs and thighs, and walked with an easy, confident grace. Cara's husband, Phillip, never hesitated to let Cara know that he liked what he saw.

Showered and changed, Traci and Cara stepped out into the blustery afternoon. They walked along Bedford Avenue and stopped at the Colador Cafe.

"Great, it's not crowded," Traci said as she pulled open the heavy door.

The warmth of the interior welcomed them. As usual the locals who benefited from the café's free Wi-Fi occupied several of the tables. Laptops ruled as centerpieces on the wood tabletops.

They walked up to the counter to place their orders. Traci was addicted to their smoothies and ordered her favorite — mango. Cara did the same and added a Caesar salad. They grabbed a table along the sidewall and hopped up on the tall stools.

"I decided to go to the theater last night anyway."

Cara's eyes widened in surprise. "You? You're kidding. You went to the movies by yourself."

"Yep." She nodded.

"Wow." Cara pushed out a breath and grinned. "Well, damn, good for you."

For all of her intelligence, great personality, and talent, Traci was a victim of self-esteem deprivation. Years of living in the shadow of her flamboyant mother and absent father, and a debilitating relationship with her ex, had left her in a constant state of second-guessing herself. For her to have gone to a theater on a Friday night alone was a major achievement.

Traci grinned. "You'll never guess what happened afterward."

"Girl, after that bombshell, I am clueless."

"I had a late dinner and drinks with that guy from CoffeeMate that I've been telling you about."

"What? Wait. Hold up. You did what?"

Traci giggled. "You heard me. Is that so hard to believe?"

"You're damn right it is, and I want to hear every detail."

Over smoothies and salad, Traci recounted her night on the town.

"He sounds really nice, T."

"Yeah, I know. Almost too nice."

"Don't go there. Okay. You've had your eye on him for so long, and now that you've finally had a real chance to break the ice, don't sabotage yourself before you get started."

Traci pushed out a breath. "Yes, you're right. It's just hard, you know."

"Yeah, I do. But at some point you're going to have to give a man a chance, and yourself, too."

Traci lowered her gaze. "It's so much easier said than done."

"Give him a chance. I'll even ride shotgun with you if necessary."

"Just what I need, a grown-ass chaperone."

"At your service!"

They both laughed.

Traci spent the balance of her Saturday doing her food shopping and then cleaning her apartment. Today was "love it or toss it" day. At least once per month she went through her drawers, closets, and cabinets and tossed what she didn't need, and organized what remained. Even as often as she purged, it never ceased to amaze her the amount of foolishness that could gather in a month. Maintaining order was the thing she could control in her life, something that she could be certain of.

She'd taken the row of books down from the top shelf of her six-shelf bookcase so that she could dust. As she was putting the books back, a photograph fell from between the pages and fluttered to the floor. She bent to pick it up and her stomach knotted, the way it always did when she saw it. It was a picture of her taken on the steps of the church after her wedding. She had a wide-eyed look, almost as if she was alarmed.

She should have been alarmed. She should have listened to her instincts. She should have heeded the warnings. *Should have . . . should have. Humph. Should have.* But she didn't. And so she'd walked down that aisle, out of that church door and straight into hell. Well, not right away. She stayed in purgatory for a while.

She couldn't tell anyone. She was too ashamed and guilty and weak, and a part of her somehow believed that she deserved it.

Traci stared at the face of the expectant woman in white. That was four years ago, after three years of hell. Sometimes, though, when those internal scars started to itch and burn, it felt like yesterday.

Traci stared at the picture for a moment more. She should toss it and rid herself of the ugly reminder. But she needed to be reminded so that she would never again be that woman in the picture. She shoved the picture into a different book this time and returned them all to the shelves.

It had begun to rain by the time she got to the CoffeeMate on Sunday, a perfect day to get some writing done. But the real reason that Traci braved the rain and the chill was her hope to see Noah.

She grew anxious while she scanned the menu board as if she hadn't memorized it. *Maybe he's in back,* she thought when she gave a young woman her order. *Or maybe he's on break.* Any minute now he would pop up with that sexy smile and those eyes that held promises. But he didn't. She sipped her coffee, ate her Danish, and typed gibberish on her computer, but Noah never showed up. After two hours she packed up, with the intention of walking back home, but instead, since the rain had stopped and the skies had cleared, she decided to take a walk down to the North Fifth Street Pier.

It appeared that there were plenty of other locals who felt the same way. The sidewalks were dotted with singles and couples and strollers along the commercial streets that led to the pier.

Traci let her mind drift while she meandered along, checking out shop windows and sidestepping running toddlers, when she heard her name being called. Her heart stilled in her chest. She glanced up and into the eyes of the man in front of her. Her stomach roiled.

"Not going to speak?"

She swallowed over the dry knot in her throat. "Hello, Jason."

"That's the best you can do."

Her heart was beating so fast she began to get light-headed. Every ugly name she'd been called and unspeakable things that had passed between them during their three-year marriage whirled in her belly like an approaching cyclone.

"Well," he demanded in that voice that always led to something worse.

She started to move past him and he grabbed her arm, as if with a blink he could yank it out of the socket. "I'm talking to you. No need to be rude."

"Get off of me, Jason," she said through clenched teeth.

He tugged her closer so that her body was flush against his arm; she prayed that he didn't feel the runaway train of tremors that ran through her.

His narrow eyes snaked over her. He smiled. His dimples flashed. "You look good. Like I remember."

"Jason . . ."

"I just wanna talk."

"There's nothing to talk about."

He gripped her harder and she winced.

"Hey, Traci, there you are."

She glanced over her shoulder and nearly burst into tears of relief.

Noah stepped up to them, but his gaze remained fixed on Jason until he slowly eased his grip on Traci's arm and finally let go.

Traci took a step back. Noah slid a protective arm around her waist and planted a light kiss on her cheek. "Thought we were going to meet at the pier."

She swallowed and blinked rapidly to keep the tears at bay. "I . . . was on my way. Running late."

Noah turned a hard gaze onto Jason. He stuck out his hand. "Noah Jefferson." He stood a good head above Jason.

"Jason Logan."

"So, Jason, you in the habit of grabbing women in the street?"

Jason's sandy-toned skin darkened. His jaw rocked. He held up his hands in mock resignation. "No harm, my man. Just saying hello to my ex."

"Hmm. You have a funny way of saying hello. So how 'bout if you evah see Traci again, you bypass the pleasantries and just keep walking." He gave him a hard pat on the arm. "Nice to meet you, Jason. Come on, baby."

He ushered Traci away before Jason had a chance to respond.

"You awiight?" he asked the moment they were out of earshot, his years on the street rushing to the surface.

Traci was shaking from the top of her head to her feet. All she could do was nod her head. If she said a word, she would burst into tears.

Noah held her a little closer. "It's okay,"

he said in a rough whisper. "I'm gonna take you home and you can tell me who that mofo was. Cool?"

Traci looked up at him and the warmth in his eyes belied the hard edge of his voice. Cara's words echoed in her head: *Give him a chance.*

"Okay."

Noah hailed a cab. "Forty South Second," he told the driver.

Once inside the cab Noah gave her plenty of space. He didn't question her, try to hold hands, or make idle conversation. Instead his solid presence was more calming than anything he could say.

By the time they pulled up in front of her building, she almost felt like herself. Noah paid the seven-dollar fare and they got out. Traci walked toward the gate.

"Hey, I'm not going to come up. I only wanted to make sure that you got home safely. We can always talk some other time . . . if you want to."

"Thank you," she managed. "But I was . . . hoping, I mean, you came all this way. Come on." Her smile wobbled, then settled.

He gave a slight shrug. "Cool." He followed her upstairs. "Didn't tell me it was a third-floor walk-up," he jokingly huffed when they stopped in front of her apartment.

Traci laughed. "I'm used to it." She unlocked the door.

CHAPTER FIVE

"Nice," Noah commented when he stepped in and looked around. "It's you." He took off his coat.

"I'll take that," she said, reaching for his coat. "What do you mean it looks like me?" She opened the hall closet, grabbed a wooden hanger, and hung up his coat and then hers.

"Orderly, and together with a flair." He turned to her and smiled.

"I guess that's a compliment. Want something to drink?"

"What's on the menu?"

"Hmm, iced green tea, tap water, and some wine."

"Wine."

Traci smiled. "Be right back. Make yourself comfortable."

Noah strolled over to her two bookcases. He believed that you could tell a lot about a person by what they read. Traci's bookcase was an interesting blend of noir mysteries, literary classics, books on the arts, biographies on playwrights, but what surprised him was the row of books on political ideologies and world affairs. She had books on Angela Davis, Che Guevara, Garvey, Roosevelt, Obama, and Clinton, as well as biographies on Saddam Hussein, Napoleon, Churchill, and Caesar. What he could tell from Traci's choices was that she was invested not only in her passion for plays, but invested in the intricacies of world affairs and the people that impacted societies.

"Here you go."

Noah turned. Traci was behind him with his glass of wine in her hand.

"Thanks. You read all of these?"

"Yep." She took a sip of her wine and sat down. "One of my fetishes is book buying. There isn't a bookstore that I don't love."

"I feel the same way about vinyl."

"Albums?"

He nodded and sipped his wine. "Avid jazz and blues collector. Unfortunately, record shops like bookstores are harder and harder to find."

"Hmm, very true." She sat on the couch.

Noah followed suit and sat opposite her on the armchair. He leaned back against the cushion and crossed his right ankle over his left knee. He glanced across at Traci. "You don't have to talk about what happened . . . but what's the deal with that guy?"

Traci lowered her head. There was no point in trying to avoid the conversation. She pretty much knew it would come. It was why she'd invited him upstairs. She wanted to tell him. She wanted to test the waters and see if he would sink or swim, once he knew.

She drew in a long breath and exhaled slowly. "He's my ex-husband for starters."

Noah's brows rose for an instant, but he didn't comment.

"We were married for the longest three years of my life." She lifted her chin and looked off into the past. "In the beginning Jason was the perfect man. He filled in all the empty spaces — the man that was never in my life. I suppose I was looking for a father figure, a man to take charge and take care of me. Jason was all of those things."

"But then something went wrong."

She nodded, looking off into the distance. "It was subtle at first. It started with small things, outbursts over nonsense — a missing sock or no cold water in the fridge, the way I cleaned the kitchen or the outfit I wore. When I worked on my play, he would always find something to argue about, until I just stopped. Then it was a push here, a grab there." She tugged on her bottom lip with her teeth, reached for her glass of wine, which she'd set on the coffee table and tossed it all back in a long gulp. "I didn't tell anyone, not even Cara — at first. I was ashamed. Some part of me believed that it was my fault, that there was something about me that made him behave that way. It was the reason why my father — whoever he was — didn't want me." She snorted a laugh. "That's what I thought. So I stayed too long."

Noah listened, fuming silently inside. What he wanted to do was find the bastard who hurt her and beat the hell out of him. He knew all too well the effects of not being wanted, of living in uncertainty based on the intentions of everyone around you. He was the poster boy.

"How did you get out?"

"Dislocated shoulder."

Noah's nostrils flared. His entire body tightened. "What?"

She slowly shook her head. "Cara was my emergency contact. A nurse at the hospital decided to call her when Jason brought me in. He told everyone that I'd fallen." Her eyes suddenly filled with water. She sniffed and blinked rapidly. "Cara showed up with her husband, Phillip. To this day I don't know what Phillip said to Jason, but I went home with them that night and I never went back to Jason." She pushed out a breath. "That was four years ago."

Heavy silence hung between them. Traci's heart thundered while she waited for his reaction.

"He didn't break you." He looked right into her eyes. "He tried, but he couldn't. He tried because he's weak and he saw a strength and purpose in you that he couldn't see in himself. Cara is a good friend." He offered a soft smile that elicited one from Traci as well. "I hope to meet her one day."

Traci's throat was so tight she couldn't speak. Instead she pushed up from her seat and went into the kitchen to get the bottle of wine so that he wouldn't see the tears of relief spilling over her lashes.

When she returned, Noah was standing at the window, looking at the evening unfold.

"Thank you for saying what you said," she said softly.

Noah turned. His hands were in his pockets. His eyes slowly moved over her. He crossed the room to stand in front of her. "No need for thanks. It's all true and it only makes me think even more of you, not less."

47

"More wine?" The halo of a smile framed her mouth.

"Sure."

They spent the rest of the evening really getting to know each other, where and how they grew up: Traci, raised by her single mother; Noah by a long list of foster parents until he settled with the Harpers. Traci was born and raised in New York, while Noah had Southern roots in New Orleans, the city he would always consider home. His roots in the South inspired his love of blues and jazz. They both loved all areas of the arts: books, movies, plays, and music. Noah was better traveled than Traci, having been to South America, Paris, Nigeria, the Caribbean, and Mexico, compared to Traci's trips to the Poconos and her one visit to the Bahamas. Noah clearly stated that Disney World did not count as world travel.

As the evening wore on, they found themselves in Traci's small but efficient kitchen preparing tacos for dinner.

"I think I have some shredded cheese in the drawer at the bottom of the fridge."

"Yep. Cheddar. How 'bout some tomatoes?"

"Absolutely." She poured a can of black beans into a small pot, seasoned them, then put the flame on low to let them simmer. "I have a half a chicken or we could do a quick pepper steak. I need to defrost the meat."

"Cool by me."

In no time they were eating at the kitchen table, laughing and talking as if they'd always known each other.

"So tell me more about this play of yours. What is it about?"

She breathed heavily. "Well . . . it's about a woman who experiences a series of setbacks and her search for personal fulfillment. What I continue to have trouble with is the arc of the character. I can't seem to get her where she needs to go."

He studied her for a moment, contemplating what she'd said. "Maybe it's because you are still searching," he said sagely.

"What makes you think it has to do with me?" she asked, curious about his assessment.

He rested his forearms on the table. "We all infuse parts of ourselves into our art. Think about musicians, songwriters, painters, actors. They all draw on their experiences to make their art come alive in three dimension. I know that I do when I play."

"Play?"

He nodded and smiled. "Alto sax."

"Get out. Really?"

"Yep. Maybe you can come and listen to me play sometime."

"I will definitely make it a point to check you out. When will you play again?"

"I'm not sure, but I'll let you know. Maybe you can bring your friend Cara. Or . . . we could make it a date. You and me." He looked hopefully into her eyes while his thumb gently caressed her knuckles.

Traci's stomach did that dance thing. She licked her bottom lip. "I'd like that."

"Me too." He blew out a breath. "Let me help you clean up. It's getting late." He got up from his seat and started taking the empty plates to the sink.

She wanted to drag the moments out, didn't want him to leave as they worked side by side in easy harmony like a choreo-graphed dance, movements in sync with barely a missed step. A touch here, a smile there, a brush of hips or fingertips stirred the embers that warmed just beneath the surface and all it would take for full-blown flames was for Noah to turn to her, let his hand glide down her arm, gently ease her toward him, and let the sensation of mouths connecting find the release that they both struggled to avoid.

Traci heard her own tiny gasp when he

50

did exactly what she imagined and the world around them disappeared as his face, those eyes, that mouth, came closer to hers.

"I'm going to kiss you," he said on a ragged breath.

Traci held her own. Her heart thundered. His mouth, warm and moist, brushed her lips, testing, teasing, waiting, and she gave in, let her body meld against him as his arm slid around her waist, pulled her closer, and his mouth covered hers fully.

Electric energy surged through her veins and she felt her knees wobble. Her breasts pressed against his chest and her nipples drew taut.

Noah's long fingers combed through the back of her hair and drew her deeper into the kiss while his tongue probed for entry.

Her lips parted and she tasted him, the sweet spice of his own essence blended with the seasonings of their meal. She inhaled him. Delicious.

Noah slowly eased back. His dark eyes had grown ink black. She wanted to count the long, thick lashes. The corner of his mouth curved upward. "I should go," he said in a voice so deep it stirred her pelvis.

But even as he said the words, she felt his arousal rise against her. She wanted him, but she wasn't ready to make that leap. Not just yet.

She took a half step back, lowered her head, then looked directly into his eyes. "Thank you for everything today."

He placed a kiss on her forehead. "Anytime." He backed away, then turned to walk into the living room.

Traci tugged in a shaky breath and gripped the edge of the sink for momentary support before following him. He was putting on his coat. She met him at the door.

"Next time, my place."

"Okay," she agreed, and was filled with the giddiness of "next time."

"Are you busy next Friday?"

She thought for a moment. Other than her Pilates class and some writing, she knew there was nothing of importance on her calendar. "No, I don't think so. Why?"

"Good. Hold the date. There's an art exhibit opening in SoHo that I'd like to see and I think you might enjoy it. Maybe it'll give you some inspiration for your play."

She smiled. "Okay."

"Great." He hesitated a moment. "Get some rest." He turned to leave, stopped, and turned back. He took his cell phone out of his pocket and handed it to her. "Put your number in."

Her hand shook ever so slightly. She tapped in the number, clicked SAVE, and handed it back.

"I'll call you." He dropped the cell into his pocket, then clutched both her arms and dragged her into one last kiss, which literally took her breath away. When he released her, they were both starry-eyed. "Good night."

All Traci could do was stare at the door as it closed behind him. She stood there in a mini-trance before shaking her head to clear it.

"Damn," she whispered. It was going to be a long, lonely night.

CHAPTER SIX

Her workdays at school breezed by and she was fully beginning to believe that she had some real talent in her class. The final project for the end of the fall semester was to stage a short one-act play that the students would write and produce. They were really getting into the writing, which inspired her writing as well.

But it was the evenings that she had finally begun to look forward to again. Each evening Noah would call and "check on her," as he put it. He wanted to know about her day, her students, and how she was progressing with her play. Once, he brought up Jason.

"I know this may be hard to talk about, and you probably want to put it all behind you, but . . . if that dude gives you any trouble, any . . . you let me know. Understood? Don't hesitate. Don't second-guess. I mean that. Promise me."

She'd wavered for a moment. Knights in shining armor were only in fairy tales. Her life was far from that, but here he was anyway. "I promise," she'd murmured, even though she wasn't sure that she meant it.

"Cool, now about Friday . . ."

"Girl, I leave you unattended for a hot five minutes and you got a new man," Cara teased as they left the YWCA following their Pilates class. "See, it's a good thing we didn't go to the movies together." She grinned. "There is a method to my madness."

"Yeah, right, like you had something to do with it."

"Well," she dragged the word out. "Not directly, but you know what I'm saying." She buttoned her coat. "So tell me more." She hooked her arm through Traci's.

"Hmmm," she sighed. "He loves everything that I do. He's a sax player on the side and has dreams of opening a café-type club. He's sexy as hell and kisses like . . ." She actually moaned and Cara laughed and nudged her in the ribs. "And . . . he stopped Jason in his tracks."

"Whoa!" Cara stopped walking. "There is no way you're going to gloss over that. What the hell happened? And why didn't you call me?"

Traci revisited that Sunday afternoon in clear but halting detail. If she knew nothing else about Cara, it was that she always sensed when Traci was evading or lying, so there was no point in doing either.

Cara murmured something unrepeatable under her breath. "That bastard. What is he doing around here anyway?"

"I don't know. I thought he was in Florida."

"So now he knows you're here. He hasn't tried anything since, has he?"

"No!"

"You would tell me if he did?"

"Yes. I would."

"Well, thank goodness Noah was there. Who knows what that asshole would have tried?" She hugged Traci close.

"We were out in public. There wasn't much he would have done."

"Regardless. You never know." She shook off the icky feeling of thinking about Jason Logan. "Anyway, when am I going to meet Mr. Wonderful?"

"He did say he'd like to meet you, too."

"So, how 'bout we take a stroll over to his spot so I can give my stamp of approval before your hot date tonight."

Traci pursed her polished lips to the side. "You twisted my arm."

They walked over to the CoffeeMate just as it began to sprinkle. When they stepped inside, they were immediately welcomed with warmth and the delicious aromas.

"Is he here?" Cara asked without moving her lips.

Traci nudged her in the rib. "Can we at least get inside first?" She casually took a quick look around and her stomach did that dance thing when she spotted Noah emerging from the back.

Noah seemed to sense her presence and his gaze landed right on her. His smile lit his eyes.

"You don't even have to tell me. That's him." Cara hummed in appreciation.

"Yeah," Traci said under her breath. "You want something?" she asked, heading toward the line of customers.

"I'll have what you're having," she teased.

Traci snickered. "Cara, you're a married woman."

"But I ain't blind." She chuckled and gave Traci a light shove in the back to move her along the line.

Traci was finally in front of Noah and she felt like a giddy teenager.

"Hey," she said softly.

"Hey, yourself. The usual?"

Traci nodded. "And the same for my friend Cara."

Noah's gaze shifted to the woman standing next to Traci. "Hello, welcome to CoffeeMate. Nice to meet you."

"Thanks, and you as well. Oh, and I'll take a blueberry muffin to go along with whatever she's having." Cara grinned.

"You can pick your purchases up at the end of the line." When no one was looking, he gave Traci a wink. Her insides curled in response.

"I usually sit at that table in the back," Traci said once they had gotten what they'd paid for. She led the way.

Girrrrl, Cara said under her breath the instant they sat down. "That is one fine brother — that skin and those eyes and those locs. Humph." She peeked around a few tables to scope Noah out again. "Not to mention that he's got your back. You hit the jackpot, my sister."

Traci knew she'd had a thing for Noah months ago when she'd come in and watch him and long for their brief moments of banal conversation. She'd imagined them being together, but the reality was better than anything she could think up on her

58

own. But every time she felt herself getting close, lowering the walls of fear and doubt, she found herself backing off. If where they were now was any indication of where their relationship could go, she should be ready to jump on for the ride. She wasn't.

"What's wrong?"

Traci blinked Cara into focus. She shifted a bit, reached for a napkin, and shrugged off the question. "Nothing. Why?"

"Because I've known you for a zillion years and I know when something is bothering you, and worse when you're lying to me."

Traci wrapped her fingers around her cup of mocha latte.

Cara tipped her head to the side. "Well, talk to me. What is it?"

"Noah is a great guy. He's smart, and funny, and well traveled, and sexy. He's easy to be with."

"But . . ."

"So was Jason in the beginning."

Cara's expression softened. "T, I know Jason did a number on you, but every man is not like Jason."

"My rational self knows that, but my spirit says something else."

"This guy, Noah, is the first man that you've dealt with in the past two years that actually makes you smile, makes you feel good. I hear it in your voice and see it in the light in your eyes. Since Jason you haven't had any significant relationship with a man."

Traci lowered her head, then shook it slowly. "I've tried," she said softly. She looked up into Cara's understanding eyes. "I'm scared."

Cara reached across the table and covered Traci's hand with her own. "Say it. Say it to me. What are you scared of, sweetie?"

"That he'll hurt me. That he will be this wonderful man that I can trust and believe in and then he will hurt me, mentally and physically." She pushed out a breath, and flashes of her nightmare marriage played in her mind. "There, I've said it. I'm afraid. Nothing is as it appears. Nothing and no one."

"You really believe that, don't you?"

"Yes, I do. I'm a product of it." She shook her head. "If I give in, I mean really give in and let Noah into my heart and he hurts me . . . I don't think I could recover from that, not again."

"So what are you going to do for the rest of your life? Live in fear and doubt and . . . alone?"

"I have my work, my students." She offered up a feeble smile. "My best friend."

"You deserve that and more, but it will never happen if you don't give yourself a chance to experience it. Just because you've been knocked down doesn't mean that you don't get back up, T. You're a survivor. You've proven that."

Traci sighed heavily, then took a long swallow of her latte. "I don't know."

"And you never will if you don't give it a shot."

CHAPTER SEVEN

By the time Traci and Cara left CoffeeMate, and returned to their apartments, the rain was coming down hard and fast.

Traci peered out the window and wondered if she and Noah were still on for the art show opening. When she was with Jason, the slightest change in the weather, the people, or the time, which might shift their plans, would set him off, and somehow, no matter what the external cause, it became her fault. She shuddered and turned away from the window, but she didn't have much time to dwell on it because her cell phone rang.

She picked the phone up from the table and her heart banged when she saw Noah's name on the screen. She pressed the TALK icon and held her breath, waiting for the inevitable.

"Hey," she greeted.

"Hey, yourself. It's a mess out there."

She swallowed. "I know."

"So I'll be there to pick you up at seven. Dress comfortable. It's a real casual event. Then I figured, once we left the City, we could drive back to Brooklyn to Open End afterward for a late dinner and some music."

She was so relieved that she almost cried. "Okay," she squeaked. "I'll be ready."

His voice lowered. "I'm looking forward to seeing you, Traci."

"Me too," she murmured.

"Cool. See you soon, babe."

Traci held the phone to her chest long after the call disconnected. *Give him a chance,* she repeated over and over as she prepared for her evening.

She painstakingly chose her simple but classy outfit: a starched white shirt, her fitted black jeans with short ankle boots, a simple silver cuff bracelet, small silver hoop earrings, and dabs of her favorite scent behind her ears and on the insides of her wrists. She twisted and pinned her spiral curls up into a loose topknot, which gave it the look of slightly unkempt on purpose.

Traci faced the full-length mirror that hung on the back of the bathroom door, appraised herself from every angle, and had to admit that she was satisfied with what she saw. She added several coats of mascara to her lashes and swipes of tinted lip gloss to her lips and she was ready just as her doorbell rang.

Suddenly the confidence that she'd just had began to crumble. When was the last time she was out on a date? She couldn't remember. Did she even know how to act? *Don't be silly,* her inner voice warned. *It's no different than the other times that you've spent with him.* But it was. This was an official date.

The bell rang again and she flinched. She drew in a breath, took a last look at herself, grabbed her coat and purse, and trotted downstairs.

She pulled the front door open and there he was, just like the knight in shining armor, equipped with not a lance and a horse but holding a huge umbrella. And the delighted smile on his lips upon seeing her said more than words ever could.

Traci shut the door behind her and Noah wrapped his arm around her waist, pulled her close and kissed her under the dome of the umbrella. For several moments, as his tongue gently explored her mouth, they were the only people in the world.

"Hey," he whispered against her mouth as he broke the kiss.

"Hey, yourself," she managed.

"Ready?"

She nodded.

He held her hand and shielded her from the cold, whipping rain. When they got to the bottom of the stairs, he pointed out his Navigator and they made a dash for it.

"You okay?" Noah asked while he shook out the umbrella before tossing it into the backseat. He slammed the door shut.

"Yeah," she said with laughter in her voice. "Didn't expect all that."

"Chance of showers," he quipped.

Traci fastened her seat belt and settled back. His car smelled like him, deep and sexy. It was nothing overpowering, just present. Inwardly she smiled.

Noah put on his signals and pulled out. "I heard a lot of good things about this exhibit. Hope it lives up to the hype."

"Do you go to exhibits often?"

"Hmmm, when something strikes me. I'm not into 'the greats,' as they say, more of the locals and up-and-comings artists. They take chances. Make you think." He snatched a look at her. "What about you?"

"I haven't been to an exhibit in ages. But I do agree, I am not all that moved by 'the greats,' either. Don't get me wrong. I think Rembrandt, Van Gogh, Da Vinci, are great and set the stage for all those that followed, but the new artists have taken the foundation and built it to another level with the incorporation of a variety of media."

"Exactly! That's the thing about art. It's not monolithic but a reflection, a disturbance in the everydayness."

Traci looked at him in admiration. "I feel the same way. Whether the art is literature or music or drama or visual arts, it should stir something, upset the status quo in a way that makes the viewer take a step back and say 'wow.' "

"Couldn't have said it better." He turned to her and smiled as they pulled up to a red light.

"Hey, see that building over there. The Chadwick?"

"Yeah, been closed for a few years."

"I saw a couple of local plays there before it closed. Fell in love with it. That's where I've been envisioning staging my play. Right there." She pushed out a sigh. "Can't get around the reality of the cost of getting it opened and refurbished, but . . . a girl can dream."

Noah started to say something, but held his tongue. Nothing was set in stone yet and he wasn't about to rock the boat. Instead he said, "No bright lights of Broadway?"

Traci laughed. "No. I want to bring it to

the community, have it accessible. I remember years ago, seeing *For Colored Girls . . .* right at the Billie Holiday Theatre in Restoration Plaza on Fulton Street. I thought that was the greatest thing. I want to do the same."

"I remember that. I went to one of the last showings."

"How crazy is that? Two ships passing in the night."

Noah glanced at her just before pulling off. "That finally came ashore . . . together."

Traci's heart raced. She fiddled with her purse. *Careful, Traci, Noah is too easy to fall really hard for.*

The art exhibit called "Blurred: A Search for Humanity" was an eclectic blend of black-and-white photos, mixed media, and live art — people who were part of the exhibit that spoke to the audience — all of which addressed the idea of identity and the notion that with the blurring of lines, humanity would soon be one universal color and their sex interchangeable.

The gallery was packed with the curious and the art enthusiast, along with the media who all wanted a piece of this avant-garde new artist, Dweli.

When Traci and Noah emerged from the

showing, they both looked at each other and simultaneously uttered "wow," in utter awe of what they'd seen.

"That's some powerful stuff," Noah said as he got behind the wheel of the car.

"I'm at a loss for words, to be truthful. I mean the entire exhibit speaks to the changing times and the impact of the decisions we make regarding us as humans and individuals."

"A lot to think about."

"If the world actually became the homogenous utopia that Dweli envisions, it would certainly relieve us of a lot of problems as a society."

"Hmm, true, but I think what was the most telling were the few holdouts, the ones who maintained their identities and struggled to reclaim the old order."

"Modern version of a brave new world."

Traci nodded in agreement. "A lot to think about."

"Yep. I hope you're hungry. I'm starved and I know the music tonight will be on point. The band is crazy phenomenal."

Traci grinned. "I'm with the driver."

When they returned to Brooklyn from SoHo and arrived at Open End, the classy bar was jumping. The large entry had a line of people waiting to check their damp coats. Beyond the check-in, to the left, the long bar began and was lined from end to end with customers. Opposite the bar was the wide-open space filled with rectangular and round tables and several banquettes. There was a midsized raised stage that faced the bar and seating area. The band and a well-known local singer named Dawne were at the end of a set. When she ended her signature song "Love," the crowd went crazy.

"I've heard about her," Traci said, pleasantly surprised that she was the featured artist. "Cara is always talking about this indie artist named Dawne. Loves her music. I think I'm a fan."

"I'll introduce you a little later."

"Say what?"

He grinned. "I know people who know people," he teased.

They finished checking their coats and were greeted by one of the hostesses.

"Good evening, Mr. Jefferson. Your table is ready."

Traci gave him an "excuse me" look of amusement.

He held her hand as they walked behind the hostess, who led them around the maze of tables and people, until they reached the reserved table in the center of the seating area. The hostess plucked the reserve card from the table.

"I'll send your waiter right over."

"Thanks," Noah said.

Did he always get treated this way, or was he trying to impress her? Her guard went up. When she and Jason first got together and he was courting her hard, he always did things like this to impress her, try to make her feel special. It was all part of his sick game plan.

Noah placed his hand on hers and she jumped. "You okay?"

She blinked rapidly and forced a smile. "Yes, fine. Sorry. My mind was wandering for a minute." She turned her full attention on him.

His eyes squinted. "Sure?"

"Positive."

"All right." He picked up his menu and leaned back in his seat. "You want a drink?"

"Since I'm not driving," she teased, "I'd like an apple martini."

"Not a problem."

Before he could look around, the harried waiter stopped at their table and quickly took their orders for drinks and crab cakes for appetizers.

"This is a really nice spot," Traci said,

looking around. "I can't believe I haven't been here before."

"I'll let you in on a secret."

"What?" she said, lowering her voice.

"My best friend owns it." He winked.

Traci twisted her lips. "That's what's up with all the fancy treatment."

"Kinda. He wants to meet you."

"You told him about me?"

"Of course."

Her heart began to skip, then run. "Oh." She lowered her gaze.

"Should you be a secret?"

"No . . . I mean . . ." She shrugged. She never met any of Jason's friends and over time he'd weaned her away from her friends until she was isolated and alone. He always used the excuse that they were busy or that she didn't have the right outfit — or whatever justification he could concoct.

Noah took his index finger, placed it under her chin, and lifted it to compel her to look at him. "I want everyone to know about you and me — about us. I want them to see that I'm crazy about you and getting crazier by the day."

Traci could hardly breathe.

Noah smiled at her, then leaned over and lightly kissed her lips. "Us," he whispered, "for as long as you'll have us."

The waiter returned with their drinks and appetizer, saving Traci from having to respond.

"To a great evening, with many more to come," Noah said, raising his glass of scotch.

Traci tapped her glass to his and took a tiny sip. Her eyes closed in delight. "Delish," she murmured.

Noah winked.

The waiter returned to take their order just before Anthony wound his way around the tables and stopped at theirs. He clapped Noah on the back.

"Hey, man, glad you could make it."

Noah stood and they exchanged the black handshake of the day. "Have a seat for a minute."

Anthony pulled up a chair.

"Anthony Fields, this is Traci Long. T, this here is my main man from back in my college days. Frat brothers. And he's the owner of this wonderful establishment," he added in admiration.

"I pay him to say all that good stuff," Anthony teased as he turned all of his attention onto Traci. He extended his hand. "Good to finally meet you. Noah bends my ear about you all the time," he half-joked.

Traci felt her face flush with embarrassment. She swallowed and then her smile bloomed. "Nice to meet you, too. Your spot is incredible. Congrats."

"Thanks. Looking to expand. Soon, hopefully. But I won't bore you with all that. Enjoy your evening and whatever you want is on the house." He pushed up out of his chair and turned to Noah. "You sitting in tonight?"

"Naw. Think I'm going to stay in customer mode tonight."

"Cool. If you change your mind, let me know."

Noah nodded and Anthony walked off.

"So this is where you come to play?"

"Mostly. Every now and then I hook up with a small band in Harlem and play up there."

"I'd love to hear you play sometime."

"I'll keep that in mind for next time."

Traci sipped her drink and tried to put the pieces of Noah together. He seemed to have so much ambition and potential. He'd graduated college. His best friend was a business owner. And yet, Noah served coffee every day and occasionally played with a band. True, he talked about his dream of having a café with an entertainment space, but the couple of times that she broached the subject, he found a way to steer clear or talk around it. Now, this wasn't to say that what he did for a living would change her feelings about him. It was an honest living. What it did, however, was have her question his drive. Was he only a dreamer and not a doer? Men who talked a good game were a dime a dozen. Been there, done that. She hoped that Noah wasn't one of them. She wanted to believe that he wasn't.

She pushed those thoughts aside and let herself melt into the charm that was Noah. His laughter, the light touches, the spark in his eyes when he spoke to her as if she was the most important person in the world.

It had been a long time since she'd been made to feel utterly special to someone else. And the fact that it was Noah only intensified her feelings for him, combined with the perfect atmosphere, delicious food, and incredible music. She couldn't ask for more.

"You were so right about the singer," she said once Dawne's set was over. "She is amazing."

Noah grinned. "Ready to meet her?"

The flush of excitement lit her eyes. "Yes!"

He pushed back from the table, came around to help her from her seat, and once again took her hand. Slow warmth rolled up her arm.

Noah led her around the table to the side

of the restaurant and down a narrow hall to the dressing room of the performers.

He tapped lightly on the door.

"Come in."

Noah stepped in first and brought Traci in behind him.

"Hey, lady."

"Noah!" Dawne got up from the cushy love seat and darted over for a hug. The petite powerhouse stepped back and looked up at him. "It's been a while. How are you?"

"Can't complain."

"You should have let me know you were here. I would have loved to have you on set."

Noah chuckled. "Maybe next time." He turned his gaze on Traci. "Want to introduce you to a new fan. Traci Long, this is Dawne."

Dawne extended her manicured hand. "Any friend of Noah's is a friend of mine. Glad you liked the music."

"You are amazing."

She smiled demurely. " 'Preciate that. You guys want something to drink, eat?" she asked, pointing to the spread on the side table.

"No, we're good. Gonna let you unwind. I just wanted to holler at you and introduce my lady." He squeezed Traci's hand and her heart thumped.

"You must be some kind of special," Dawne said to Traci. "This guy here, he doesn't bring *anyone* around. Trust." She gave Traci a wink.

Traci's cheeks heated. Her stomach did that flutter thing. She stole a glance at Noah, who smiled back at her to confirm what Dawne confessed.

"Guilty as charged." He draped an arm around Traci's shoulder, then leaned down and kissed Dawne on the cheek. "Take care. When are you back in town?"

"Hmm, I head out to Atlanta in the morning for a short stint, then I'll be back in about two weeks."

"I'll try to catch up when you get back."

"Do that," she said, pointing a finger at him. She turned to Traci. "Really nice to meet you."

"You too."

"I had an amazing evening," Traci confessed when Noah pulled to a stop in front of her building. "And meeting Dawne . . . wow. Thank you."

"Anytime. I hope you know that." He drew closer. "I want to spend more time with you. I want you to know me. I want to know you. You with that?"

She swallowed. "Yes. I'd like that."

His mouth lifted into that half grin that made her insides quiver. He leaned closer, and so did she, until their lips touched. A current of desire whipped through her at the contact. Noah's mouth was like a live wire that sizzled and sparked. When he dipped his tongue into her mouth, she sighed in pleasure. He pulled her closer and a part of her wanted to leap across the gearshift and into his lap as desire bloomed.

"Damn, woman," he muttered as he pulled away. He cupped her face in his palm. "You make me crazy."

She licked her lips and tasted him again. "So do you," she whispered.

"Go, before . . ."

"Before what?" she dared to ask. Her heart pounded.

"Before I forget that I'm a gentleman and this is a car parked on a public street and not a bedroom."

Traci took a breath and eased back. "We'll talk tomorrow?"

"Yeah, definitely."

She clutched her purse to her chest. He disengaged the locks on the door. She reached for the handle and sat on the fence of indecision, but only for a moment.

"Why don't you come up?"

His eyes widened. "You sure?"

She nodded.

Noah turned off the car. The rain had stopped. They got out.

CHAPTER EIGHT

Traci's legs shook as she mounted the stairs to her top-floor apartment. Halfway, she second-guessed her decision. But it was too late now. She felt him behind her. She fumbled for the key in her purse, finally found it, and opened the door.

Before she had a chance, Noah helped her out of her coat, letting his hands linger on her shoulders before he placed a kiss on the back of her neck. A shiver ran along the length of her spine. She arched her back and mentally moaned.

Her voice shook. "Can I fix you something?"

Noah turned her around to face him. He held her arms and looked into her eyes. "I'm going to say this so that we're real clear. I want you in the worst kinda way. I want to make love to you until the sun comes up. I want to hear you call my name and me call yours. I want to do things to that banging body of yours that you will want me to always do. But . . . only if you're sure. Only if you want me as badly as I want you."

Traci took a calming breath. She reached up and draped her arms around his neck. "What are you waiting for?" she said against his mouth. She took his hand and led him to her bedroom.

The moment they crossed the threshold Noah took her into his arms, pulling her hard against him. His mouth covered hers in a breath-stealing kiss. His fingers played along her back and cupped her plump behind to pull her closer. His erection pressed against her belly. He bent his knees so that he could push up between her legs. She moaned and rotated her hips against him. He sucked in air.

Traci held on to his biceps as they bumped and grinded against each other. Then with his large hands firmly planted around her rear, he lifted her off her feet. She wrapped her legs around his waist and he walked over to the queen-sized bed. They tumbled onto the thick teal-colored down quilt.

Noah wasted no time in beginning his long-awaited exploration of her body. He deftly unbuttoned her white blouse to reveal the lacy black bra that barely contained the swell of her breasts. He planted tiny, hot kisses along their arch. He slipped off one strap and then the other, then tugged the cups downward. An involuntary groan rumbled deep in his throat.

He sat up and pulled her up with him. "I need to see all of you," he said in a gravel-laden voice. He unhooked her bra, tossed it aside, then unbuttoned and unzipped her jeans.

Traci rose up onto her knees and wiggled her jeans down over her hips.

"Stand up."

She did.

Noah pulled the jeans all the way down. Her lacy panties matched her bra. He softly moaned and nuzzled her center, making her nearly collapse against him. She gripped his broad shoulders. The warmth of his breath whispered along her inner thighs, followed by swipes of his tongue. Her eyes squeezed shut and her fingers dug deeper. He continued his tease all the way down her legs. He then lifted one foot and took off her ankle boot. He tossed it and followed suit with the other foot, then removed her jeans and panties. They wound up in a heap on the floor.

Noah eased back a bit so that he could take her in, from the top of her wild curls to the bottom of her feet. Hungry eyes, shadowed by lowered lashes, took snapshots of her to store in his memory for those rare times in the future when they would be apart.

"You are so beautiful," he murmured while he stroked her thighs. "Lay back," he commanded.

Traci gingerly lowered herself down, praying that she wouldn't tumble over in the process, then stretched out on her back.

Noah began at her ankles, kissing the insides; then slowly and deliberately he moved up her legs, teased behind her knees, laved and nipped the inside of her thighs, until the muscles in her stomach fluttered uncontrollably. She gripped the sheets in her hands when he reached her center. He pressed his mouth against her, and licked her like dessert. Her body arched as if shot with a surge of electricity. She was going to explode — any minute. She bit down on her bottom lip to keep from screaming.

He parted her thighs wide and held them in place to give him all the access that he desired. He suckled the tiny fruit until it was hard and pulsing against his tongue. Her whimpers pushed past the hold that she had on her lips and floated like musical lyrics into the air.

Noah draped her thighs across his wide

shoulders and slipped his finger into her deep, wet opening. Traci's scream was raw, rising from the depths of her being as her hips jerked upward. She sputtered words and sounds that Noah couldn't make out in between her cries of his name. All that mattered was pleasing her, taking her to heights that she would not soon forget.

Traci felt so hot. She felt as if her body would self-combust. Wave after wave of exquisite heat raced through her limbs. She couldn't put words to what Noah was doing to her body because she couldn't process anything more than feeling. She felt alive, and powerful, and submissive, all at once. She wanted this feeling to go on and on, though she knew nothing this good could last forever. But she was intent on experiencing every possible sensation before she gave in to the inevitable release that was building like a firestorm and tearing across what was once dry land.

Noah slid a second finger inside her and she gasped as her wet walls closed and opened around them. He rose up on his knees and unfastened his pants with his free hand while he continued to pleasure her. "Open your eyes," he said, his voice as hard as his cock when her lids fluttered upward and saw what he had waiting for her.

Traci's lips parted, but no sound came out. Her heart raced. She wanted him. She desperately needed to know what he would feel like inside her. She lowered her legs, leaned up, and stretched out her hand and wrapped her fingers around his width. Noah sucked in air through his teeth. For a moment his eyes drifted closed and he embraced the feel of her hand around him.

Slowly she stroked him, up and down, while intermittently letting her thumb graze over the head to awaken the tiny dewdrops that slicked its surface. She'd done as he'd asked. She'd opened her eyes and now she saw the effect of what she was doing to him reflected in the jutting veins in his neck, the flaring of his nostrils, the pulsing of his cock, and the dark, dangerous look in his eyes that only intensified her own desire. Yet, through it all he continued his ministrations on her.

Noah reached to the side of the bed, where he'd tossed his slacks. He dug in his pocket and took out his wallet. He gave it to Traci.

"Take one out."

Traci swallowed. She flipped open the wallet and found a string of three condom packets behind his money. She pulled them out and put the wallet on the nightstand.

She handed the condoms to Noah.

"No. I want you to do it."

Traci hesitated. She'd actually never done this before. She'd watched, but never done it. "I don't . . ."

"Tear one apart from the rest."

She did and then put the remaining two on the nightstand.

"Now just tear off the top with your teeth."

She felt around for the contents inside the gold packet then put the corner of it in her mouth and ripped off a section. Noah smiled.

"Take it out."

Traci gingerly pulled out the condom.

"Go ahead, put it on me," he said so low that his words were almost lost.

Traci looked up into his eyes and saw the desire that matched hers that only seemed to intensify with this very intimate act that had turned into erotic foreplay.

"Just place it on the head and slowly roll it down. Leave a little room at the top." He grinned mischievously when her eyes flashed to his.

Traci kept her eyes trained on him, relishing the expression of delight on his face as she slowly, very slowly, rolled the latex over him. She made a game of it, rolling it down a little, then stopping to cup his swollen sacs, then rolling again, stopping to place a kiss on his belly.

Noah gritted his teeth. He totally enjoyed the game she was playing, but he was tired of playing now. He wanted her. He wanted release, and he would have it.

He gripped her wrist and stared hard into her eyes as he urgently assisted in the sheathing.

Traci grinned. "Are you okay?"

"No," he groaned, "but we're going to fix that."

Traci giggled and flopped back against the pillows. "Okay," she whispered with a taunting look in her eyes.

Noah uttered something deep in his throat. He reached behind her and snatched up a pillow, then shoved it under her hips.

Traci's breathing escalated. Noah was momentarily transfixed by the rise and fall of her breasts. He lowered his head and took one of the dark brown nipples into his mouth.

"Ooohhh." Traci thrashed her head against the pillow.

He attended to the other side and back again. "Open your legs for me, Traci. Just for me," he whispered into her ear.

The simple request nearly made her come.

She did as he asked. She spread her legs as wide as she could and bent her knees.

Noah groaned. He held the weight of his throbbing penis in his hand and slowly pushed past her opening.

Their first contact sent shocks through them both and they moaned in unison.

Noah gritted his teeth as he pressed deeper. The wet heat of her, the tightness of her, the feel of her wrapped around him, sent him hurtling toward the edge. Only sheer will held him back. He needed to please her, to hear her scream in release, before he let go. So he took his time, stroked her slow and deep, teased her with kisses and caresses, until she was a single vibrating mass of sensation. He could feel her need rise in the way her body began to tense, her moans began to grow louder and more rapid, the sheen of perspiration that coated her body, and the way her breasts had swollen. The only sounds were their moans and the slap of damp flesh.

She was so wet and slick, but so tight, that he wanted to scream in his own pleasure. It was like being with a woman for her first time; yet he knew it wasn't, not by the way she rocked her hips, lifted her breasts for his kisses, or locked her knees against his waist.

Then there it was. Her neck arched and her belly flexed. Her fingertips pressed into his back.

He slid his hands under her behind and pulled her hard against his thrusts.

"Noah!"

Her body shook and the grip and release of her insides around his member were so hard and fast that it sucked the essence out of him, sending him spiraling. He wasn't even sure what he'd said other than calling on a higher power through his teeth as the flood of his release made him infant weak.

Traci wrapped her legs fully around him and pulled him tight against her.

Their hearts pounded like crazy. Their breaths were just a beat above gasps. Aftershocks zipped through them, jerking his still-hard penis and pulsing her vagina until they were utterly spent.

"Damn," they both muttered, then broke out in satisfied laughter.

Noah reached between their joined bodies and made sure that the very used condom made its exit along with him.

"Bathroom is first door on the right," Traci said.

Noah grinned and padded out of the room to the bath. Traci watched in utter pleasure at the magnificence of the man from the toned wide shoulders down to the tapered waist, narrow hips, tight just-right ass and great legs. And that was only from the back. She nearly salivated when he returned and she gained a full-frontal view. *OMG* was the only coherent thing she could put together in her mind.

He came to her with a warm washcloth and a towel and, without a word, began to wipe her down. The simple act was so caring and tender that tears sprang to Traci's eyes.

"What's wrong?" he asked. A deep frown etched a line between his eyes.

She sniffed and suddenly felt ridiculous. "Nothing," she croaked. "Just happy."

Noah's smile was slow and then the warm light returned to his eyes. He leaned closer and gently touched her lips with his. "That's all I want for you — to be happy." He stroked the loose hair away from her face and then pulled the sheet up to cover them. Traci curled on her side and Noah spooned with her. He draped his hand across her waist, gave her a tender kiss on the back of her neck before they both drifted off to sleep.

CHAPTER NINE

"So," Traci breathed as she lifted a slice of crispy bacon toward her lips. "You know my sordid past, what about you, any ladies in waiting?"

Noah snorted a laugh. He took a sip of juice and thought about what he would tell her and how much. He set the glass down. "There was somebody, once."

"Only once?" she teased.

His lowered lashes hid his eyes. "Just once." He tried to joke and held up one finger. "Anita. About five years ago. She wanted to head down the aisle."

He paused for so long after that admission that Traci had to nudge him to finish. "So what happened?"

"Let's simply say that she was with me because of who she wanted me to be rather than who I was."

Traci frowned. "And what was that?"

Noah shifted his jaw. He looked away. "It

was a long time ago."

"Maybe she saw potential," she hedged, actually mouthing her own thoughts.

His head whipped in her direction. "Meaning?" His brows drew together.

Traci swallowed down her response when she saw a mixture of hurt and anger shift places with each other on his face.

She shrugged lightly. "Nothing. Really." She waved off any further response as her protective instincts kicked in. This was how things always began, then escalated with Jason. She would make some innocent remark and he would take it from zero to sixty.

Noah watched her shrink away and could have kicked himself for being so utterly blind. He reached for her, but she hopped up from her seat and took her plate to the sink. Noah came up behind her. He placed his hands on her tight shoulders. He pressed his forehead into her hair.

"I'm sorry."

She inwardly flinched. Jason was always sorry, too.

"Hey, don't worry about it. It's fine. Really. No apology necessary."

Noah turned her around to face him. Traci kept her focus on the floor. He lifted her chin with the tip of his finger.

"Yeah, there is." He paused. "I'm not him.

I'm not going to flip out on you." He drew in a long breath. "Look, I'm not good at this whole opening-up thing. I'm not that guy. I figured out since I was a kid that letting people know that you needed them or that you cared too much would bite you in the ass in the end. Seen it happen."

"Between the two of us we seem to have enough baggage to open a luggage store."

That made him laugh and the tightrope of tension loosened.

"So look . . . I'm not going to make any promises of happily ever after. I can't. It's not me. But . . . if you want a man to be in your corner, support your dreams, show you a good time, keep the boogeymen away, make crazy love to you . . ." He held out his hands, palms up. "Here I am."

"So basically he blew your socks off in bed and then pretty much told you that he's only 'sort of the one,' as long as you don't want the full monty," Cara said with a clear line of sarcasm in her voice.

Traci listened to Cara with one ear and her Pilates instructor with the other. She planted her palms facedown on her mat and lifted her legs to a forty-five-degree angle and held it for a count of fifteen as directed.

"You don't have to make it sound so awful." Traci exhaled as she lowered her legs.

"Not awful, just real."

They turned on their stomachs and executed a series of leg and hip lifts before completing the wind down.

"Sounds like you're going to stick it out."

Traci mopped her face with her towel. "I think I am."

They walked toward the dressing room.

"But why, when you know it's not going anywhere?"

"For the time being I like what we're doing, enjoying each other. No strings, no expectations." She blew out a breath. "Besides, people change all the time."

Cara grabbed her shoulder. "Girl, don't even go down that road because you're setting yourself up to be let down. People don't change," she insisted. "And if you stick with it, believing that you can change him . . ."

Traci stopped in her tracks and turned to her friend. "I've been eyeing this man for months, fantasizing about him and now he's finally here. I want to be happy, Cara. It's been so long that I've felt happy in a relationship that I look forward to the next day. Noah makes me happy. He reminds me that I'm a woman to be cared for." She sighed and slowly shook her head. "I'm not ready to give that up. I'm going to enjoy it as much as I can for as long as I can." She got out of her clothes and walked to the shower, leaving Cara with an expression of worry on her face.

As promised, Noah always made time for Traci, whether it was giving her extra attention when she frequented the CoffeeMate or the hours they spent on the phone on the nights that they weren't in each other's beds, or on their eclectic dates that could be anything from sitting on the pier to watching old black-and-white movies, hanging out at Open End, visits to museums and spoken-word clubs, cooking for her, or making love to her. All of it made it very difficult for Traci to believe that Noah wasn't falling for her as hard as she was falling for him.

The only odd part of their relationship was Noah's hours of disappearance on Sundays. He wasn't at the shop, he wasn't with her, and he didn't call or come by. It bugged her, made her curious, or maybe "suspicious" was a better word. At first she thought it was only in her head, but as she looked closer at what was happening between them, she knew she wasn't imagining things. Where did he go every Sunday and what did he do? Who was he with?

"Why don't you just ask him?" Cara said.

Traci shifted the phone between her shoulder and her ear. "I don't want to be that kind of woman."

"What kind of woman would that be? One who asks for answers on the things she wants to know about?"

"Not funny, Cara. You know what I mean. Someone who is always checking, needing to know where her man is twenty-four/seven."

"So you consider him your man?"

"Yes," she said a bit hesitantly.

"A man that you don't really trust?"

"I never said I didn't trust him."

"Not in those exact words, but you clearly have some kind of suspicion."

Traci rolled her eyes, even though Cara couldn't see her. "Anyway," she huffed, "how is everything else?"

Cara laughed lightly. "Fine."

They talked a few minutes more until Traci gasped at the time. Noah would be there to pick her up in a couple of hours and she needed to get ready. They were going to see Misty Copeland in *Swan Lake* and she couldn't wait.

"Girl, I gotta go."

"Have a ball. One thing I have to give to Noah, he sure knows how to wine and dine.

The prices for those tickets are crazy."

Traci laughed. "Later, girl."

The entire area surrounding Lincoln Center was lit up with the lights of the holidays, which were rapidly approaching. Entering Metropolitan Opera House, however, was like stepping up for the Oscars. Everything gleamed and sparkled from the teardrop chandeliers to the diamonds that dripped from wrists and ears. The rarified air was scented with outrageously expensive perfumes and colognes. It had been a while since Traci had been to Lincoln Center, and that was for the free outdoor summer movies. This night was a true experience and she was thrilled that she'd splurged and gotten her designer dress — on sale — at a small boutique in Williamsburg.

Noah held her lightly around the waist as they followed the line into the seating area. "You are stunning," he whispered into her ear. "Would it be awful of me to say that I can't wait to peel you out of your little black dress?"

Traci flushed. "I'd be insulted if you didn't."

"Aww, naughty girl." He kissed her behind her ear, lingering for an extra moment to inhale her scent.

The usher showed them to their seats. Traci was fully expecting that they would be in the balcony or, at best, the second mezzanine. She was wrong. They kept walking until they reached the orchestra, second row center.

Traci held down her surprise and tried to play it cool, as if getting second-row orchestra seats was an everyday occurrence. But her insides belied her outward calm. She bubbled with excitement. She couldn't believe it and knew for a fact that these seats easily went for five hundred dollars *each* for opening night. How in the world could Noah afford them on a manager's salary at a coffee shop? She side-eyed him, and when he turned and gave her that smile, and squeezed her hand, she made up her mind that at least for tonight she would keep all of her doubting questions away and just enjoy the experience.

"I . . . I can't even put into words what that was like," Traci said as they exited the theater. "She was magnificent," she said, totally awestruck by Misty Copeland's performance.

"The American Ballet Theatre knew what they were doing when they named her principal dancer."

"After seeing her I want to change my professor to ballerina!" She did a little twirl, much to onlookers' delight.

"I could see you now, spinning, leaping, doing those splits. You already have the moves, babe," he teased, and pecked her lightly on the cheek.

She nudged him in the side. "Very funny." She paused for a moment. "As great as it is, it's sad to realize that in this day and age we are still saying the 'first African-American . . . whatever.' "

"Hmm, I know."

They were contemplative for a moment.

"One of these days, hopefully in our lifetime, that won't be the case."

"Hopefully. But" — he pulled her close — "in the meantime we can celebrate the moment."

"For sure." She smiled and kissed him with the intention of it being no more than a gesture, but Noah suddenly pulled her flush against him and kissed her as if they were the only people in the world. And it didn't matter that they were in the middle of the Plaza and hundreds of theatergoers were watching.

"I've been wanting to do that all night," he whispered against her mouth. He held her firmly. "Sitting next to you, feeling you beside me, inhaling you, watching your expression, your happiness, and only able to touch your hand or your thigh, was making me crazy for you." His gaze scrolled her face.

Traci's heart raced so quickly that it was hard to breathe. "Let's go home."

Noah's dark eyes flashed in the night. "Let's."

CHAPTER TEN

Noah stretched and blinked against the intruding light of a new day. He turned his head toward the clock on Traci's nightstand. It was almost seven. He glanced over at her still-sleeping form. He hated to leave, but he had things to do. All of his planning was coming together and he didn't want to screw things up now. He had to stay on top of the progress. Anthony was going to meet him at his place at nine so that they could head out to Philly and get back to Brooklyn at a reasonable hour.

He quietly eased out of the bed, careful not to wake Traci while he dressed. Once he was finished, he stood over her sleeping form, debated about letting her know that he was leaving, then finally decided to send a text to her phone for her to find when she got up.

Anthony volunteered for the two-hour drive

and the buddies took his SUV for the weekly road trip.

"So how was the ballet?" Anthony asked with a note of amusement in his voice.

"It was really great."

"I'm still trying to picture you at the ballet."

Noah chuckled. "I know. Me too. But I was there."

"Well, when you set your mind to impress a woman, you go all out. I'm pretty sure she was blown away by those seats that cost you a grand."

"I think so. But Traci is too classy to speak on it that way."

"But, man, if you're trying to be all low-key, don't you think buying ballet tickets for a thousand dollars would set off some warning lights? Where does she think you would get that kind of money working at a coffee shop?"

Noah glanced out of the passenger window. "Saved up," he quipped.

"Yeah, right. Not the fact that you're the CEO of the CoffeeMate franchise and could have bought the entire orchestra if you wanted. I've never known you to intentionally go out with a stupid woman and I'm pretty sure that Traci is far from it. She's going to start asking questions and you're either going to come clean or you're going to lie."

"I'll deal with it when the time comes."

"I say you tell her before she finds out some other way."

"When I'm ready. I need to be sure. I'm not going down that road again, man."

Anthony blew out a breath. "I hear you. Just don't F-up if she really means anything to you."

"She does," he quietly admitted. "More than I thought she would."

"Then, like I said, don't F-up." He made the turn onto the Pennsylvania freeway.

By the time they arrived on the south side of Philly, it was almost noon. Traffic was bad and the rainy mixture didn't help.

Noah had gotten the building for a steal. It was an abandoned three-story brownstone that sat on the edge of commercial and residential space. What was also great was that it was totally accessible by public transportation and there was a small parking lot less than a block away.

They entered on the ground level that would host the café. The contractor had completed the entire first floor: hardwood floors, a horseshoe counter, and high ceilings with recessed lighting that gave the space the feel of a nightclub. There were banquettes that lined the walls and space in the center for tables. All that was left to do was bring in the furnishings and equipment.

"Mr. Jefferson, Mr. Fields." Herman the foreman stepped out from the back room, wiping his face. "I was getting ready to call you."

"Yeah, sorry, Herman. We ran into a bit of traffic."

Herman peered out of the paneled window. "Hmm, getting bad. Well, let's review so that you can get back on the road."

As they moved from space to space on the first floor, they checked off items on the punch list and got the all clear. Then they went up to the second floor, taking the staircase behind the café. What Herman was able to do, according to Noah's request, was to install a side door for direct access to the rooms upstairs that would be available from the outside.

The second level was for pure, intimate dining. Each table setting was designed with partitions for the ultimate in privacy. Chandeliers provided the lighting. Speakers had been strategically placed to pipe in soft music. Again it was all about ambience.

The top floor was a total entertainment space, complete with a full stage, lighting, a dynamic sound system, room for sitting and dancing, and, of course, a bar and small kitchen that would provide a house menu.

In total it would employ at least one hundred people, if not more, provide a venue for up-and-coming artists and established ones, as well as serving as a local hangout for the community. And it was discreet. The fact that it was a brownstone blended right in with the surrounding community and was part of the visual landscape rather than a sore thumb.

Herman turned to Noah and Anthony with a look of expectation in his eyes.

Noah stuck out his hand. "You've done a helluva job here, Herman. I knew I hired the right man."

"Thank you, Mr. Jefferson."

Noah took the punch list from Herman and gave it his final approval. His pulse raced. This was it. He'd finally done it. Now the planning for the grand opening had to be put in motion.

"You did it, man," Anthony said as they drove back to New York. The rain was coming down harder now.

"Yeah." Noah smiled. "Only wish I could have found something comparable in New York."

"I know. Real estate in the Apple is crazy high. You got a good deal on this, and knowing you, this is going to be even more successful than the franchise."

"That's the plan."

"And how is Traci going to fit into all of this?"

"When the time is right . . ."

"Where does she think you are every Sunday, visiting nursing homes or something?"

Noah's brows drew together. He thought about the text he'd sent her and all the other bogus excuses he'd used for never being around on Sunday. She'd not pushed the subject. She'd asked him once or twice what he did on his day off and he tossed out something generic like "just relax," "take some time for me," or "nothing special." He wanted to tell her who he really was and what he was doing, but there was that part of him, that damaged little boy that didn't quite recover from rejection, from wanting to be a part of someone's life, only to have it taken away time and again. And the one time, the one time when he let down his guard and gave someone a chance to show him what love was, she proved to him that what he'd felt and believed all along was true.

As much as he cared about Traci, wanted to love Traci, he found himself still unable to cross that invisible barrier. He would never allow himself to be that vulnerable to anyone ever again.

Anthony shot him a quick glance, knew he wouldn't get an answer so he kept further comments on the subject to himself.

The pounding rain only added to Traci's irritated mood. From her seat by the window she looked out on the darkened street pounded by the pouring rain. She'd awakened to find Noah gone. All he left behind was his scent on her pillows, a throb between her legs, and a text message: T, Had to head out. Didn't want to wake you. Have a good one. N

She shouldn't have been surprised; it was Sunday, after all, but that didn't take away the sting or the disappointment. For some ridiculous reason she'd imagined that since they'd gone out on Saturday night, instead of Friday, and that he'd spent the night at her house, that *this* Sunday would be the day that he stayed.

She didn't want to believe that Noah was doing something underhanded or seeing someone else, but at this point she wasn't sure what to believe and maybe she should listen to Cara's advice and just come right out and ask him. But her traumatic experiences of asking the most benign questions had silenced her, had successfully cut off her ability to speak about what was on her mind and in her heart, because to do so resulted in physical and verbal assaults. She'd had several years of freedom from the abuse, but the scars remained just below the surface.

Traci slightly pushed the sheer curtain aside to get a better look below. She needed to run to the corner store and pick up some flour, when suddenly her entire body heated and a flush of prickling dread rose like a rash along her arms and back.

Jason was outside, across the street, staring at her building. She blinked several times and looked again to be sure that she wasn't imagining that the six-foot-plus man in the brown overcoat, which she remembered buying him for a Christmas gift in another lifetime, was pacing across the street, oblivious to the rain, and periodically looking up toward her window.

Her breathing hitched in her chest as if she'd been running. What was he doing here? How did he find her? She felt paralyzed. The old fear had taken hold and held her in place. What should she do? She dug her phone out of her pants pocket. Her hand shook as she began to tap in Noah's number, but when she looked again out of the window, Jason was gone and all she got on the other end was Noah's voice mail.

"He was really outside?" Cara said, tugging off her damp coat and hanging it on the coatrack. She took off her boots and walked barefoot into Traci's living room.

"Yes."

"You're sure?"

"Yes! You don't think I know Jason when I see him?" she yelled.

"Okay, okay," Cara said softly. "I'm sorry." She went to the kitchen, got two glasses, and poured them each a glass of wine. She handed Traci her wine and they both sat down.

"Any idea how he found out where you live?"

Traci tucked her feet beneath her. She slowly shook her head. "Been wracking my brain for the past hour."

"You think Loretta would have told him?"

Traci's face tightened as she sipped and sipped her wine. Loretta Palmer was her mother and she never understood how Traci could have left a "good man" like Jason. He worked hard, took care of the home, had a

108

nice car and a fat bank account, and he didn't run around, she'd ranted when Traci told her that she was leaving him. It didn't seem to matter to Loretta that Jason abused her daughter. *"Sometimes a woman had to 'make concessions' to keep a good man,"* she'd said. *"If I had, maybe your no-good daddy would have stayed."* From that moment to this one Traci hadn't spoken to her mother other than on the requisite holidays.

"It's the only explanation," Traci finally said. "After he saw me that day by the pier, he probably called her. And knowing how charming Jason could be, and how tone-deaf my mother is, she probably gave my address to him, thinking she was doing some kind of good." She rolled her eyes in disgust.

Cara pushed out a breath. "Well, you can't stay locked up in the house."

"I know that," she snapped. She squeezed her eyes shut. "I'm sorry . . . again."

Cara held up her hand to dismiss the unnecessary apology.

"I'm not going to let him run me out of my house. Not again."

"Well, for the time being, you're staying with me. He's not out there now. Pack a bag, get your school stuff, and we'll go to my place."

■ ■ ■ ■

A little more than an hour later, Traci was settling into Cara's guest room. When Noah called her as usual for their late-night chat, she never mentioned what had happened or that she was at Cara's apartment and not her own. If he could have secrets, then so could she.

CHAPTER ELEVEN

Thanksgiving had arrived. Noah had convinced Traci that he was hosting Thanksgiving at his loft and she could invite whomever she wanted. Since the night of Jason's appearance on her street, the previous week, Traci had not returned, at least not alone, and she offered no explanation to Noah why he couldn't come over. Instead she stayed at his place and pretended that all was well with the world. Yet, every sound made her jump. She was constantly looking over her shoulder whenever she went out and her body stayed in a state of high alert. None of which was lost on Noah.

"You want to tell me what the hell is going on with you?" Noah finally asked after she'd nearly leaped out of her skin when he came up behind her to kiss her.

"Nothing. You surprised me, that's all." She continued chopping the tomatoes and cucumbers for the side salad. Everything else for the very elaborate meal, as Noah promised, had already been taken care of by him. The entire loft was filled with the aromas of a Thanksgiving feast.

He clasped her hand to stop her movements. She wouldn't look at him. "T, talk to me. What is it? You've been somebody else for days now." He paused and then slowly the real possibility dawned on him. "Has he bothered you again? Your ex."

Her nostrils flared. "No." That much was true.

"Then what is it, baby? Whatever it is, you can tell me."

She cranked her neck to the side and stared up at him. "Maybe I'll tell you when you finally tell me what's really going on with you, where you vanish to every Sunday, and why, if I ever dare to ask about it, you evade a real answer." She folded her arms defiantly and waited.

"Whatever you're thinking, that's not what it is."

"Humph." She snorted a laugh and turned away.

Noah blew out a frustrated breath and briefly shut his eyes. "Traci, look . . ."

The doorbell rang. The guests had arrived.

"We'll talk about this later." He tossed the hand towel on the counter and went to answer the door. The first to arrive was Anthony and his lady friend, Jessica, who was a dead ringer for Alicia Keys. Before they got settled, the bell rang again. This time it was Anthony's cousin Myra, and her latest significant other, Aaron Clark, a broker on Wall Street whom she'd met during her company's fund-raising gala. Traci had invited Cara and Phillip, but they'd committed to going to Phillip's family's house upstate.

"Get settled, everybody, and put in your drink orders," Noah cheerfully announced after he'd made the introductions. "Whatever you want, we got it."

"This is a fabulous place," Myra said, looking around the mammoth space, with its all-the-way-to-heaven ceilings and enormous windows, which looked out toward the Williamsburg Bridge and the Manhattan skyline. It was furnished straight from a page in *Architectural Digest*. After he'd opened his fourth CoffeeMate in lower Manhattan, he'd had a decorator come in and turn his echoing cavern into a warm and inviting living space with earth-toned furnishings, rugs strategically placed, small sculptures on tables and in nooks, and dazzling paintings on the walls. Traci always wondered how in the world he could afford something like this, and Myra sidled up to her to ask the same question.

"Girl, this place is . . . I don't have words," Myra said. "This has got to cost a pretty penny and I don't care what kind of deal he got," she whispered through her teeth.

Traci often thought the same thing, but kept her opinions to herself. At the moment, even if she did want to engage in speculation, she didn't have it in her today. She had more pressing issues weighing on her, like what in the hell was really going on with Mr. Perfect?

"What can I get you, ladies?" Noah asked while he put an arm around Traci.

"Wine is fine for me," Myra said.

"Me too," Traci murmured, and subtly slid from his hold. She walked, along with Myra, over to Jessica, who was looking at one of the paintings. The three women made small talk while Billie Holiday's "God Bless the Child" played in the background.

After a round of drinks and seafood appetizers, the couples made their way to the kitchen, where a meal fit for royalty was laid out from end to end on the long counter and the side tables that Noah had set up.

"Buffet style, folks. So help yourselves and dig in," Noah said. "Load up and then come on over to the dining area."

Once everyone was seated, they held hands and Noah blessed the food. Then it was Anthony who injected one of his family's traditions: Everyone had a chance to say what they were thankful for. Anthony was thankful for his health, good friends, and the success of his business. Jessica was thankful that she had a great family. Myra was thankful for her health. Aaron was simply thankful for his six-figure job and that the recession had receded. Then it was Traci's turn.

She ran her tongue across her lips. "I'm thankful . . . that we're all here today," she said solemnly.

Noah looked at her, but she wouldn't look back. He cleared his throat. "Well, I'm thankful that I didn't burn the turkey or the ham." Everyone around the table laughed. "But, seriously, I'm thankful for my friends old" — he eyed Anthony — "and new, and most of all . . . I'm thankful that Traci walked into the CoffeeMate, into my life, and made me a better man. I can't imagine my days without her."

Traci looked at him from beneath her lashes. Her eyes filled, but she sniffed back tears. That was as close as he'd ever come to declaring how he felt about her. But the pessimist, the wounded Traci, saw it as a ploy to sweet-talk her into forgetting about their standoff in the kitchen.

"Now let's eat!" Anthony declared.

For the next few moments the only sound other than the music was the clicking of silverware and moans and sighs of delight at the meal.

They were just about finished when Aaron lifted his fork and pointed it in the direction of Noah. "You said the CoffeeMate earlier."

Noah looked up from his plate. "Hmm, ummm."

"I thought I knew you, but I wasn't putting it together at first. You're *the* Noah Jefferson."

Everyone at the table turned their attention on Noah.

"What do you mean?" Traci asked.

Noah tried to wave it off. "It's nothing." He stared hard at Aaron, who clearly did not get the memo.

"This brother is the founder and CEO of one of the most successful coffeehouse chains in the Northeast, outside of Starbucks." He grinned as if he'd just hit Lotto.

Noah's jaw clenched.

Anthony lowered his head. "Shit," he muttered.

"CEO?" Traci was trying to process the information. "What is he talking about?"

"We'll talk about it later. Not important," Noah said. "Hey, refills, anyone?" He stood.

Anthony picked up on his cue. "Yeah." He held up his glass and nudged Jessica, who, in turn, asked for a refill as well.

Traci turned all her focus on her near-empty plate, but she wasn't eating. She suddenly pushed back from her seat, picked up her plate, walked into the kitchen, and confronted Noah.

"Are you going to tell me what he's talking about?"

"Traci . . . we'll talk. I'll explain everything. I promise. But not now."

"What else haven't you told me?" she pressed.

Noah pushed out a breath. His voice rose. "Not now."

Reflexes caused her to flinch.

He reached out to touch her and she drew away, turned, and walked out.

"Traci!"

She kept walking.

When she returned to the dining room, she announced that she wasn't feeling good and would have to cut the evening short. "I'm really sorry, everyone." She looked around the table and offered a tentative smile.

Noah returned as Traci was at the closet

to retrieve her coat. He came up to her and spoke in an urgent whisper. "Traci, don't do this. Whatever you're thinking, that's not what it is."

She snatched up her coat. "You have no idea what I'm thinking." She put on her coat and took her purse from the closet shelf. "You're no different from the rest." She pulled open the door and walked out.

Noah didn't bother with his coat and went out behind her.

"Traci, wait."

"Noah, go back to your guests and leave me alone." She hurried off and pushed through the building door and out into the street.

For several moments Noah stood in the frame of the doorway, then turned and went back inside.

When he returned, the festive mood was nowhere to be found.

"We're going to get going, too," Myra said. "Thanks for a wonderful dinner."

Noah's smile was forced. "Sure. Thanks for coming."

He walked Myra and Aaron to the door. "Thanks again."

He returned to the dining room and began collecting the empty plates. Anthony followed him into the kitchen, leaving Jessica in the dining room.

"I won't say I told you so . . ."

"Then don't," he snapped.

"What did she say before she left?"

Noah's jaw clenched. "That I was just like the rest."

"Ouch. Well . . . give her a minute to cool off, then call her. You need to just be up-front."

Noah didn't respond. He loaded the dish-washer.

Anthony clapped him on the shoulder. "It'll work out."

"Yeah," Noah grumbled. He didn't really think so.

CHAPTER TWELVE

Traci walked for about five minutes with no cab in sight. By this time it had started to snow lightly. What was she thinking by walking out like that? She was anxious about going back to her apartment, but she had no choice. Before Cara left to go upstate, Traci had told her that she would be staying at Noah's place. So much for that. She kept walking and realized that for the most part she was the only one on the street. This was the height of the Thanksgiving evening and everyone who had family or friends was gathered around a table or in front of televisions enjoying the company. She was alone. Her eyes burned. Her throat tightened. Her instincts told her from the beginning that it would be this way. It always started out good.

She had at least six more blocks to walk to her apartment and the snow was coming down harder and faster. She paused on the corner for a few minutes in the hopes of spotting a cab. No luck. She tried Uber and all the drivers were busy.

By the time she came up on her street, she was a cold, wet, crying mess. She quickened her pace, with her head bent against the swirl of cold and snow. She just wanted to get inside, get out of her wet clothes, sit in a hot tub, and forget about this day and Noah.

Traci looked up at the windows of her building. No lights were on. No one at home. She dug in her bag for her keys when she was grabbed by the arm and spun around. Her bag went flying. Her gasp caught in her throat.

"Where's your boyfriend?"

"Get off of me!" She tried to pull away, but his grip grew tighter.

"We need to talk."

"There's nothing to talk about."

"Us. That's what there is to talk about. I'm not done with us. I don't care what the court said."

Her heart raced. Her eyes darted around, looking for an out.

Jason held her arm and reached down, pulling her with him to pick up her keys. "Open the door."

Once he was inside, there was no telling

what he would do. He pushed her toward the door, and then the next thing she knew, the grip on her arm was released. She spun around and Noah had Jason on the ground.

"I told you once before to stay away from her!" He reached down and grabbed Jason by his coat collar and raised his fist to hit him again.

"Noah. Don't! It's not worth it."

Noah flashed her a dangerous look from over his shoulder before shoving Jason back to the ground. "Stay down," he ordered, and pointed a warning finger. "Go on upstairs," he told Traci. "Leave this door unlocked." His tone left no room for argument.

She fumbled with her keys, hesitated, then opened the door and went inside. When she reached her apartment, she was shaking like a leaf. She sat on a kitchen chair, afraid to move as the scary scene replayed in her head. If Noah hadn't shown up when he did . . . She didn't want to even think about it. A shiver ran through her. She wasn't sure how long she'd sat there, but the knock on her door jerked her to the present.

On wobbly legs she went to the door and peeked through the peephole. Her heartbeat slowed. She unlocked the door. For a moment Noah simply stood there, staring at her. "Are you all right?" he asked from between clenched teeth.

She nodded and swiped away the tears of fear and relief.

Noah pushed out a breath and gathered her in his arms. "I swear if anything would have happened to you . . ." His jaw clenched and he squeezed his eyes shut.

She wept openly, shaking and sobbing in his arms. Noah managed to usher her inside and get her out of her wet coat. He sat opposite her on the side chair, while she curled in the love seat.

"Thank you," she whispered.

"There's nothing to thank me for. I should have never let you leave by yourself in the first place." He paused. "Did he hurt you? Did he threaten you?"

"Not physically. He insisted that we needed to talk, and that our relationship wasn't over, no matter what the court said." She sniffed and hugged herself tighter.

"He won't be bothering you again."

Her troubled gaze jumped to look at him. "What did you do?"

"Don't worry about it. He won't be back. I promise you that."

She didn't have it in her to debate the point. For now all she could muster was to take him at his word. After what just happened, her reason for leaving Noah's loft in the first place seemed insignificant. Especially in light of the fact that had she told him that she'd spotted Jason outside of her apartment, and that she'd been staying at Cara's simply to "pay him back" for his missing Sundays, none of this would have happened. Warning bells rang in her head. She was doing it again, blaming herself. If she was ever going to move on with her life, in any real way, she knew that she was going to have to get beyond that. Old habits are the hardest to break.

Traci sat up a bit in her seat. "I'm sorry about running out like that, and I'm sorry for not giving you the space that you asked for. But I don't want to be lied to . . . even lies by omission. I need to be with someone that I can trust. And it's really hard for me to make that leap. I don't want to always hold my breath waiting for the other shoe to drop. I'm tired of being afraid of my own voice, my own wants, and living on the edge with the belief that if I say anything, ask for anything, want anything . . . I'm going to pay some kind of price." Tears welled in her eyes again. "I just can't."

Noah rested his arms on his thighs and linked his long fingers together. He lowered his head for a moment, then looked across at her. "Look, I don't know where our relationship will eventually go, Traci. All I know right now is that I want to give it a real shot and that means being up front about some things."

Traci wiped her eyes.

"Aaron was right about me. I'm not the manager. I *own* the CoffeeMate franchise. There are twenty locations, so far, along the Northeast. No one knows. Well, no one that I work with, except Anthony, of course. When I'm away on Sundays, I'm usually at one of the locations or at the new enterprise that I've been working on in Philadelphia."

"But why would you keep it a secret? I don't understand."

"Like you said once, we both have baggage. My experience was a bit different from yours. Living from home to home, I never felt secure. It was like whatever I had could be taken away from me any minute, that people only wanted me for the money they could make off of me in foster care. It created a world of distrust in me about everyone, until I went to live with the Harpers." He breathed deeply. "I started to feel that someone believed in me and didn't want me for what I could line their pockets with, and then when they died, it threw me for a major loop. I turned away from everyone

125

except Anthony. I dug into my work, determined to make my own world. And then I met Anita. She made me think that I could trust her, that she was in my corner." He snorted a laugh and looked away. "But she was only in it for what she thought she could get. She was looking down the length of the rainbow." He shook his head in disgust. "After that, I turned off and shut down." He looked into her eyes. "Until I met you. So yeah, I'm a little jaded and cautious, too."

Traci blinked slowly. "I should have told you that I saw Jason standing out in front of my building a few weeks ago. It was a Sunday. I knew you weren't around, so I called Cara. I wanted to prove something, I guess. I figured if you were keeping secrets, then so could I. I've been staying with her ever since."

"Wow . . . we're a real pair."

Traci flashed a weak smile.

"So how about from here on we stay honest with each other whether it stings or not?"

She searched his face. "Okay."

He pushed up from his seat, crossed the room, and stood above her. "We're going to be spending every night together, either here or at my place." He grinned. "So where do you want to stay tonight?"

Her cheeks heated. "Wherever you are," she said softly, and meant it.

"I'm going to go home and pick up some things to bring back here. Why don't you get some of your things together and we can take them to my place." He reached for her hands and pulled her slowly to her feet. "Is that cool with you?"

She looked into his eyes. "Yeah, I think it is."

He slid his arm around her waist and pulled her close. "You need some help in the bedroom . . . I mean getting your things?"

"I would love some help," she said by way of invitation.

Noah's eyes darkened. A slow smile moved across his mouth. "At your service."

Noah shoved Traci's bag onto the backseat of his Navigator. He checked the street. He didn't want any surprises. He got in. "Buckle up." He shifted the truck into gear.

"What did you mean by your enterprise in Philadelphia?" she asked. The comment had just registered with her.

"I was wondering when you were going to ask." He went on to tell her that it was the project he'd talked with her about. It was finally complete and he was hoping for a

Christmas opening.

"Noah! Oh, my goodness. That's fantastic. What!" she screeched in delight, and pounded her feet on the car floor.

Noah laughed. "Yep. Done. Just need to get it staffed and have the furniture delivered."

"Wow," she said in admiration.

"We'll go see it this weekend."

She snapped her head to look at him.

"I want to know what you think."

She swallowed. "Okay."

"And, Traci, don't ever be afraid to ask me anything. I may not always say what you need to hear, when you want to hear it, but I won't ever make you feel like you can't talk to me . . . about anything. I promise you that." He reached across for her hand and brought it to his lips. He placed a soft kiss there. "Promise."

They arrived at Noah's loft and he emptied out one of his drawers for her things and hung the rest in the closet. "If you need more room, there's plenty," he said, once her clothes were put away.

"Let's stay here tonight."

"You won't get an argument from me," he said, coming up behind her. He kissed the back of her neck. "I don't intend on letting you out of my sight."

Her body tightened.

Noah turned her around to face him. "What is it?"

She couldn't look at him. "Jason used to say that."

"I'm not him. You're not Anita. It's not that I don't want to let you out of my sight because I want to control you. It's because I'm not myself when I'm not with you." His gaze moved slowly over her uncertain expression. "Can you get with that?"

She pressed her lips together. He was asking her to trust him, to put her faith in him and come along for the ride, even if he was uncertain about their destination. "Can't have you going around not being yourself," she finally said.

Noah's eyes crinkled at the corners. "Why don't we seal this deal of ours," he said, and backed her toward the bed.

"How do you propose we do that?" she taunted.

"Hmm, let's discuss it," he said, speaking against her neck. She moaned softly. He nibbled the lobe of her ear, while his thumbs brushed the underside of her breasts. "I figure if we really take our time . . ." His hands skimmed her waist, then cupped her behind in his palms. "If we really work it," he said, tugging her against the bulge of his erection, "we'll come up with a satisfactory resolution for both of us." He kissed her.

Her neck arched to give him access to the tiny pulse that beat there. Her heart jumped and banged when his tongue tasted her there. A little lick, a little nibble, just enough to make her whimper for more.

Noah walked her to the bed. She stopped when the back of her knees hit the mattress.

"Take off your dress."

Traci blinked several times before reaching for the side sash that held her wrap dress in place.

"Take your time," he coaxed, his gaze hooded by his long lashes.

Traci's eyes flashed. Her mouth flickered with a smile. Slowly she unknotted the sash and let it fall. Inch by inch she opened the dress to expose more and more bare skin.

Noah hummed deep in his throat.

She shrugged and let the dress fall from her shoulders and onto the floor. Noah's nostrils flared. He stepped closer, but only touched her with one finger. He traced the outline of her bra, the way it curved like half-moons. He let his finger trail ever so slowly down her center, until he reached the band of her panties. He traced that as well, from left to right, then the outline of

130

the flimsy garment between her legs. Her inner thighs trembled. Her breathing elevated.

"You can take the rest off now."

She reached behind her and unhooked her bra, peeled it off, and tossed it aside.

Noah's gaze roamed hungrily across her. "You're not done."

Traci tucked her bottom lip between her teeth. She hooked her fingers around the band of her panties and shimmied them down over her hips, then stepped out of them.

"Damn," he groaned as he looked at her from head to toe. "You're so beautiful. Perfect." He reached out and touched her breast, so tenderly as if it were a found treasure. His thumb brushed back and forth across her nipple, continuing until it stood hard and erect. He repeated himself on the other side, then drew a puckered nipple into his mouth.

Traci moaned and gripped the back of his head, thrusting her needy breast into his mouth. He took his time, moving from one side to the other, all the while he was cupping her sex in his palm, and gently patted it, awakened it, stirred it, prepared it for him. His palm was slick with her desire.

Noah snaked down her body, marking his

territory with hot kisses along her torso, until he reached her center. He was on his knees for her. He clasped her hips and suckled her.

Traci cried out and gripped his shoulders.

Noah teased and nibbled, licked and sucked, until Traci's nails bit into his back and her toes gripped the carpet. Her body jerked in intervals as the charge of release pulsed through her. When she was finally spent and limp against him, Noah picked her up and carried her to the bed.

He reached into the nightstand and quickly rolled on a condom. Traci looked at him through partially opened eyes.

"That was . . . amazing," she managed.

"You up to a little more?"

She nodded with a smile.

Noah moved toward her, braced himself above her for a moment. He parted her thighs wider with a sweep of his knee, when suddenly Traci pressed her hands against his chest to stop him. His brows drew together. "What's wrong?"

"Lay down. On your back."

He hesitated for a moment. In all the times that they'd made love, Traci had rarely, if ever, taken the initiative. He was more than willing to comply.

Traci straddled him, rose up a bit on her

knees to position him. Slowly she lowered her hips and took him in. The air rushed out of her lungs. She took him all the way in and then froze, allowing the fullness of him to settle. Then slowly and deliberately she rode him. Her body was no longer hers. It moved and undulated of its own free will. She was only the conduit for pleasure.

She felt free, utterly free, for the first time in her sexual life. With each thrust of her hips against his hard cock, she released another reservation that had emotionally held her in place. She had a voice. She wasn't a victim. She was worthy to be loved. Her mind and her body were her own. No one would take that away from her ever again.

Noah watched as Traci's body rocked and banged against him, the way her breasts bounced and swayed with each movement. He watched her claim her power and it was a major turn-on for him. This was what he wanted. He wanted her to demand what was hers, to take what she wanted because she deserved it.

Her back arched. Her hands pressed down into his thighs as she hurtled toward the finish line and Noah was determined to take her there and beyond. He gripped her hips so that she could barely move except to take his hard thrusts.

The cry of his name stretched out across the room. She bucked wildly, needing to be free. Noah waited until the perfect moment and loosened his hold. Traci cried out and rocked her hips feverishly against him until she brought them both to blinding satisfaction.

"That was . . ." Noah couldn't find the words.

"I know."

"I hate to say this, but I'm starved."

Traci giggled. "Me too."

"Plenty of leftovers."

"Last one to the kitchen cleans up," she declared, pushed him aside, and darted out to the kitchen.

They wound up making sandwiches and brought them back to bed.

"I need to ask you something," Traci said once they were finished.

They lay spooned in the darkness.

"Anything."

"What did you say to Jason?"

"I told him that I come from the street. I didn't believe in calling the po-po when I could handle it better. And that he'd be better off with the police than with me if I ever saw him again or found out that he was anywhere near you — even by accident."

Traci smiled into the darkness.

CHAPTER THIRTEEN

"Oh, my God, T. What is on Jason's mind?"

Traci shook her head as the two friends walked side-by-side with their Christmas shopping bags through the slushy Brooklyn streets.

"Girl, I don't want to think about it."

"Seems like Noah got a helluva lot going for him. Not only is he fine, but he's crazy rich and can whip some ass when necessary."

Traci bit back a snicker.

"And clearly he cares a lot about you, Traci. He gave you the key to his apartment, unpacked his baggage, and accepted yours. Now that everything is out in the open, give it a real chance. I'd say he was a keeper."

"We're going to see his place in Philly on Sunday."

"Nothing like living your dream," Cara said.

"Yeah," Traci wistfully agreed.

It was snowing lightly on the Sunday morning when Noah, Traci, and Anthony headed out to Philadelphia. The roads were pretty clear and they made good time. Traci didn't know quite what to expect when they arrived, but her imagination never conjured up the reality of what she saw.

The club was, as Noah said, a reconverted three-story brownstone. The furnishings were being delivered. Noah gave Traci the full tour and she listened to his enthusiasm as he outlined his vision. Traci saw Noah in a new light. Yes, she knew and accepted that he was a wealthy and successful businessman, but now she witnessed up close and for real the man behind the growing empire. He was focused and no-nonsense. He knew what he wanted and got it. Yet, his interactions with the deliverymen and the vendors were as professional as if he had been dealing with CEOs from Fortune 500 companies. That said a lot about the kind of man Noah was. He treated everyone with an equal amount of respect and he got it back in return. He asked for her input about staging the space and what she, as a patron, would like to see. It meant a lot to her that he took what she suggested, weighed it, and actually implemented some of her suggestions. Jason would have never done that. Ever. Noah was a man of many talents and he loved her.

"Good that you fessed up, man," Anthony was saying. He put his feet up on the ottoman and took a long swallow of beer. "And next time you plan on rolling up on somebody, you need to tell a brotha. Thought I was your ride or die."

Noah chuckled. "Yeah, man, for sure. Had no idea that fool was gonna be there." Just thinking about it ticked him off all over again. "All I had on my mind when I went tearing out of here was getting things straight with Traci."

"I think she's good for you, man."

Noah's brow rose in question.

"Yeah, I do. Since you've been with her, you actually seem happy and not tunnel-visioned on work. You're easy again — almost human," he added with a chuckle.

"Very funny."

"Anyway, you sitting in tonight, right?"

"Yeah, last set."

"Cool." He put down his empty beer bottle and stood. "Okay, I'm out. I need to get over to the club. I'll see you later."

"Yeah." Noah got up from the couch and

walked Anthony to the door. "Around nine."

Anthony put on his coat. "Later, man." They shared a handshake and a one-armed hug and then Anthony left.

" 'Almost human,' " Noah murmured while he locked the doors. Maybe that was the reason why he was feeling the way he was feeling about Traci Long.

"Now I see why you can play that sax the way you do," Traci said as she snuggled against Noah later that night in bed.

"Why is that?" he said with laughter in his voice.

"Cause you definitely know how to manipulate that sweet tongue and those luscious lips," she said boldly and confidently.

"Hmm, is that right?" He rolled her onto her back and stared into her eyes. "I was thinking I needed a little more practice."

"Really? Where are you planning to practice?"

He ran a finger from beneath her chin down to her belly. "All over you for starters."

"Be. My. Guest."

"I think I will." And he practiced his craft for the next hour.

"Why don't you just move in here?" Noah

said as he held her close. He kissed the back of her neck.

Traci stiffened. "Move in? You mean give up my apartment completely?"

"Yeah."

He pressed his palm flat against her stomach and cupped her breasts with his other hand.

"Noah . . . that's a big step."

"I know."

She tried to look at him from over her shoulder. "Can I think about it?"

He paused. "Yeah, sure," he finally said. He loosened his hold.

"Noah . . . why do you want me to move in with you?"

He pushed out a breath. "Look at me."

Traci turned around.

"I'm falling in love with you, Traci."

The air stuck in her throat. "Love me?" she whispered.

"Yeah." He brushed the hair away from her face. "That's why I want you with me. I've been fighting it, figuring it was just great sex — although the sex is off the charts — but that's not it. I love you and I want you to know that you mean more to me than someone to spend the night with."

"Not because you feel you have to protect me?"

"That's what a man does for the woman he loves."

Her throat tightened. "Noah . . ."

"Think about it." He kissed her on her forehead. "In the meantime let's get some sleep." He kissed her on the lips this time, draped his arm around her waist, and closed his eyes.

Sleep for Traci was elusive. Throughout the night Noah's declaration played in her head. *Love.* All the old insecurities came flooding to the surface. Jason said he'd loved her, too. All that he did was because he loved her, he'd said. But love hurt. For her, love always hurt. Her mother's love hurt and her ex-husband's love hurt. She squeezed her eyes tight and pressed her fist to her mouth to muffle any sound. *"Give him a chance,"* Cara's words whispered in her ears. Even with all that she now knew about Noah, the man, she didn't know if she could.

There was only one more week before the school semester ended and the holiday season was in full force. Traci still hadn't given Noah an answer to his proposal of moving in with him. More important she had yet to say the three magic words herself. Since that night he hadn't brought it up

141

again or tried to pressure her in any way. She was grateful for that, but it still kept her on edge. She feared that at any moment the elephant in the room would make its presence known and she would finally have to respond. Cara told her that she deserved to be truly loved; and if she didn't give herself a chance to experience it in full, she would always regret it.

Traci dismissed her class, congratulated them on a successful semester, and wished them a wonderful holiday. She packed up her things, and her thoughts quickly shifted to the fact that she had yet to select a Christmas gift for Noah. What did you give a man who apparently had everything: talent, multiple businesses, clothes, a car, and a fabulous apartment? She had barely two weeks before Christmas to come up with something. She checked the time on her cell phone. The dean had asked that she stop by his office after she dismissed her class. She hoped that he made it quick, since she had shopping to do.

She walked down the corridor and took the stairs to the ground floor, where the administration offices were located.

"Hi, Stephanie," she said to the office clerk. "Last day at last," she said with a smile. "Plans for the holiday?"

"I'm heading out of town to visit my folks in North Carolina. You?"

"I'll be here, but the time off will definitely do me good. Is the dean in? He wanted to see me."

"Yes, go right in. He's expecting you."

"Thanks. Happy holidays."

"You too."

Traci walked toward the dean's office and waved to several of the office staff members on her way. She knocked on the partially opened door.

"Come in."

"Hello, Dean Hanson."

He pushed up from his seat and stood. "Traci, please have a seat."

Dean Hanson was always cheerful and outgoing, lighting up every space that he entered, but today there was a reserve about him that was a bit out of character.

Traci hesitantly sat down.

Dean Hanson resumed his seat. He folded his hands on top of the desk and looked directly at her. "I won't beat around the bush. You have definitely been an asset to the college. I've gotten great feedback from some of your students."

Her heart began to pound and the room suddenly grew overly warm.

He cleared his throat. "We've reviewed our

funding for the spring semester and we had to make some hard decisions. Unfortunately, we have to cut the theater arts program."

What he was saying wouldn't register. "Sir?"

"I won't be able to renew your contract for the spring, Traci. I'm very sorry. I know this comes at an awful time with the holidays and all, but it can't be helped. We've had to let several of the adjuncts go." He paused. "I'm sorry." He opened a folder on his desk and pulled out a sheet of paper. "I've written you a recommendation letter, and with your skills I know that you will find something to showcase your talents." He handed over the paper.

Traci stared at it, but the words simply danced on the page. She lifted her chin and forced a smile. "I appreciate that, Dean Hanson."

He stood. The meeting and her career had come to an abrupt end.

Traci managed to shake his hand, gather her things, and leave without falling apart. As she walked through the halls to the front door, the reality that it would be for the last time hit her, along with the cold blast of air when she stepped outside. What was she going to do? She did have money in her savings and her salary covered her living expenses, with little extra to spare. But how long could she live on her savings?

She started walking to the train station, oblivious to the sights and sounds of the approaching holiday. Her train ride was a blur and she nearly missed her stop. When she got off the L train, she walked aimlessly, knowing that she wasn't ready to face being alone in her apartment. She thought about going to the CoffeeMate and seeing Noah, but he would know immediately that something was wrong and she wasn't ready to face him yet, either.

When she looked up, she was in front of the Chadwick Theater. She stood on the opposite side of the street and was stunned to see men working on the building, hauling out worn chairs, tattered curtains, and old wood. She didn't know whether she was happy that it was apparently going to open once more, or saddened by the notion that yet again someone was living his or her dream and hers continued to slip further away.

Traci sat in her chair by the window and looked out on the hustle and bustle below. She was going to have to find another job and quickly. Maybe she had enough to get her through January, but beyond that . . .

Her cell phone buzzed and shimmied across the table. She got up to get it, saw that it was Noah calling, and let the call go to voice mail. She put the phone back down, only for it to ring again. This time it was Cara.

"Hey," Traci said.

"Gee, don't sound so enthused. What's up? You should be thrilled with the last day of classes."

"My last day, period."

"What does that mean?"

Traci went on to tell Cara about her meeting and the outcome.

"Oh, T, I am so sorry. I don't even know what to say, girl. You want me to come over later?"

"No. I just want to be by myself for a bit. I have to think some things through."

"Did you tell Noah?"

"No. I don't want him feeling sorry for me and trying to come to my rescue. I need to figure this out on my own."

"T, I know your financial situation. I know you love teaching, but the pay ain't great. Maybe you should really consider Noah's offer to move in," she hedged.

"For all the wrong reasons, Cara. I don't want my decision to be made because I'm desperate."

"When are you going to be honest with yourself?"

"What do you mean?"

"The bottom line is you are still scared silly. You are terrified of getting close to anyone because of the asshole ex of yours. Not to mention mama dearest. But, T, Noah's not like that and you know it. He loves you. He's shown it. He's proven it. You simply don't want to accept it. But if you don't, you're going to lose a good man. And good men, men that are willing to stand up and be real men, are hard to come by. Don't let the past stop your future."

"I am scared, Cara." Tears slowly slid over her lashes. "When I'm with him, the joy I feel is inexplicable. I want it. I want it to last . . . but every time I think, 'I can do this . . . ,' the past flashes in front of me." She sniffed and wiped her eyes. "I do love him," she whispered. "But I'm so afraid that once I admit that to him, I'm vulnerable all over again."

"Sweetie, love is being vulnerable. Putting your heart and your spirit in the hands of someone else is all about vulnerability, about trust. That's part of loving someone, trusting that they will treat your heart and your spirit with tenderness. You have a real chance to experience that with Noah, if you let him in." She waited, and when she didn't get a response, she said, "Well, that's my lecture for today. I know you'll make the right decision. Call me if you need me."

"Thanks. I will." She disconnected the call and put the phone down on the table. *I love him.* She'd actually said the words out loud, and the admission was like a boulder being lifted off her chest. A glimmer of hope, something just out of reach, danced in front of her. Now she had to decide if she was going to grab it or not.

CHAPTER FOURTEEN

"You're really quiet tonight. I thought you would be overjoyed that school is over. Now you can work on your play during the break," Noah said as he put his feet up on the footstool and took a swallow of beer. "Everything okay?"

Traci drew in a breath and slowly released it. "I . . . got let go today."

Noah sprang upright in his chair. "What?" The storm clouds brewed in his eyes. He was ready to take on whoever had done this.

She nodded. "Yep. Budget cuts, I was told. So I don't have a job after today."

He mumbled some expletives, then looked at her. "What do you want to do?"

Her brows rose and fell. "I don't know yet. That's what I've been thinking about all day."

"Why didn't you tell me first thing?"

"It wouldn't change anything."

"Hey, look, I've lost more jobs than I've

had. Maybe it's one of those crazy blessings in disguise. The last time I lost a job, I promised myself it would never happen again. I would be my own boss. Now may be the time for you to chart your own course, you know."

"I suppose."

"Don't suppose. Do it. What do you want to do more than anything? Your dream?"

A shadow of a smile lifted her mouth. "Stage my play."

"Now you have the time to do that. To concentrate on getting it finished and producing it."

"You make it sound so easy. I still have to live," she said half jokingly.

"That's what you have me for."

She stared at him.

"We're a team, baby. Me and you. Whatever you need, I got you."

Her throat tightened. She blinked back tears.

"My offer is still open. Move in with me. Then your apartment and all the expenses that go with it will be off the table."

"I didn't tell you it so that you can feel sorry for me. I'm not a charity case."

"Okay. I'm sure I can find a way for you to pay for your keep." He grinned mischievously.

She playfully rolled her eyes and twisted her lips in contemplation. "Okay," she finally said. "But I'm going to have to break my lease, and that's going to be an issue and —"

"I'll take care of it," he said without hesitation.

Noah got up and crossed over to where she was and sat on the arm of the chair. He played with the curls of her hair.

"So you know I'm all about business," he began.

She glanced up at him with a wary eye.

"And in business we always seal the deal."

She bit back a grin. "Oh, really."

"Yeah, so I was thinking, you know, we need to seal this deal of ours."

"And how do you propose we do that?"

He took her hand and pulled her to her feet. "Come with me and let me show you."

As promised, Noah took care of everything, from arranging for movers to pack up her stuff and bring it to his place, to paying off the five-month balance of her lease. He didn't question; he didn't hesitate; he didn't blink. He just did what needed to be done, and all he kept telling her whenever she would begin to protest against his generosity was "We're a team. I got you."

151

Day by day she began to believe. She allowed herself to be healed by his love for her. She looked forward to each morning and every night because she knew without a doubt that Noah would be there. She'd never before felt so complete and secure. This was how love was meant to be, what she'd been waiting for. It was hers. What could she ever hope to give him in return?

On Christmas Eve morning Noah and Traci finally decided to get a tree before they were all gone.

"I haven't had a tree since before college," Noah said as he hauled the tree into the loft.

"I can't remember the last time I had a tree." She shut the door behind them.

Noah turned to her. "We're starting a new tradition. Me and you." He leaned down and kissed her lightly on the lips. "Now, where should we put it?"

"Right in front of the window."

"You got it."

They spent the rest of the afternoon decorating, talking, laughing, and listening to music. Then they began preparing their spread for Christmas dinner. It would just be the two of them, but because it was their first Christmas together, they were going all out. They had everything from fresh collard greens, string beans, sweet potatoes, rice and beans, honey ham, to turkey and home-made stuffing.

Noah was a master in the kitchen and now she found out he could also bake. He prepared a cherry cheesecake for their dessert because she'd once told him that it was one of her favorites.

By evening the loft was glimmering with Christmas tree lights, accompanied by the scent of evergreen and the tantalizing aroma of the meal to come.

"I think after all of our hard work we deserve a hot bath and a drink."

"I totally agree," Traci said, walking up to Noah and wrapping her arms around his waist. She looked up into his eyes and saw the love raining down on her. "Thank you," she whispered.

"For what, baby?"

"For everything. For being you, for letting me be me, and for showing me what love really is." Her heart pounded. She caressed his cheek. "I don't know what I could ever do in return." She paused. "I love you, Noah. I love you."

For a brief instant he shut his eyes and then looked down at her and cupped her face in his hands. "You've just given me the greatest gift — your heart. And I promise you that I will cherish and protect it, and you, for as long as you'll have me. You'll never regret loving me, Traci. I'm going to make sure of that."

He covered her mouth with a searing kiss that stole her breath and unleashed her heart. She wanted to scream from the mountaintops, run through the snow-covered streets, and shout it out to the world. Her soul burst free and she gave to him, with every ounce of her being, the magnitude of her joy.

They made love all through the night, slow and easy, hard and quick, then back again. Traci couldn't tell him enough times of her love for him, so she tried to show him with each kiss, caress, roll of her hips, and whispers of his name. It was nearly 3 a.m., by the time they collapsed into an exhausted but satisfied sleep.

Around six o'clock Traci's eyes fluttered open. She peeked over her shoulder. Noah was sound asleep. Gently she eased herself out of his hold and tiptoed out of the bedroom. She wanted to get his present before he woke up.

She eased open the hall closet, pushed aside the coats and one of her boxes that hid her present, and pulled out the large brown-paper wrapped gift. She was so excited to see his expression that she couldn't wait until he woke up. Holding it in front of her naked body, she hurried back to the bedroom and stood on the side of the bed.

"Noah . . . Noah."

"Hmmm," he mumbled, but didn't open his eyes.

"Noah, wake up."

He blinked several times before he came fully awake and could focus on what was in front of him. He rubbed his eyes. "What time is it?"

"Six-thirty."

"Merry Christmas," she said with a big grin. She pushed the gift forward.

Noah sat up in bed. His eyes lit up like a little kid when he realized what was going on. "What is it?"

"Open it, open it."

He untied the string and then tore the paper away. His eyes widened. "Traci." He looked at her, then back at the Basquiat print. "This is . . . baby . . ."

"You like it?" She grinned with happiness.

"Like it! Are you kidding? This is a collector's piece. How in the world did you manage this?"

"I have my ways, too." Since she didn't

have the expense of her apartment, she'd used a chunk of her savings to purchase the artwork. But Noah would never have to know that. It was a major expense, but he was worth every dime.

His eyes roamed across her nude body, then back at the painting. "I don't know which is more beautiful — you or the painting," he teased.

Traci picked up a pillow and playfully tossed it at him. He grabbed it in midair and flung it aside. He took the print off his lap and gently placed it on the floor; then he reached up and unceremoniously pulled her down on top of him, much to her delight.

"Knowing that you love me was my gift." He cupped her cheek. "The print makes it even sweeter because I know you did it from the heart. That means more than you'll ever know." He swatted her behind. "Come on, you need clothes for my present. Get dressed."

"Can't you at least tell me where we're going?"

"Hmm, nope," he teased, and turned the corner when the light changed. "Just relax. We'll be there in a minute."

"Be where?" she innocently pressed.

Noah laughed. "Ahh, you think you're slick. I'm not giving up the intel."

Traci folded her arms and huffed, feigning annoyance. She glanced out of the passenger window and her head jerked back when she realized where they were.

Noah pulled the Navigator to a stop and cut the engine. "Come on."

They got out and Noah took her hand. They crossed the street to stand in front of the Chadwick Theater.

"Noah, what is going on?"

He reached into his inside coat pocket and pulled out an envelope and handed it to her.

"What is this?"

"Open it."

She unsealed the envelope and unfolded the sheaf of documents. It was the deed to the Chadwick Theater and her name was listed as the owner, free and clear. She shook her head to clear it and read the first page again.

Her hands shook. She looked at Noah, who was grinning with anticipation.

"Noah?" Her heart was beating so fast she could barely breathe. "Is this . . . you did this?"

"It's yours, your very own theater. It's not Broadway, but it's a start."

She didn't even try to hold back, but

broke down in body-shaking tears. Noah gathered her in his arms and held her tight. "I hope those are happy tears."

Traci sniffed hard. "I . . . I don't even have words. Noah, oh, my God."

"Wanna see inside?"

"Yes, yes!"

He took a set of keys out of his pocket and held them up. "You open up your theater," he said softly.

Traci took the keys with shaky fingers. After several tries she was finally able to unlock the door.

Everything smelled brand-new, from the paint to the wood. Noah turned on the light to the lobby. It was small and cozy, with a glassed ticket booth. On either side of the lobby were restrooms, and behind the thick wooden doors was the theater. Traci was beside herself.

She placed her hand on the knob and looked behind her at Noah, who gave her a smile and a nod of encouragement. She tugged in a breath and pulled the doors open. There it was, her dream spread out in front of her. The one-hundred-seat theater had been totally refurbished from the red velvet seating to the stage lighting and control booth. The curtain was already open to showcase the stage.

Traci gingerly walked down the steps, past the seats and to the stage. She walked across the front, then up the side stairs and stood in the center of the stage. She looked out at the chairs that would one day be filled with theatergoers who'd come to see her work. This is what she'd dreamed of, and Noah had made her dream come true, and not because he wanted something in return, but because he loved her. Plain and simple.

She stretched out her hand. Noah descended the steps, then came up to join her on stage.

"Happy, baby?"

"Happy doesn't explain how I feel," she said, looking into his eyes. "I love you, Noah Jefferson."

"Love you back. You can make this be what you want. It's yours, no strings attached. The taxes are paid for up to a year. I figured that would give you enough time to do your thing and get it off the ground."

She was giddy with excitement. So many thoughts and ideas were running through her head at once. All she could do was nod. This man of hers was amazing.

Suddenly she whooped with joy and literally jumped up in Noah's arms. "How can I ever thank you for all this?" she shouted, her voice clear and rising to the rafters.

"You already have."

"How, how could I ever?"

"You gave me the gift of your love, baby. That's all a man like me needs."

She angled her head and kissed him slow, deep, and sweet — sealing their new deal.

"Well, I hate to break this up," he said against her mouth, and slowly set her on her feet, "but let's say we go home and celebrate?"

"Hmmm, I like the sound of that."

CHAPTER FIFTEEN

Noah had postponed the Christmas opening of the club until New Year's so that it wouldn't overshadow her excitement. It was just one more thing to love about him.

"Girl, I can't say 'I told you so' enough times," Cara said as they shopped for their New Year's outfits. "Damn, who buys a woman a whole darn theater?" She laughed, but with amazement.

"I know. I'm on cloud nine. Things are finally coming together. I feel good inside and out every day. That man brings me joy, Cara. You know what I mean?"

Traci was so happy she felt as if most days she was floating on air. While Noah was busy putting the final touches on the club and working on publicity, she was finally writing, really writing. The play had finally come to life for her because she'd discovered what it was missing — heart.

"So what are your plans for the theater?"

Cara picked up a black dress and held it in front of her.

"I'll be finished writing and revising by the end of January. Then I want to start with table reads. I'm going to use students from the college first and then put out a casting call. I've also been thinking that on the theater downtime, I could teach classes there for the community and open it up for use by other local playwrights. In between writing and revising the play, I've been working on my game plan. Watching Noah in action as he's built his business, and now expanding for the club, has been the kind of lesson that you can't get in a classroom. And he's all for it. He offers suggestions, but never tries to impose his ideas."

"Traci, I love it! It's what you've always wanted."

Traci grinned. "Yes, it is," she said softly. "Now help me find something to wear."

Noah and Anthony had left to go to Philly early in the day to prepare and make any last-minute adjustments before they opened for dinner at seven. Anthony was supplying the music and had arranged for the cooks and bartenders. Working with Noah on his project was priming him for expansion as well.

Traci drove in with Cara and Phillip. When they arrived at six-thirty, there was already a line outside waiting to get in.

"Wow, if this is a reservation-only event, imagine the kind of crowd the club will get when it's open to the public," Phillip commented.

Noah had advised Traci to come to the side entrance when they arrived to bypass the line. The trio walked around to the side of the building and down three steps. Phillip knocked. Moments later the door was opened by a young man dressed in black shirt and slacks.

"Ms. Long?" He looked from Cara to Traci.

"That's me," Traci piped up.

"Right this way." He stepped aside to let them in. "Mr. Jefferson has a booth reserved for you in the lounge area and your dinner table is ready when you are."

They stepped inside and the electricity in the air was palpable. As early as the evening was, everything glittered, from the guests, who had stepped out in style, to the décor.

"Is Mr. Jefferson available?" Traci asked as they were being escorted to the lounge on the second floor.

"I'll let him know that you're here."

"Thank you."

They got settled and were immediately served with a bottle of champagne.

"Wow. I'm impressed," Cara said.

"That's how he does things," Traci said, "in a big way and with style," she added with a note of pride.

"Listen to you," Cara teased, and nudged her friend.

Traci grinned. "Yes, who would have thought it?"

"Hey, baby!" Noah came up behind her and kissed her behind her ear. She turned and grinned up at him and took his hand, which he'd placed on her bare shoulder. "Welcome, welcome," he greeted the trio. "For you guys everything is on the house, so no worries. Okay?"

"Noah, everything is amazing," Cara said. "Congratulations."

"You have a real winner here," Phillip added.

"Thank you. I'd love to stay and hang out, but duty calls. Anything you need, just ask." He leaned down and kissed Traci again. "You look incredible," he whispered. "See you later."

In no time the tables were filled, drinks flowed, food was served, and the band was pumping. The singer Dawne was the main act for the night and the crowd was in musical love with her. Opening night was an absolute success. And as the clock drew closer to midnight, the excitement rippled throughout the three levels.

At one minute to midnight Noah finally appeared and swept Traci away from her friends. The countdown began. Noah and Traci stood in the middle of the dance floor, with controlled chaos swirling around them.

Traci was giggling like a schoolgirl. "I'm so proud of you!" she shouted.

He held her hands against his chest. "I wanted to do this at Christmas," he said into her ear. "But I wanted this gift of love to have its own moment."

"Do what? What gift?"

"This." Out of his tuxedo jacket pocket he took a ring that rivaled all of the glitter of the night.

Traci stopped breathing.

10, 9 . . .

"I love you, woman, and I want to spend the rest of my life showing you just how much. We can do amazing things together. I believe that. Me and you."

8, 7 . . .

His gaze roamed over her face. Tears of pure joy sprang in her eyes. She knew that this time would be different, because Noah was different and finally so was she. He'd opened her world and healed her heart and soul.

5, 4, 3 . . .

"Me and you," she whispered. "Yes, yes."

2, 1 . . .

"Happy New Year!"

Noah slid the diamond onto her finger, and as they always did, they sealed their deal. And it sounded as if everyone was celebrating their joy.

■ ■ ■ ■

HOLIDAY SPICE

FARRAH ROCHON

■ ■ ■ ■

CHAPTER ONE

"Who needs a fat guy in a Santa suit?"

Miranda Lawson stood at the edge of Booth 48 in Istanbul's famed Spice Market, the viewfinder on her Nikon D3s positioned over her right eye. She honed in on the shot, her camera poised a foot away from a handcrafted scarf that draped along one of the booth's sturdy posts. It was myriad bold pinks, bright oranges, and the slightest trace of turquoise. The lights shimmering from the arched ceiling of the centuries-old building glinted off the gold lace that edged the borders of the *yemeni,* the traditional Turkish scarf. The colorful fabric embodied the very essence of Istanbul's rich culture, creating the perfect frame for the shot Miranda wanted to capture.

She adjusted the camera's lens, bringing the shop owner, who stood just a few feet beyond the scarf, into focus. Miranda snapped the picture just as the leathery-skinned man handed a smiling patron a sachet of spices.

"Oh, that's beautiful," Miranda murmured underneath her breath.

It was a postcard-worthy shot, which is exactly what she was going for. She'd taken so many awe-inspiring photos over the past two days that she would probably have to flip a coin to figure out which ones to send to the magazine editor once she got back home. Maybe it was finally time for her to put together her own travel book, or at the very least start up that blog she'd been contemplating for the past few years.

Miranda snapped a couple more frames of the shoppers inspecting the goods at this particular booth before foraying deeper into the crowded marketplace. The clamor of thousands of shoppers speaking in deep Turkish accents blended with the hustle and bustle of commerce taking place at a frenetic pace. The sounds were sweet music to Miranda's ears, drowning out thoughts of what she would be hearing right now if she were back home in Portland: strands of "Jingle Bell Rock" being piped through grocery store speakers, the crinkling of wrapping paper stretching over gifts, greetings of "Merry Christmas" from strangers at every turn.

No thanks.

But you said this year would be different!

Miranda tried to ignore the annoying voice in her head, but it would not be silent. After all, her conscience was right. She *had* said that this year would be different.

This year marked a turning point for her. She had a decision to make. Either she finally let go of the tragedy that changed everything fifteen years ago, or she accepted that it would rule her life forever. For months she'd prepared herself for the holiday season, resolved that *this* would be the Christmas when she finally moved on.

But things weren't working out as planned.

Instead of enjoying what was once her favorite holiday, Miranda had accepted a last-minute job, hopping on a flight to a non-Christian country where it would be unlikely to encounter cheerful dancing elves, Salvation Army bell ringers, or fake trees covered in messy tinsel.

Call her a coward, but when it came to suffering through another Christmas or working, she'd choose work every time. She would much rather be in one of her favorite cities in the world, doing exactly what she was doing right now: capturing the essence of Istanbul through her camera lens.

Besides, the opportunity to completely avoid the holiday had been taken out of her hands this year. Her best friend, Erin, cajoled Miranda into promising to celebrate Christmas Day with their family, using every underhanded trick at her disposal, including the fact that it was the couple's brand-new baby girl's first Christmas.

Miranda could still hear Erin's voice in her head.

How will you explain to your goddaughter that you missed her first Christmas?

Goodness, she was *such* a pushover.

Miranda was scheduled to arrive back in the States on December 23, and as she'd just been shown a few minutes ago via a text from Erin, she had a place waiting for her at a table so crowded with poinsettia leaves, gold-dusted pinecones, and stout candles, Miranda wasn't sure it would hold up under the weight of an actual meal. Everything just oozed Christmas.

Yay.

Thank goodness she had a reprieve here in Istanbul. Hopefully, over the next day and a half, she could summon up the courage to get through the upcoming holiday.

Cupping the barrel of the lens in her palm, Miranda once again peered through the eyepiece, shrinking the massive seventeenth-century bazaar to the small scene she could only spot through her viewfinder. She centered the frame on the miniature mountains of colorful spices lining the entrances of the booths. Shaped like the pyramids of Egypt, the aromas of the rich, jewel-colored spices permeated the air, filling the space with the scent of cumin, smoked paprika, and Indian saffron.

"Pretty scarf for the pretty lady?" One proprietor smiled, thrusting a bright red scarf toward Miranda as she walked past his small storefront.

"No, thank you," she answered in English. This was her fifth visit to Istanbul in the last four years, but she'd decided after her second trip not to attempt to speak the language. She totally butchered it whenever she tried.

She held up her camera, seeking his permission before taking photos. His smile widened and he stood proudly among the handmade trinkets that were clearly targeted to the millions of tourists who visited the ancient city every year. Miranda snapped several pictures of the gold-plated lanterns hanging from the eaves of the narrow shop and the brightly colored fabrics that draped along the ceiling.

"Thank you," she said.

"Bakiniz," the man said, holding out a tiny ceramic doll for Miranda to see.

She took it from his hand, thinking it would make a cute Christmas gift for her new goddaughter, Angelica.

Wait? Was she really Christmas shopping?

Miranda braced herself for the onslaught of unease. She waited, fully expecting her skin to crawl and her breaths to quicken.

But none of that materialized, which was the most shocking thing to have happened in quite a while. At one time, the thought of doing anything that even hinted at celebrating this holiday was enough to make Miranda break out into hives. For years she'd refused to even acknowledge Christmas. Despite her agreeing to be part of this new tradition for her goddaughter, Miranda still wasn't fully on board. She'd been contemplating ways to get out of Christmas at Erin's for weeks, practicing her cough.

But the fact that she didn't hyperventilate at the thought of buying a Christmas gift gave her a sliver of hope that things were finally getting better. Maybe after fifteen long years, she'd finally gotten to a place where she could put the past and the pain behind her. She'd long ago stopped believing in Christmas miracles, but if one were to happen, she was all for it.

174

She held the camera up to her eye again, observing the marketplace through the shrunken scope of her camera lens, searching for nothing in particular. She would know the shot she wanted to take when she spotted it. The camera's constricted viewpoint had a way of bringing into focus the things she could not see when looking at the larger picture.

As she panned across the various booths, Miranda stopped short, the air whooshing out of her lungs.

Whoa!

Standing in the center of the red frame of her viewfinder was a gorgeous, late-night-fantasy-worthy work of art. He stood in front of one of the booths that sold spices, loose teas, and *lokum* — the sweet treat staple known to the rest of the world as Turkish Delight.

And he was staring directly at her.

One thing that immediately struck Miranda was the fact that he was clearly American — a bit of a rarity in Istanbul at this time of year. But the fact that he was *African American* was even rarer. Encountering a fellow African American during the Christmas season was definitely not something she would have expected.

His gaze remained on her as his fingers

caressed the dried flowers. He brought a bright red bud to his nose, his eyes never leaving hers.

The warmth that suddenly passed through Miranda had nothing to do with the heat radiating off the numerous bodies crowding the narrow pathways, and everything to do with the stranger looking at her with a subtle intensity that heated her skin.

He wore a green sweater paired with a cinnamon-colored leather coat that stopped midthigh. The green looked good against his smooth, light brown skin. He had strong cheekbones, full lips, and a neatly trimmed goatee. Miranda had never been one for facial hair, but in that instant, she threw away all her previous notions on the subject and decided that facial hair was her new favorite thing.

She and the mystery man continued to stare at each other. A mere ten yards separated them, but it could have just as well been a thousand. Whenever someone blocked their shared line of vision, he was still staring at her when the space cleared. The next time it happened, there was a smile waiting for her when the handsome stranger came back into view. One edge of his full lips tipped up ever so slightly, causing her heart to beat faster within her chest.

Miranda surreptitiously sucked in a breath and returned his smile. He nodded in acknowledgment, his amber eyes gleaming in amusement.

A cart carrying several thick rolls of colorful silks rolled between them, then stopped, completely blocking her view.

"Ms. Lawson?" Miranda turned to the woman walking toward her from a nearby booth. She looked at the number above it. This was the booth she'd been looking for.

"Yes," she answered. "Please call me Miranda." She held her hand out to the woman.

"Merhaba," the woman said with a bright smile. Miranda returned the greeting. She, at least, remembered how to say hello.

She looked back toward her mystery man, but the cart with the fabrics remained there, blocking her view.

Oh, well. It was fun while it lasted.

It's not as if she could spend all day playing staring games with the handsome stranger anyway. She had a job to do.

Miranda didn't bother with one last look. She'd just remember the smile on his face and be satisfied with that.

Kyle Daniels paced back and forth in front of the main gate of the spice bazaar. He stopped and peered inside the arched entry-way, his heart pumping faster just at the thought of spotting the knockout he'd made eye contact with a little over an hour ago. He studied the steady stream of people entering and exiting the ancient building, but not one of them had golden brown skin or hair done in a sexy, messy bun.

Kyle shoved his hands in his pockets and cursed himself yet again for losing sight of her. He'd tried leaving the booth after she'd finally dropped that camera from her eye and looked at him, but the shopkeeper was insistent, and it wasn't in Kyle's nature to be rude to someone who'd been helping him. After a promise to the shopkeeper that he would return for the pomegranate tea buds, Kyle had finally started toward the beauty, only to find her gone. He'd spent the past hour searching through dozens of shops, hoping to spot her. *Needing* to spot her.

But she was nowhere to be found.

A horde of questions had swirled through his mind over the last hour. Who was she? What was she doing in Istanbul just a few days before Christmas? Was she here on vacation? Was she traveling alone, or was her husband or boyfriend back at her hotel? Was she an expat living abroad? Kyle knew there were quite a few here in Turkey. He'd read several blogs by American expatriates in Istanbul and surrounding areas during his preparations for this trip.

What were the chances of finding someone like her in a city halfway across the world? And what were his chances of finding her again? A sickening feeling filled his gut at the thought of that brief glimpse across the bazaar being their only encounter.

Just as all hope started to seep out of Kyle's body, the mysterious beauty emerged from the entrance of the bazaar and turned right.

The relief that washed over him was so intense it nearly knocked his legs right from under him.

Determined not to lose sight of her again, Kyle's long strides quickly ate up the distance between them. He was still a couple of yards behind her when she stopped walking and turned.

His footsteps halted, and for several brief moments, Kyle just stared.

She was even more beautiful up close. Her pronounced cheekbones stood out, high and perfectly shaped. They were by far the best feature in a face that was made up of a ridiculous amount of gorgeous features.

"This sounds trite," Kyle started, "but I

thought I'd never see you again." He put forth a hand. "I'm Kyle, by the way."

The barest lines creased the corners of her eyes as they lifted with her smile. She captured his outstretched hand.

"Miranda," she returned.

Her voice had a husky, hoarse quality that he hadn't expected. It was so sexy it made his stomach tremble with instant want.

"That's a beautiful name, Miranda."

"Thank you. So is Kyle." She gestured back toward the entrance to the Spice Market. "How did you know I'd come out of the main gate?"

"A lucky guess," he answered with a shrug. He leaned over slightly, and in a lowered voice, he said, "Personally, I think it means we were fated to meet."

One plucked eyebrow cocked over her deep brown eyes. " 'Fated,' huh?"

Kyle shrugged again. "You can call it fate. Or persistence. I had every intention of tracking you down."

She moved the massive camera hanging from her neck to the side and folded her arms across her chest. "And exactly what makes you so confident that you would have found me in a city of this size?"

"I already told you, I'm persistent. Where did you go off to anyway?" Kyle asked, matching her pose. "You were standing there one minute, and then you just vanished. I looked all over for you."

"I went into one of the shops," she said.

He shook his head. "Try again. I searched the nearest twenty booths, you were nowhere to be found."

"That's because I was in a back room," she said. She held up her camera. "I'm working. I went back there to take some shots of the shop owner's setup."

Kyle nodded. "So your work takes you all the way to Istanbul?" he asked. "Or are you here permanently?"

He stopped breathing for a moment as he awaited her answer.

"Just visiting," she said.

For the second time in a span of ten minutes, he experienced a dizzying rush of relief. He'd known of her existence for less than two hours, so the fact that she didn't make her home in Istanbul shouldn't mean anything to him. But it did. At the very least, he wanted them to live on the same continent.

"Actually, I'm visiting for the sixth time," she continued. "My work brings me here a lot."

"You're practically a local."

"I wouldn't go that far," she said with a

husky laugh. God, he loved her voice. "But I do enjoy Turkey, and I especially love Istanbul. It's an amazing city. Full of history and some of the warmest people you'll ever meet."

As if on cue, the giggles of a group of kids playing kickball stirred in the air around them. Miranda glanced over at them and smiled, then looked past the kids, toward a huge mosque with a half-dozen minarets.

"So," Kyle said, afraid that she'd been reminded that she was heading somewhere else when she walked out of the marketplace. "Where do you normally reside when you're not ducking into back rooms of the Spice Market?"

She returned her attention to him and gave him a do-I-look-like-I-was-born-yesterday look.

"I'm pretty sure I don't know you well enough to share that kind of information," she said.

"Smart woman," Kyle returned with a nod. He'd always found smart women sexy. "I guess that means we need to take some time to get to know each other better." He held a hand out. "Can I interest you in a cup of coffee?"

She looked upon his proffered hand with more caution this time, as if she wasn't sure it was a smart move to touch it. After several moments ticked by, she finally took his hand in hers.

"I'm more of a tea drinker," she said with a wry lift to her lips.

"Tea it is," Kyle returned, his day suddenly feeling a thousand times brighter.

Their hands clasped, they walked due north, past the imposing main entrance of the seventeenth-century edifice, which Kyle had learned during his visit yesterday was known as the New Mosque. They made their way to the famed Galata Bridge. A number of fishermen lined one side of the steel structure, their fishing lines submerged into the Golden Horn, the body of water separating the newer part of the city from what was once ancient Constantinople. At least that's what the guidebook he'd picked up from the airport said.

Kyle had circled this bridge as a "must-do" activity. Never had he imagined he'd do it hand in hand with one of the most beautiful women he'd come across in ages.

"This way," Miranda said.

They headed underneath the bridge, where dozens of restaurants and shops lined the waterway. It was a sight unlike any Kyle had ever seen. Once they had their mint tea in hand — a requisite, according to Miranda

— they settled at one of the many outside tables with views of the majestic cityscape. Miranda pointed out several structures as they sipped piping hot tea and munched on a dessert the street vendor had called *tulumba*. After Miranda took a bite of the sticky cone-shaped cookie soaked in a sugary syrup, she licked her fingers.

Kyle just sat there for a moment, completely mesmerized. His subconscious must have picked this particular pastry from the street vendor so that he could see her do just that.

Miranda perched her elbow on the table and settled her chin in her upturned palm.

"Okay," she started. "I wasn't ready to reveal this information about myself just yet, but how about you? Where can one find you when you're not tea-shopping in Istanbul's Fatih District?"

"Colorado," Kyle answered. "A town called Golden, just west of Denver."

"I've heard of it," she said. "I think I passed just south of there on my way to Beaver Creek a few years ago."

"Probably so, if you took I-70 into the mountains," Kyle said with a nod. "So?" he asked.

She cocked her head slightly. "Oh," she said. "I'm in Portland."

"That wasn't so hard, was it?"

Her cheeks turned the barest hint of rose and Kyle was seconds away from declaring himself in love.

"By way of Columbus, Ohio," she added.

"A Midwesterner. So, how did you end up working in Istanbul?" He gestured to the camera that still hung from the strap around her neck. The fact that she had yet to take it off told him how important it was to her. "I'm assuming you're a photographer?"

"Freelance," she said. "I'm doing a shoot for a travel magazine. It's a Valentine's Day feature. The top ten most romantic places to visit in Istanbul."

"And the Spice Market is one of them?"

"Actually, that was for the gag reel. I'm sure you noticed all the shops selling Turkish Viagra."

"I did," he said with a laugh. "And before you ask, no, I didn't buy any."

"I wasn't going to ask," she said, her husky laugh carrying on the breeze that traveled across the water.

"How long are you here for?" he asked as he drank down the last of his tea.

"I have one more day of touring the city before I leave on Friday."

"Just in time to be home for Christmas."

She shrugged and looked out toward the water.

"My Christmases tend to be low-key. I'm supposed to spend it at a friend's this year." She held up her phone. "A friend who has no regard for international texting rates, which is why I'm sending her my cell phone bill when it comes in."

Kyle crossed his arms on the table and leaned for ward. "Well, I happen to have another day of touring Istanbul before I head back to Colorado. Maybe we can do it together."

"Tour the city?"

Kyle nodded. "You know your way around, and I haven't really had the time to do much sightseeing."

Her forehead dipped in inquiry. "So you're not here on vacation?"

He shook his head. "Like you, I'm here on business."

"What kind of business do you do? If you don't mind me asking."

"Not at all," Kyle said. "I'm a brewer. A couple of my buddies and I started brewing our own beers. I came to Istanbul to seek out new flavor ideas."

Her eyes lit up with interest. "I'm pretty sure you're the first brewer I've ever met," she said.

"Are you a beer drinker?"

"Not at all," she said, her lovely cheek-bones becoming even more pronounced with her huge smile. "But I still find it fascinating."

"It was a hobby that turned into something more. I had the time off from my full-time job — I own a small tech firm." Well, he *owned* a small tech firm, but he wasn't about to get into all that. "I decided at the last minute to come to Istanbul after seeing a program about the Spice Market on the Travel Channel."

"Really? The Travel Channel?"

Kyle shrugged. "The host was pretty convincing. However, I haven't seen much of the city. Would you mind if I tagged along with you tomorrow? I know you're working, but I would love it if you can show me around while you take your pictures."

Miranda ran her finger along the rim of her teacup, her eyes glinting with amusement. "Do you make a habit of inserting yourself into other people's lives?" she asked.

Kyle leaned for ward and, in a lowered voice, said, "When the person is as beautiful as you are? Yes, I do."

The smile that curled up the edges of her lips was enough to make his entire day. He needed to see more of it. So much more of it.

"I can't believe I just fell for that line," she said with a laugh. "But I totally did. Meet me at the north entrance of the Topkapi Palace at nine o'clock tomorrow morning."

She started to rise. Panic flushed through Kyle's veins. He wasn't ready to say goodbye just yet.

"Let me buy you dinner tonight," he said, coming around the table and taking her hand in his.

Amusement mingled with regret as her expression softened. "I'm sorry," she said. "I'm meeting a client for dinner, a local travel company that's interested in starting up excursions in the United States. I need to get back to my hotel so I can upload the shots I took today before I head out to dinner."

"Should we exchange phone numbers?" Kyle asked, pulling out his cell phone.

"I just felt comfortable enough to tell you that I'm from Portland. The phone number exchange isn't going to happen just yet," Miranda said, again with that throaty laugh.

She leaned forward, and for one heart-stopping moment, Kyle thought she was going to kiss him. She bypassed his mouth, her lips brushing his ear as she whispered, "Thanks for being so persistent. I'll see you tomorrow."

Kyle just stood there, watching with awed fascination as she meandered through the throng of people underneath the bridge. He'd come to Istanbul with two goals, to discover new, unique flavors for Bros Who Brew's spring lineup, and to get his mind off the fight he'd had with his dad at Thanksgiving. A fight that led to Kyle choosing not to go back home to Chicago for Christmas.

But finding Miranda?

That was a stroke of luck he hadn't anticipated, but one he was all too eager to accept.

CHAPTER TWO

Miranda woke to the strange, yet comforting sound of the call to prayer at the mosque a few blocks from her hotel. She stared up at the ceiling, bracing herself for the agony she'd come to anticipate on this day.

It hit her square in the chest, knocking the breath from her lungs. So many people said it would lessen with time, but fifteen years later, and the pain still stunned her with its ferocity. Miranda permitted herself a full twenty minutes to indulge in the sobs that would not be staved. She rarely cried anymore, but on this one day, it was allowed.

Once her body had recovered from the shattering sobs, she forced herself to get out of bed. Lord knows she could sit and wallow in her sadness all day if she allowed it.

But she'd vowed that this year would be different, and she was determined to make it that way.

"You had your cry," Miranda whispered into the silent room. "Now it's time to move on."

She thought about what awaited her in just a few hours, and an honest-to-goodness smile stretched across her lips. It's exactly what she needed to help shoulder the agony that often accompanied today's tragic anniversary. She craved the distraction that Kyle Daniels would bring to her world today.

Miranda climbed out of bed and took more time than usual getting ready. Instead of putting her hair up in the sloppy topknot she usually relied on while on a job, she brushed the relaxed strands and captured them in a loose ponytail that hung over her right shoulder. She dressed in a pair of worn jeans — that's the only thing she had with her — and a white turtleneck underneath a purple sweater. As she swiped lip gloss over her lips, she cursed herself for not bothering to bring makeup. Being on the other side of the camera, she just never worried that much about how she looked.

"You caught his eye yesterday, so apparently he doesn't mind how you look, either."

She regarded her reflection in the mirror and decided this was the best she could do.

She checked the side compartment of her

camera bag for extra batteries and a backup SD card, even though she knew she'd put both in there last night. It was a habit she wasn't inclined to break.

With the bag strap comfortably stretched across her chest, she went downstairs and hopped on the tramway, exiting a few minutes later at the busy Sultanahmet stop. Miranda had saved this area of the city for last, because it was always the most crowded. She started for Topkapi Palace, making her way through the clusters of tour groups that clung together, crowding around their flag-waving tour guides. The yeasty smell from the street vendors selling *simit,* a circular bread dipped in molasses, triggered hunger pangs, reminding Miranda that she'd skipped breakfast.

A different kind of hunger took over when she looked toward the palace entrance and spotted Kyle.

He strode toward her, his steps smooth and confident. And she experienced the same rush of heat she'd felt when she laid eyes on him yesterday.

"Good morning," Kyle greeted.

"You are the most adorable tourist ever," Miranda said, gesturing to the guidebook in his hand.

"I don't know when or if I'll ever get back

here. I want to make the most of my one and only sightseeing day."

"We'd better get started," she said. "There's no way to see all of Istanbul in one day, but I'll do my best to make today one you never forget."

They entered through the palace's massive Imperial Gate and quickly made their way to the second courtyard, with its tree-lined walkways that traveled out from the second gate like spokes on a wheel. Miranda had watched the weather forecast carefully, and knew she'd have an abundance of natural sunlight today, but the sun seemed more brilliant than usual. She captured breathtaking shot after breathtaking shot of the well-maintained gardens.

"I think I have enough of this section," she said. "Do you want to tour some of the structures before moving to the next court?"

"Not if it will put you behind," Kyle said.

"Let me worry about my work," she said, taking his hand. "You worry about seeing as much of Istanbul as you can before the day is over."

Having visited several times already, Miranda played tour guide, pointing out various buildings as they made their way through the courtyard. They dipped into the Imperial Treasury, where the armory museum was now located, then moved to some of the most valued pieces in the palace, including the famed Emerald Dagger and the 86-carat Spoonmaker's Diamond.

"This," Miranda said, "is the entrance to the Imperial Harem. It has more than four hundred rooms."

Kyle's brow rose. "As in a *harem* harem?"

Miranda barked out a laugh. "Is there more than one kind?" As they ventured farther into the space, she gestured to the various rooms with their opulent marble walls. "The harem contains the sultan's apartments, along with an entire corridor of apartments for his many wives and concubines."

"Guess they liked keeping it all in the family back then, huh?"

That wrenched another laugh from her. Never in her wildest dreams could Miranda imagine that she'd spend even a moment of today laughing. Never on this day.

But Kyle's humor was infectious, and she would be eternally grateful for the distraction he'd provided.

They moved onto the fourth courtyard, which usually contained thousands of tulips.

"Thankfully, I have some shots of the tulips from the last time I visited," Miranda said as they walked along the stone pathways.

"How much international traveling do you do for your job?"

"Pretty much all of it, at this point," she answered. "If I get the job with the travel company I met with last night, I'll have more work in the States, but it doesn't really matter where I work, as long as the work continues to come in." She looked up at him and grimaced. "I used to work for a small newspaper, but print papers have pretty much gone the way of the dinosaur. These days, reporters are snapping pictures on their iPhones. It's okay," she said with a shrug. "I've gotten pretty steady work from several high-profile travel magazines. If you flew any of the large U.S. carriers, there's a good chance some of my shots were in the magazines in the seatback pockets."

"So you're in the major leagues when it comes to this stuff?"

"I like to think so," Miranda said with a laugh.

"Have you always wanted to do photography?"

"Yes." She smiled, remembering happier times. "Ever since I got my first camera at twelve years old. At first I wanted to own my own studio. You know, taking cute baby pictures or graduation photos. But I love what I do, and wouldn't give it up for anything. I've been a bit of a nomad since college, so it fits."

"It's strange that you would choose to work during the Christmas holiday."

Several moments stretched between them before Miranda said, "I can say the same thing about you."

"Touché," he answered.

Miranda prayed he wouldn't press further. It had been such a great morning; she didn't want to ruin it by thinking about her reason for always working during the holidays. Kyle seemed okay with her question dodging. He changed the subject, asking instead about some of the other places she'd visited in her travels.

Once they left Topkapi Palace, it took less than five minutes on foot to reach the Hagia Sophia. Miranda pointed out its Byzantine architecture from the outside, but the lines to enter the famed holy place were too long.

"I guess you'll just have to make your way back to Istanbul," she told Kyle.

Five minutes later, as they came upon one of Turkey's most famous structures, Miranda explained that an interior tour of the Blue Mosque was a must-do, no matter how long the lines were. She wrapped the scarf she'd tucked into her bag around her head, and slipped off her shoes before entering the mosque. The iconic building, with its stunning mosaic tile work, was as breathtaking as it had been the first time Miranda visited.

Kyle took the plastic bag the attendant had given Miranda for her shoes, and held both of theirs in his hand.

"Such a gentleman," Miranda whispered. "I like that."

His eyes sparkled with amusement as he glanced over at her, but as they continued into the building, those eyes filled with wonder. Miranda studied his profile as he looked around the mosque.

"This is amazing," Kyle whispered. "The detail is remarkable. How many tiles do you think it took to cover these walls?"

"I don't know, but I'll bet Google will tell us," Miranda whispered. "We'll have to look it up when we leave."

They slipped out of the mosque just as the midday call for prayer began and Miranda guided him to a street vendor so they could grab a quick lunch. Kyle eyed the cart's vertical meat-laden spit with wariness.

"I don't know about this," he said. "I'm

not a huge fan of street food. I had a bad experience with a gyro in New York."

"You're in another country. Be adventurous," she teased, holding out the sandwich for him to try. "This is called *doner*. It's fabulous."

His brow arched. "Okay, but I'm not responsible if this day suddenly takes a very bad turn."

"I promise, if anything doesn't sit well with you I will take full responsibility."

"Will you also sit by my side when I lose my lunch?"

"I'll even rub your back."

He slapped a hand to his chest. "A woman after my own heart."

Miranda's head snapped back with her laugh. She couldn't remember the last time she'd laughed this much around Christmastime. Especially on *this* day of all days. She waited for a feeling of guilt to seize her, but it never came.

All she felt was . . . joy? Is that what this was?

After lunch, in which Kyle managed to eat two *doner* kebabs, Miranda talked him into helping her with work.

"You look the part of the inquisitive traveler," she said. "Why don't you stand just a few inches to the right. I want to get

198

the roof of the Hagia Sophia in this shot."

"Do I get paid for this?" Kyle asked as he slipped his hands in his pockets as Miranda instructed.

"Consider it payment for being your tour guide today," she answered, snapping shots in rapid succession.

"I didn't know there was a cost." He started walking toward her, his stroll slow and steady.

Miranda lowered the camera. "Do you have a problem with my price?"

He shook his head. "Not at all." He stopped just a few inches in front of her and brushed the back of his finger across her cheek. "I'm willing to do anything you want me to do. Name it and it's done."

The air around them sizzled, charged with a heady mixture of exhilaration and need. Miranda silenced the part of her conscience that tried to point out that she'd known him for less than a day. What did time matter when they were both leaving tomorrow? She had him now. And now was enough for her.

"So," Kyle asked, his voice plunging an octave, "what is it you want me to do, Miranda?"

His thumb made its way across her lips, triggering a burst of intoxicating tingles in its wake. Her entire body trembled with the excited rush of anticipation as he lowered his head.

Ambulance sirens bellowed from just a few yards away, knocking both her and Kyle out of the spell that had come over them.

Miranda stumbled back a step.

"We . . . uh." She cleared her throat. "We should probably get going if we're going to see the cistern before it closes for the day."

She turned to leave, but Kyle caught her hand and pulled her back to him. He caught her by the waist, and tilted his chin down so that his eyes met hers.

"You call the shots here, Miranda. You know that, right?"

She nodded. She knew the decision was up to her; she just had to figure out how far she was willing to take this. They had only one day together. Was she willing to throw caution to the wind and live out every fantasy with him? Or should she heed the voice in her head trying to remind her that, when it came to men, going from zero to sixty in a matter of minutes was not the way she operated? She liked to take things slow.

You don't have time for slow.

Well, now. There was no mistaking which path the little devil on her shoulder wanted her to take.

Kyle brought a hand up to her face, his

fingers caressing her jaw. "Have I thanked you for today?"

"There's no need to thank me," she said.

"Yes, there is. You didn't have to invite me along. You could have said good-bye yesterday and that would have been the end of it."

She bit her bottom lip, the effort to suppress her smile was futile. "I'm happy I didn't," Miranda answered.

Kyle's answering grin sent a ripple of sensation along her skin and Miranda had a feeling the little devil would win this round.

His arm remained around her waist as they strolled back north toward Sultan Ahmet Park. Just to the west of it stood the inconspicuous entrance to the Basilica Cistern. Having visited a number of times before, Miranda knew that the innocuous entrance was misleading. What awaited them in the hollow cavern beneath the city streets was a sight so magnificent that it took her breath away every time she saw it.

They were greeted by hauntingly soothing classical music being piped in from hidden speakers. Kyle followed closely behind her as they walked down the stone steps into the bowels of the cistern. Miranda chuckled at his reaction once they reached the platform where visitors stood to admire that stunning architectural marvel.

"Are you serious?" Kyle said. He turned to her. "What is this again?"

"The Basilica Cistern," she answered. "It's an ancient aqueduct system that dates back to the Byzantine Empire."

"The Byzantine were pretty badass, weren't they?"

"Yes, they were," Miranda said with a laugh. "This particular cistern used to supply water to the city, including the Topkapi Palace, which we visited earlier this morning."

The vast space was dark and damp, but dim lighting revealed rows of thick columns that created passageways for the water that flowed underneath the city. There were hundreds of them, all lined up in neat succession.

Miranda and Kyle walked along the wooden walkways that snaked throughout the underground cistern. She showed him the Peacock Column, with elaborate peacock feathers etched into its centuries-old sides. They walked several yards farther and came upon the famed Medusa pillars.

"This is amazing," Kyle said. "To think that these structures have stood for centuries."

"It makes you realize just how young

everything in the States is, doesn't it?"
Miranda said. "It's one of the reasons I love
to travel. There's so much to see — so much
world history that remains standing, even to
this day. I want to bring it all to life for those
who will never get the opportunity to see it
with their own eyes."

Kyle cupped her jaw in his hands, his
thumbs rubbing soothingly along her neck.
"I love your passion," he said. "I'll bet it
comes through with every picture you take."

"I hope it does," she answered.

Her eyes settled on his lips as darkened
shadows played across his face. Their tene-
brous surroundings created a sense of
intimacy that Miranda couldn't deny. It was
as if they were alone in the quiet underground chamber.

"What are some of your other passions,
Miranda?" Kyle whispered, his lips within
inches of hers. Despite the dimness, she
could see the way his chest heaved in and
out with his labored breaths.

She was the first to make a move. Leaning
into him, Miranda pressed her palm against
his chest and tipped her head up for his kiss.

The moment his lips connected with hers,
everything around them ceased to exist. It
had been regrettably long since she'd felt
this way about anyone, but there was no

denying the combustible attraction between them. He lit a fire in her that had been extinguished a long time ago. The excitement she felt when she was with him was intoxicating, but it was nothing compared to what she now felt, having his pliant mouth upon hers.

Miranda melded her lips against his, learning the feel of them, relishing in their soft strength. He kissed like a man straight out of her dreams, not rushing her, letting her set the pace. When his arm circled her waist and his hand rested at the base of her spine, she wanted to push it a few inches lower, so that he cupped her bottom. Instead, she closed the distance between them, until her body was flush against his.

His tongue trailed along the seam of her lips, licking at the edges, urging her to open her mouth. Once she complied, the kiss went from slow and sweet to a fervid, fiery joining of lips, teeth, and tongues.

He tasted like heaven itself.

He was a gift from above. He had to be. What other reason could there be for this tempting stranger to be placed in her life on this very day that had caused her so much heartache in the past. Surely, God had given her the gift of Kyle Daniels.

And she wanted to enjoy her gift for

however long she had him.

His touch was almost more than she could bear. If not for the fact that they were in public — however secluded they may be in the bowels of the darkened cistern — Miranda wasn't sure she would have stopped herself from taking this kiss several steps further. She wanted to take him all the way to her bed.

And she would.

The decision was hers to make, and she'd just made it. They had less than twenty-four hours before they would part ways. If Kyle truly was a gift, she needed to take advantage of their short time together.

Finally, after what seemed like forever, but wasn't nearly long enough, Miranda ended the kiss.

The soft lights reflecting off the quiet pool cast a gentle glow over Kyle's face, making him even more devastatingly handsome. He didn't let go of her. Instead, he dropped his head to her forehead, his eyes closing shut as he inhaled a deep breath.

"If I'd known you would taste like that, I would have kissed you the moment you walked out of the Spice Market yesterday," Kyle said.

"I wouldn't have let you," Miranda said. "Baby steps, remember?"

"I leave tomorrow. I don't have time for baby steps."

"Patience," she said with a throaty laugh. "We still have too much of Istanbul to see."

Taking him by the hand, she guided him out of the cistern. Now that she knew exactly how her night would end, Miranda didn't feel the need to rush. Kyle didn't know it yet, but it was going to be a very merry Christmas for both of them.

"Why aren't you taking any pictures?" Kyle asked as they strolled down the street that looked like something in the heart of a typical American metropolis. Brand-name stores like Gucci and Cartier lined each side of the wide avenue, their windows dressed up for the holidays.

"Because that's not the reason we're here," Miranda said. "This is a slight detour that we're taking for your sake."

He looked over at her. "My sake?"

"You mentioned that you were missing the usual Christmas sights. This is the closest you'll get to it here in Istanbul. Being a Muslim country, the holiday isn't widely celebrated, but some places still decorate for the New Year. The ornaments and lights are very close to what you'll see in the States."

He stopped walking and turned to her. "Are you for real?" Kyle asked.

Her face lit up with her smile. She looked at her arms and down the front of her body. "I was pretty real the last time I checked," she said with a laugh.

"You know what I mean," Kyle said. "To do something like this for me? I didn't know anyone could be this kind anymore."

She tipped her head back, her warm brown eyes swimming with compassion. "I understand what it's like to miss something that's dear to your heart," she said. "If giving you a little taste of Christmas helps, then that's what I'll do."

Kyle dipped his head and captured her lips in a swift, sweet kiss. "A little taste of this helps even more."

Her throaty laugh drizzled down his spine like warm honey. Kyle still couldn't believe that he'd had to travel halfway across the world to find someone like her.

They strolled for several more blocks, past store windows lined with heavy green garland, twinkling lights, and colorful ornaments. Miranda demanded that they stop at a gourmet chocolate shop with a brilliant window display of various candies made into a Christmas tree. They treated themselves to some of the most decadent chocolate Kyle had ever sampled. While he bought a couple more pieces to go, he noticed Miranda on her cell phone, slowly pacing in front of a table of half-dipped dried fruits.

"Is everything okay?" Kyle asked as he approached, handing her another chocolate.

She nodded. "My best friend, Erin, she's a new mother, and for some reason, she's always calling me for advice, as if I somehow know better than she does."

"Is this the one you're spending Christmas with?"

She nodded, taking the chocolate he held out to her and popping it into her mouth. She released a deep moan, her eyelids drifting closed as a look of complete bliss came over her face.

Kyle was completely mesmerized. He wanted to be the one to put that look on her face.

"This is going to spoil my dinner, but I can't bring myself to care," Miranda said. "And speaking of dinner," she said, an alluring smile lifting the corner of her sinfully sweet lips, "I've got a surprise for you. Are you ready for the one thing I just have to do before leaving Istanbul?"

"I've been anticipating it all year."

She rolled her eyes and caught the sleeve of his leather jacket. "Come on."

Forty-five minutes later, they were back in the heart of the city, near the Galata Bridge, where they'd shared tea yesterday.

"Haven't we seen this already?" Kyle asked.

"I'm going to need you to just trust me on this one," Miranda said. "I haven't steered you wrong yet, have I?"

She had him there. He'd seen more of Istanbul in this one day with her than he could have ever imagined.

They boarded one of the numerous ferryboats that lined the waterway.

"Welcome to your Bosphorus dinner tour," a woman dressed in a flowing gown greeted them.

"Before you ask, yes, this is a part of the job," Miranda said. "Dinner by candlelight while drifting along the Bosphorus Strait is, by far, the most romantic thing one can do while in Istanbul."

"So you would still do this tonight, even if I wasn't here with you?" Kyle asked as he took the seat next to her.

"Yes," she answered, "but it wouldn't be nearly as enjoyable."

The greeter guided them to a table on the left side of the ship. Both chairs were on the same side, with the far edge of the table butted up against the ship's railing. It afforded them both an amazing view of the remarkable landscape.

They were served drinks and an assortment of traditional Turkish *meze,* which Miranda explained was basic appetizers. She pointed out various sights as the sun set over the water.

"Did you get the chance to visit the Asia side of Istanbul, or have you spent the entire time on the European side?" Miranda asked.

"Never got to Asia." Kyle shook his head. "Pretty pathetic to come to the only city in the world that is located on two separate continents and not visit both sides. Though, to be honest, I didn't know much about Istanbul when I booked this trip. I looked online for good places to travel where I could find different flavors, and Turkey was one of them. The Spice Market in particular."

"You really came all this way just to shop in the Spice Market?"

Kyle shrugged. "And to get away from home for a bit," he said. He looked over at her and shrugged. "Family issues. I needed a breather."

Miranda eyed him with a hint of wariness. "When you say 'family issues,' you don't mean between you and your wife, do you?"

"No, no, no," Kyle said with a laugh. "Not

married. Never have been." He chuckled at her visible sigh of relief, but then sobered. "My dad and I got into it over Thanksgiving. I decided it would be better to skip Christmas with the family this year and let things cool off a bit, you know?"

Kyle was proud of the way he was able to speak with such nonchalance, as if it wasn't killing him inside, thinking about his brothers and sisters gathering at their childhood home, just outside of Chicago. As if the fight he'd had with his dad was some insignificant thing that would soon blow over, instead of a dispute that had created a chasm between them that grew more and more as each day passed.

"So, did this trip do the double duty that you'd hoped it would? Giving you some inspiration for new beer flavors, while also taking your mind off your troubles from back home?"

"It did so much more than that," Kyle said. He set his wineglass on the table and captured her hand, placing a gentle kiss across the backs of her fingers. "It gave me an unexpected gift when I looked up from a bushel of tea leaves and spotted one of the most beautiful sights I've ever seen in my life."

Her cheeks instantly turned a lovely shade

of red, and all Kyle could think about was how other parts of her body would look with that same blush.

"And to think that I nearly skipped the Spice Market yesterday."

"Did you?"

She nodded. "I told you that it was more of a gag with the Turkish Viagra. The only reason I even had time to visit is because I finished up my shots from Pierre Loti Hill earlier than I'd first anticipated."

"But didn't you have a meeting with one of the shopkeepers there?"

"It was a last-minute thing," Miranda said. "She wasn't even supposed to be in town this week."

"That seals it," Kyle said. "There's no longer a doubt in my mind that this was fate. We were meant to meet."

"I'm not a big believer in fate," she admitted. "But I'm not sure there's any other explanation."

"I won't accept another explanation," Kyle said, placing another kiss on her fingers. "It was meant to happen."

She leaned over and rested her chin on his shoulder. "Well, if the Fates did have something to do with it, I owe them one," Miranda whispered against his neck.

Once they were done with their meal, Kyle

took her hand in his again and refused to let go. They were treated to a traditional Anatolian belly dance show, but if someone were to ask him about it, Kyle wouldn't have been able to recall a single thing. He only had eyes for Miranda.

Thoughts of leaving tomorrow crept into his mind, despite his attempts to shut them out. If she didn't have to head home as well, he would have changed his flight to a later date. It would be worth it — whatever the cost — to spend just one more day with her.

Instead, he would make the most of these last few hours.

After the show, they moved to the bow. The frigid wind coming off the water cut through him, but the beautiful lights of the city more than made up for it. Kyle stood behind Miranda and wrapped her body inside his jacket. He tucked his chin against her neck and pressed a trail of light kisses along her jaw.

"I've thanked you for today, haven't I?"

"More than once," she said, a smile in her voice.

"It's still not enough. Today has been the best day I've had all year. Being in this beautiful city with one of the most beautiful women I've ever laid eyes on? It's more than I could have ever hoped for."

She looked back at him over her shoulder. "If your beer-making skills are even close to your skills at being a charmer, you and your friends are going to make a ton of money with this new business of yours."

Kyle barked out a laugh. "It's true. Today has been amazing. And it's all thanks to you. I thought this would be the worst Christmas on record, but you've managed to turn it into one of the best. It's just too bad it has to end before Christmas Day," he added.

"At least we had today," she said.

Kyle hesitated a moment, then decided he had nothing to lose. He placed his lips against her earlobe and whispered, "There's still tonight."

His breath lodged in his lungs as he ticked off five agonizingly long seconds before Miranda turned to face him. A sliver of doubt crept in as her gaze roamed his face, and some of the boldness he'd been feeling trickled away.

Kyle lifted his shoulder in the most nonchalant shrug he could muster, and said, "A nightcap seems like the perfect way to end such an amazing day."

Miranda's eyes brightened with the sexy smile that stretched across her lips. "If it's the kind of nightcap that lasts for hours and requires no clothing, then yes, it seems like the perfect ending to our day."

Knee-buckling lust rushed through his bloodstream, gripping his stomach. "Yes." He swallowed past the desire clogging his throat. "That's exactly the kind of nightcap I was hoping for."

The ten minutes it took for the boat to dock felt like a lifetime; the fifteen-minute cab ride to his hotel — an eternity. As he ushered Miranda down the hallway toward his room, Kyle's body hummed with the need to get them both out of their clothes in the quickest way possible.

When he reached the door, he stopped to take a breath. He needed to calm the hell down. Pouncing on her like a horny teenager on prom night was not the lasting impression he wanted her to take from this evening, but his grip on his control slipped away with every second that passed.

Kyle's fingers shook as he tried to slip the flat keycard into the electronic lock and completely missed the slot.

Miranda covered his hand. With a throaty chuckle, she said, "Take your time. I'm not going anywhere."

"Yes, you are," Kyle said, trailing his eyes up and down her body. "I plan to take you places you've never been before."

The lock disengaged and they barreled into the room. Clothes flew in all directions, landing haphazardly about the room. Kyle's entire body hummed in anticipation as he watched Miranda strip out of the dark blue jeans that had driven him crazy all damn day. His eyes followed their descent over her hips and down her smooth legs. Once the jeans were off, she went for the hem of her sweater, pulling it over her head. The turtleneck followed.

As she stood before him in white cotton panties and a no-nonsense bra, Kyle thought she looked better than any supermodel who'd ever strutted across a catwalk in skimpy lingerie.

"You're a goddess," he said, striding up to her and clasping his palms around her waist.

He dipped his head and took her mouth in the kind of kiss he'd wanted to give her from the minute he first saw her, his tongue thrusting past the seam of her lips with quiet force. He didn't know what it was about this woman that made him want her with a ferocity unlike anything he'd ever experienced before. She stoked the fire burning in his belly, sending it from a smoldering ember to a blazing flame in mere seconds.

Slow down, Kyle warned himself. If the

next few hours were all they had together, he wanted to last the entire time.

He smoothed his hand down her flat stomach, caressing her soft, unblemished skin. "I knew your body would look amazing, but it's even better than I'd imagined."

"Don't you think it's time I get to see how *your* body looks?" Miranda asked, tucking her fingers just inside his waistband.

Kyle made quick work of shucking the clothes from his body, and flinging them on the room's lone chair. But he didn't stop at his outerwear the way Miranda had. Their time was limited, and he was ready to take this to the next level. Besides, it wasn't as if his boxer briefs were doing a good job of concealing the erection straining to break free.

He pushed the cotton material down his legs and tossed them with the rest of his clothes; then he picked Miranda up and carried her to the bed. He placed her gently in the center of the mattress and followed her down, covering her body with his. He lifted himself up on his elbows so that he could look down at her.

"I just remembered yet another reason why this has to be fate," Kyle said. He reached over and grabbed the wallet that he'd tossed on the bedside table. He pulled a string of three condoms from it. "I put these in here at the very last minute before I left Denver. I haven't had use for them in months, but something made me do it."

"Hmm," Miranda murmured. "I think I'm starting to like this fate thing."

Kyle lowered his mouth until his lips brushed against hers. "Like it? I freaking love it."

Anticipation hummed throughout Miranda's entire being as she held Kyle's gaze. He levered himself up on one arm, rolling the condom over his erection with his other hand. Once covered, his fingers caressed her inner thigh, trailing along her skin before he pushed her legs apart and wedged himself between them.

Her stomach clutched with need as he slowly drove into her body. The twin moans they both released resonated through the air like a melody.

Miranda clutched his back, sinking her fingers into his skin, holding on for dear life as his hard length settled inside her, filling every inch of her.

"God, you're beautiful," Kyle breathed against her jaw as he trailed his tongue along her skin. He dipped his head, pressing gentle kisses down the column of her throat and along her collarbone. He kissed his way down the valley between her breasts before closing his lips around one nipple and sucking on the erect nub until it glistened. Everything inside her swam to that point of sensation. The pleasure intensified with every pull of his lips, the suction sending a lightning rod of desire straight to her soaking-wet core.

Miranda locked her legs around him, urging him to move faster. She captured his head and brought his mouth back up to hers, thrusting her tongue inside, savoring his spicy flavor. She wanted all of him. She craved what he gave her, not just physically, but mentally.

Kyle had taken this day — a day she dreaded like no other throughout the year — and made it magical. He was like a balm to a festering old wound.

"More," she moaned against his lips.

With every delicious slide of his cock, her focus on the tragedy of this day melted away. She wanted to return the favor. She needed to give him everything he was giving her, and more.

Miranda unlocked her legs and pushed against his chest with gentle insistence, urging him to flip over. Once on top, she straddled his hips, and then, taking his latex-covered erection in her hands, guided him inside once again.

Kyle's eyes closed, his head rolling back. A deep groan tore out of him as he lifted his hips and drove his thickness inside her. Miranda couldn't deny the rush of power she felt at the knowledge that she could elicit such a strong reaction in him. Bracing her hands against his shoulders, she pumped up and down his length, rising until her body nearly released him before plunging down again. He felt so good inside her she could barely stand it, yet she never wanted this to end.

"Faster," Kyle urged with a shaky breath. He grasped her hips, his fingers biting into her skin. He guided her motion, quickening their pace, lifting her up and down with increasing speed while his hips bucked, pumping like a piston.

The sensation started low in her belly, building with each second that passed, until she erupted with the violent orgasm that tore through her body.

"Oh, my God," Miranda cried out. Her limbs continued to tremble as she collapsed onto Kyle's chest. She remained there for several moments, listening to the rapid beat of his heart and relishing the feel of his erection still filling her.

Goodness, she'd needed this.

She wasn't aware of just *how much* she'd needed it until this very minute, when she realized that she never wanted to break this connection. To be joined with another human being in such an elemental way. She missed this feeling. She craved it. Relished in it.

But she also knew it was only for tonight.

The sobering thought proved a catalyst for Miranda to finally lift herself up from Kyle's body. She flopped down next to him on the bed and pulled the sheet over her lower half. She was too exhausted to worry about covering the rest.

Kyle took full advantage, bracing his hands on either side of her shoulders and dipping his head to capture her nipple again. Miranda released another moan.

"What are you doing?" she purred.

"Having dessert," he whispered, his warm breath sending chills along her skin. Her back bowed off the bed as she thrust her nipple higher into his mouth, mesmerized by the attention he lavished upon her.

"You taste divine," Kyle said as he moved to the other breast. He rolled his tongue around the tip, laving the protruding nub, soaking it with moisture. He stopped abruptly and looked up at her. "I'll bet another part of you tastes even sweeter," he said.

Miranda's stomach clenched at the hungry look in his eyes. When he started a path down her abdomen, she just knew she wouldn't survive the onslaught of sensation that was bound to take over.

Kyle flattened his palms against her inner thighs and spread her legs open; then he dipped his head and licked at her soaking-wet sex. Miranda's legs began to tremble as his tongue became more insistent, lapping with wildly fierce strokes. When he closed his mouth over her mound and sucked hard on her clitoris, her entire body went up in flames.

"Oh, God!" Miranda screamed, clutching the sheets in her fists and holding on for dear life as she came apart yet again.

She remained spread eagle on the bed, unable to move for untold moments. Her lungs hurt with the force in which the breath left her body.

She watched as Kyle took several tissues from the box next to the nightstand and used them to dispose of the condom; then he came back in the bed, lying on his back and pulling her up onto his chest.

"Merry Christmas to me," Kyle said with a laugh.

Miranda released a tired chuckle. "It's been a while since I celebrated, but if this is the year I'm going to start again, I can't think of a better way to kick off the holiday."

He trailed his fingers down her hair and along her arm. "Why haven't you been celebrating Christmas?" he asked.

Her chest tightened as indecision tumbled through her. Despite what just transpired in this bed, she didn't know him well enough to share the gory details of her life.

Yet, it was also a reason that she *could* tell him. She'd decided that this time with Kyle would be just for today. She would never see him again. Maybe discussing her past with this man who was still a stranger would be cathartic. He'd given her so much already, maybe he could also take away some of the pain that came from holding this hurt inside all the time.

In the end, Miranda decided against it. Instead of telling him the full truth, she settled for the partial.

"Work," she said. "It tends to take me away around the holidays."

"But you'll be with your friend this year, right? The one with the new baby?"

"Yes," she said with a sigh.

Kyle laughed. "Try to contain your excitement."

"I am excited," Miranda lied. It was easier to fudge the truth than to admit that she loathed the holiday season. Needing to take the spotlight off herself, Miranda turned and folded her hands on his chest, resting her chin on the backs of them. "What about you? Was the fight with your dad really bad enough to miss spending Christmas with your family?"

She caught the hurt that flashed across his face. "Just this morning, I debated changing my flight and heading to Chicago, but I think it's better if I stay away this year. My dad and I ruined Thanksgiving. I won't allow us to ruin Christmas for everyone."

"So you'll be alone this year." She knew the feeling.

Kyle tipped his chin down and looked at her, one brow cocked. "I wouldn't mind an invitation to Portland," he said.

Miranda instinctively flinched.

"I was only joking," Kyle said. "Honestly."

Miranda knew her nervous laugh did nothing to hide her unease, but his words hit her like a bucket of ice water to the face. Even if it was all in jest, it was probably time she bring this magical night to an end.

"I should get going," Miranda said. She began to push herself up from the bed, but Kyle caught her by the wrist and pulled her back down onto his chest.

"Come on, Miranda. I was just joking. I realize we don't know each other well enough for me to get an invite to Christmas."

"Yes, but I have a lot to do before my flight tomorrow. And you need to get some sleep, too, don't you? Didn't you mention that you're flying out at six in the morning?"

"I don't have to sleep at all. I've got a two-hour flight to London and then a ten-hour flight back to Denver. I'll get all the sleep I need on the plane."

"I still need to get back to my hotel and pack. It takes a lot to secure all of my camera equipment."

"Do you need help?" Kyle asked.

She grinned. "And just how would I have done it if I'd never met you?"

He brought her hand to his mouth and grazed the crest of her fingers with his lips. "Thank goodness that's something neither of us ever have to think about."

Then he asked the question Miranda had been dreading.

"When can I see you again?"

Her gaze traveled from the desk to the lamp to the floor. Anywhere but to Kyle. She knew she was taking the coward's way

225

out, but, dammit, he was only supposed to be a distraction.

"Miranda?" Kyle said, the barest hint of anxiety coloring his voice. "Come on, Miranda. You don't expect me to say good-bye to you tonight and that be the end of it, do you?"

Finally she returned her attention to him. "That's exactly what I expect," she said. She reached for his hand and sandwiched it between her own. "Look, Kyle, today has been amazing. And tonight . . . well, let's just say it will be something I think about for a long time. But it's best that we end it right here. We live hundreds of miles away from each other. Long-distance relation-ships just aren't my thing."

"Who says it has to be a relationship?" he asked. "I'll settle for a texting buddy. Hell, just a Facebook friend, if that's all you're willing to give."

Miranda rose from the bed and grabbed her underwear from the floor, quickly pull-ing them on. Kyle followed her around the room as she put on her jeans and sweater, not bothering to cover his nakedness, which was distracting as hell. She folded her turtleneck over her arm.

"Is this because of the joke I made about spending Christmas in Portland?" he asked.

She picked up her camera bag and slung it over her shoulder, then turned to him.

"It was always supposed to be just a day, Kyle. That's all I was ever willing to give." She captured his face between her hands. "Thank you for the unexpected holiday treat. You have no idea how much I needed it." She pressed a quick but firm kiss to his lips. "Safe travels back to Denver."

Five minutes later, while sitting in the backseat of the cab the doorman hailed for her, Miranda couldn't escape the unease that trickled along her skin at the way she'd left Kyle standing in the middle of his hotel room. Yet, she couldn't erase the smile that traveled across her lips as she thought about the day she'd had.

She always looked forward to traveling to Turkey, but of all her visits here, this trip would be the one she would never forget.

CHAPTER THREE

Leaning back in the plush business-class seat, Kyle tried to get comfortable for the ten-hour flight from London to Denver. He'd missed his original connection after sitting on the tarmac in Istanbul for hours due to a plane malfunction. Luckily for him, there was a spot on this last direct flight out of Heathrow.

He adjusted the complimentary noise-canceling headphones in hopes that blocking out the chatter and hum of the engines would help him get some rest. Sleep should have been easy to come by, seeing as he got hardly any last night. But it was the reason why he didn't get any sleep that kept him awake right now.

Kyle emitted a low groan.

Earlier, in the wee hours of the morning as he'd stared up at the ceiling of his hotel room, Kyle had started to believe that Miranda had been a mirage. The previous day and a half had been so magical, so mind-blowingly awesome, that it just couldn't be real.

But it had been *very* real. It had just been too damn short.

And now it was over.

How did he let her go without figuring out some way to stay connected with her? An address? A phone number? Hell, even a last name. It wasn't until he'd pulled up his phone and tried to Google her that Kyle realized he'd never gotten her last name. All he really knew about her was that she was a travel photographer from Portland. Well, and that her husky voice rose several registers when she screamed during orgasm. He'd discovered that last night.

Kyle's eyes popped open. Remembering something Miranda had mentioned during their tour of the city, he pulled the magazine from the seatback pocket and started to flip through it, looking at the photographs. Or, more accurately, at the photographer credits next to the pictures.

When he ran across a gorgeous shot of a brilliant pink-and-purple sky glowing across the rippling waters of the North Atlantic near Reykjavik, Iceland, Kyle didn't even have to look at the credit to know it was Miranda's photograph. He could tell just by the story the picture told. He'd picked up on it while scrolling through her digital pictures yesterday. She didn't just snap something because it was pretty. There had to be more behind it in order for something to catch her eye. A story to be told, a history.

Kyle looked at the photo's credit line and broke out into a smile.

Miranda Lawson.

At least he had a full name now. He vowed not to turn into some creepy stalker, but he also could not accept that the few hours they'd shared together was the beginning, middle, and end of *their* story. The connection between them had been too strong just to give up on it.

Once the flight crew was done with their instructions and the plane took off, Kyle settled in for the long flight. Sleep continued to elude him, so he tried to ease his mind by watching an in-flight movie, but it never truly captured his attention.

He peered up the aisle toward the lavatory for the fourth time, but just as he started to unbuckle his seat belt, someone closer got up and slipped in there. Deciding not to wait any longer, Kyle released the buckle and headed for the facilities in the rear of the plane. He'd been sitting for over three hours already; he needed to stretch his legs.

He was nearing the back of the plane when a tall twentysomething, with blond dreadlocks and a scruffy beard, rose and opened the overhead compartment above his seat.

"Sorry," the guy said in a thick British accent, looking down at Kyle. "I'll only be a minute."

"No problem," Kyle lied.

He stood in the aisle, shifting from one foot to another. As his eyes roamed around the plane, they fell on a familiar face.

Kyle's heart skittered to a stop.

Two rows down, in the middle seat on the plane's right side, Miranda sat with her eyes closed, her face tilted skyward as she leaned back against the headrest.

"Miranda?" he said, walking toward her now that the guy with the dreads had taken his seat.

It's when she didn't answer that Kyle noticed the earbuds in her ears. He leaned over her seatmate, who had a newspaper spread out in his lap, and gently jostled her arm.

"Miranda," Kyle said again.

She woke with a start. She looked around, blinking several times as if disoriented and trying to figure out just what was going on. Her eyes widened when she finally honed in on his face.

"Kyle? What . . . what are you doing here? I thought you left Istanbul at six a.m.?"

"My flight out of Istanbul was delayed," Kyle answered. "Why didn't you tell me you were connecting in London when I mentioned it last night?"

The stodgy man in the tweed jacket sitting next to Miranda loudly cleared his throat.

Ignoring her seatmate's irritated look, Kyle gestured toward the back of the plane. "Come with me for a minute," he said. Not because he gave a damn about the curmudgeon glaring at him, but because he didn't want to have this conversation with an audience.

Miranda glanced at the man next to her, then back at Kyle.

"I meant what I said last night," she said to him. "What we shared was lovely, but it needs to remain back in Istanbul."

No. No way.

She may want it to stay in Istanbul, but there was something larger at play here.

What were the odds of his flight being grounded for two hours on the tarmac in Istanbul? And then, of all the flights out of

London back to the States, to end up on the very same one with her?

Heck, the fact that he'd spotted her on the plane, when — with the size of this vessel — it wasn't out of the realm of possibility that the people sitting in business class would never come in contact with those in the rear of the plane.

Coincidence only went so far. When things started to bombard him the way they had when it came to Miranda, the only answer Kyle could possibly accept is that it was meant to be.

"Just come to the back with me for a few minutes," he asked.

The flight attendant, whom Kyle had noticed a moment ago out of the corner of his eye, came up to him. "Sir, we ask that you keep the aisle clear."

"Miranda, please," Kyle pleaded.

Expelling a deep breath, she unhooked her seat belt and rose from the seat, murmuring an apology to the old man as she squeezed past his legs.

Kyle nearly choked on the relief that crashed through him. He gestured for her to go ahead of him, following her to the rear of the plane where the flight attendants were preparing the meal carts.

It wasn't until he encountered the lavatories that Kyle remembered that using the restroom was his original purpose for walking back this way. There was no way he was taking a bathroom break right now, not when he had Miranda right here.

Yet, now that she was here, Kyle didn't know where to begin.

He started with the question he'd asked a few moments ago.

"Why didn't you tell me you were connecting out of London? And out of Denver," he tacked on, realizing that it should have rung a bell for her the minute he told her he was from Denver.

"I didn't think it mattered, once you mentioned that you were on the early flight out of Ataturk International. I figured you would have left London by the time I landed here for my connection."

"And Denver?"

"I have a one-hour layover in Denver."

Several uncomfortable moments ticked by as Kyle tried to think of something else to say. It occurred to him how strange it felt. Even though they'd only met two days ago, there had never been any awkwardness between them the entire time they were together. Everything had been so easy.

It could be that way again.

"I don't want this to be the end, Miranda,"

he told her. "Why are you insisting that it has to be?"

She crossed her arms over her chest and looked toward the flight attendants. All three were still getting the meals together, but it was more than obvious that they were hanging on to their every word. Kyle didn't give a damn what they heard. He would never see them again.

Miranda, on the other hand, he *did* want to see again. And again. And again.

He *had* to make that happen.

"So?" Kyle asked. "Why, Miranda?"

She hunched her shoulders. "Honestly, I'm not sure. It just seems like a complication that I don't need."

"A complication? What about the last couple of days has been complicated? They've been two of the best days of my life."

"Kyle —"

"I'm not asking to move in together." He held his hands out, imploring her to give this just a small chance. "All I want is a phone number. Just a promise that we can at least talk and get to know each other better. I want to call you the day after tomorrow and wish you 'Merry Christmas.' Is there anything wrong with that?"

Kyle took a step toward her, bringing their

bodies within inches of each other in the limited space.

He linked their hands together and gave her palms a slight squeeze.

"It may turn out that all we gain is friendship, and if that's the case, I'm fine with it. But we clicked. We can't just sever the connection we made over these past two days. Life is too short to let go of something so special. You never know if you'll ever find it again."

Caution mingled with the tiniest hint of optimism in her warm brown eyes.

"Excuse us, but we're going to start the dinner service in just a few minutes," one of the flight attendants said. "If you don't mind returning to your seats."

"Miranda," Kyle implored.

She glanced over at the flight attendants, then back to him. She released a shaky breath before a genuine smile stretched across her beautiful face.

"Okay," she said. "Follow me back to my seat. I have business cards. It has all of my contact info, even Facebook."

Relief crashed through him with the force of a typhoon.

Was it a Christmas miracle? Luck? A combination of both?

Kyle didn't know what was at play here,

and he wasn't going to take much time trying to figure it out. All he knew was that
he'd found Miranda for the second time in
two days. And he wasn't about to let her go.

By the time the distinctive peaked roof of
Denver International Airport came into
view, Miranda was finally back in control of
her breathing. Knowing Kyle sat just a few
yards ahead of her kept her rattled the entire
flight. He never returned to the back of the
plane, but Miranda suspected that he'd
likely fallen asleep once he returned to his
seat, given how little sleep they'd both
achieved last night.

The clack of seat belts being released
sounded throughout the plane the minute
the bell dinged, indicating that guests were
cleared to deplane. Miranda waited patiently
while everyone else around her jumped up
like their seats were on fire, only to stand in
the aisle for ten minutes while the travelers
ahead of them slowly exited the plane. She
joined in with the sea of passengers who'd
endured the long transatlantic flight, the
collective jet lag a tangible thing around
them.

When she cleared the gangway, Kyle was
waiting at the gate.

He hunched his shoulders. "It seemed

rude not to wait for you."

Miranda couldn't hold back her smile, charmed by his little show of chivalry. "Thank you," she said. "I just hope you don't mind sprinting through Customs. I have less than an hour before my flight to Portland starts to board."

Kyle gestured over her shoulder. "You may want to check on your flight."

Miranda turned to the floor-to-ceiling windows that surrounded the airport and her stomach dropped. It looked as if Armageddon was just on the other side of the mountain. Dark, snow-laden clouds swirled.

She threw her head back and sighed at the ceiling. "Why didn't I think of this before booking a flight that connected through Denver?" She walked over to the electronic departure and arrival screens, her eyes seeking out the flights to Portland. She spotted her flight, relieved to see that it was only delayed by twenty minutes.

"I'm okay with a slight delay," Miranda said. "It gives me a bit of breathing room to make it through Customs. Let's get there before the line gets too long."

As expected, the journey through U.S. Customs was an exercise in surviving chaos. It was the day before Christmas Eve, after all — the time of year when people bit the bullet and maxed out their credit cards for flights home so that they could be with their families.

Miranda ignored the pang of sorrow that rang through her chest.

She'd managed to make it through yesterday without losing it; she could surely make it through the rest of the holiday season. Besides, for the first time in a very long time, she actually had a reason to celebrate Christmas. Miranda had to remind herself that this year marked a fresh start for her. She could do this. She would be back in Portland by 10 p.m. and in her bed before midnight. She would spend tomorrow psyching herself up for spending Christmas Day with Erin and her family.

Yes, she could do this. She *would* do this. She owed it to herself and to her family to move on with her life finally.

She and Kyle made it through Customs without a minute for Miranda to spare. When they came to the checkpoint where only people with boarding passes for domestic flights would be allowed to pass, she felt a tightness in her throat.

"Well, I guess this is it," Miranda said, holding her hand out to him.

Kyle captured it and pulled her in closer. "For now," he said. "That's what we agreed on, remember?"

"Yes, for now," she said. She kissed him on the cheek. "Have a merry Christmas, Kyle."

He captured her jaw in his palm and slanted his lips over hers. Miranda's knees went liquid, but she managed to hold herself upright. She would try to figure out just how she was able to accomplish that feat later, once her brain was back to operating at a normal level.

"Merry Christmas," he whispered against her lips.

Just as she started to pull away, a collective groan resonated around the concourse, followed by grumbles and a few very choice words that didn't reflect the holiday spirit.

"What happened?" Miranda said, looking around.

Kyle pointed behind her.

Miranda followed his direction and let out her own choice word. The entire screen of departures had just turned red with CANCELED listed next to each flight.

"Noooo," she groaned. "This is not happening."

She and Kyle walked over to one of the flat-screen televisions mounted from the ceiling. The brunette meteorologist stood before a weather map, her hand moving over a circular mass that was steadily encroaching on the Denver area.

"I have to find out if there are any later flights I can get on," Miranda said.

"I doubt that," came a voice from behind them.

Miranda turned to find the flight attendant from their flight from London. It was the same one who'd chastised Kyle about standing in the aisle.

"From what we're being told, there will be no flights in or out of Denver for the next twenty-four hours," the flight attendant said.

"You have got to be kidding me." She turned to Kyle. "This is unbelievable."

"Actually, this is Denver in the dead of winter," he said. "It's not all that uncommon."

"Why didn't I think about this before booking through Denver?" she asked again. Miranda sighed at her own carelessness. She was usually better at planning her travels, but she'd had more on her mind than usual this year. "I guess I need to find a hotel," she said.

"Good luck finding one this close to Christmas," the flight attendant said before rejoining the rest of the flight crew.

Miranda turned back to Kyle to find him staring at her as if she'd just sprouted reindeer horns.

"What?" Miranda asked.

"Do you really think I'd let you stay in a hotel instead of with me?"

"But don't you live an hour away?"

He just continued to stare at her with that look that brooked no argument.

Miranda hunched her shoulders. "My options are pretty limited, so I guess that means I'm spending the night with you."

"It was never a question," Kyle said.

She sidled up to him, unable to contain her grin. "I had no idea you were so demanding."

"Only when it's something I really want," he answered. "But don't think that I'm expecting some sex-filled free-for-all. That's not why I asked you to come over. Demanded you come over," he amended.

Her brows lifted as a bemused smile stretched across her lips. "That's too bad," Miranda murmured, trailing her fingertips up his chest. "A sex-filled free-for-all is exactly what I was hoping for." She looked up at him. "If we're going to be stuck together in a snowstorm on Christmas Eve, we'd better make the most of it."

The smoldering look in his eyes nearly singed her. Taking her by the arm, he started for the baggage claim. "Let's get out of here."

CHAPTER FOUR

Miranda tried to keep her eyes open on the drive into the mountains, but jet lag began creeping up on her the minute her butt hit the soft leather seat of Kyle's Range Rover SUV. He'd told her that the drive usually took about forty minutes, but with the approaching storm, coupled with the fact that it was nearly Christmas Day and last-minute shoppers were on the road, it took them well over an hour.

By the time they finally arrived at his home, it was after 9 p.m., which meant she'd officially been awake for over twenty-four hours. It took all Miranda had within her just to keep her eyes opened. Yet, despite her exhaustion, her stomach still clenched with need as she followed Kyle up the stairs that led to his front door. Her eyes honed in on the way his khaki pants stretched taut over his well-shaped ass with every step he took. She wanted to sink her fingers into that firm backside and clutch him to her the way she had back in Turkey.

But not as badly as she wanted to sleep.

"I don't think I've ever been so tired in my life," she said.

Kyle looked back at her over his shoulder. "Did you get any sleep on the flight?"

She shook her head and had to stop midstep as she yawned. "No, my brain was too preoccupied with the fact that you were on the plane with me," she admitted.

Kyle's head flew back with his laugh. "Once I found you on the flight, I slept like a baby."

They arrived at the landing to find a box next to the front door.

"Surprise Christmas present?" Miranda asked.

He shook his head. "Grocery delivery. I'm happy they were able to get here before the storm. All I have in the refrigerator are bottles of the newest brew I've been working on and a box of baking soda."

Miranda reached over to pick up the box, since both his hands were filled with her bags. He'd insisted on carrying them up from the car.

"Leave that," Kyle said. "I'll get it after we're settled in."

Miranda didn't argue. Her limbs were

weak with exhaustion.

However, when Kyle pushed open the sliding front door and flipped on a switch, she temporarily forgot about her fatigue. All around them dark gray window shades lifted in a slow, simultaneous roll, revealing a breathtaking display of the Colorado Rockies.

"Oh, my," Miranda released on an awe-filled breath.

The structure brought the phrase "people who live in glass houses" to life. The entire floor was one big open space. Two steps led to a sunken living room, which housed an ultrasleek couch and nothing more. It faced a television with a screen that had to measure at least eighty inches. A massive free-standing fireplace, with an exposed vent pipe that stretched all the way to the top of the twenty-plus-foot ceiling, separated the living room from the dining room. The open kitchen took up the left side of the bottom floor. A frosted-glass wall stood behind it. Just beyond the wall, Miranda could make out what looked like stairs leading up to a second floor.

"This is amazing," she said. The words were woefully inadequate when describing this ridiculously gorgeous house, but it was the best she could come up with at the moment.

"Thanks," Kyle said. "I sacrificed space for the scenery. It's only two-bedrooms, eleven hundred square-feet."

"You're single. You don't need anything bigger than this," she said.

He nodded. "It works." He set her bag on the stone-laid floor, then went back outside to get the box of groceries. As he carried it into the kitchen and set it on the island, he said, "I forgot to mention that I converted the second bedroom into an office, so you'll have to sleep in my room with me tonight."

Miranda burst out laughing at the fake contriteness on his face, but she had to stop midlaugh in order to yawn. It lasted so long that she started to sway.

"Okay, okay," Kyle said, coming around the kitchen island and catching her by the waist. "I think it's time to get you in bed."

"I want to," she said, "But I'm so tired."

"I meant get you in bed so that you can *sleep*," Kyle said with a laugh.

Miranda could only keep her eyes open long enough to appreciate the stark beauty of the bedroom, with its minimalist design, much like the rest of the house. She walked over to the bed in the center of the room and climbed in under the covers, not bothering to take off her clothes. She felt Kyle untying her shoes, but by the time they were off her feet, Miranda was out like a light.

She awoke the next morning to an astonishing display of Mother Nature at her finest. Thick, downy white snow covered the branches of the blue spruce trees that surrounded the elevated house. The snow continued to fall in a steady shower, covering the deck that surrounded the second floor.

Miranda sat up and listened for Kyle. She didn't hear anything at first, but moments later, she heard the front door slide back into place and then the distinctive sound of footsteps coming up the stairs. He rounded the frosted-glass wall and smiled when he spotted her in his bed.

"Good morning," he greeted.

"Morning," Miranda returned with a smile.

"I don't have to ask if you slept well. I could have brought a ten-piece band in here last night and I doubt it would have woken you, once you fell asleep."

"Blame the jet lag. It sneaks up on me."

Kyle put an arm on either side of her, enclosing her in the bed, but Miranda turned away before he could kiss her.

She shook her head. "I'm yucky. At least

let me shower and brush my teeth first."

"Did you just call yourself 'yucky'?"

"It's the truth. I've been wearing these clothes since the day before yesterday."

"Fine," Kyle said, sneaking a kiss against her neck anyway. "You shower and change. I'll get started on Christmas Eve lunch."

"Lunch?"

"It's nearly noon, Miranda."

Her mouth fell open.

Kyle nodded. "Yeah, you may want to call your friend Erin. She's been blowing up your cell phone."

"Shit," Miranda said. She scooted out of the bed and grabbed the cell phone from the dresser. After assuring Erin that she hadn't been kidnapped, she called the airline to check on the flights out of Denver. As she expected, there were none, at least not until this snowstorm blew over.

She climbed into Kyle's shower. Miranda could admit to feeling a pang of regret that he hadn't joined her, but she appreciated that he wanted to make her breakfast almost as much as she would have appreciated shower sex.

Almost.

She dressed in the only remaining clean clothes in her suitcase, a pair of denim-colored tights and an off-white cable-knit sweater that ended at her knees. Then she walked down the stairs in bare feet to find Kyle putting away groceries. The welcoming smell of bacon hit her right in the face, and her stomach released a menacing growl.

Kyle set two plates with bacon, fried eggs, and toast dripping with butter on the place mats that sat on the kitchen island across from the stove.

"Look at all that lovely butter," Miranda said. "You don't happen to have a home gym around here somewhere, do you?"

"Calories don't count during the holidays," he said as he rounded the island and pulled out one of the stools for her to sit.

"I'll go along with that," she said with a laugh. "So," she said before taking a bite of bacon, "you mentioned that you're from Chicago. How did you end up in Denver?"

"I followed the tech jobs," he said. "It isn't Silicon Valley, but the tech industry is still pretty robust here."

"So you're a tech geek, huh?"

"A huge one," he said with a good-natured chuckle. "If you have any apps that deal with increasing productivity on your phone, it's more than likely that my team had a hand in it. We created over three hundred these last five years."

"My goodness, Kyle. That's an amazing

achievement. Your family must be so proud of you."

He huffed a humorless laugh. "Let's not go there."

Miranda studied his profile as she bit into her toast. This wasn't the first time he'd shied away from talk about his family, which, of course, intrigued her even more. But she was no stranger to backpedaling from talk about family, and she wouldn't force Kyle into engaging in any conversation he didn't want to have. Lord knows she wouldn't be up for it if the tables were turned.

Once they were done with breakfast, Kyle went upstairs to take a shower. Miranda used the opportunity to check out the house. She roamed around the downstairs area, learning about him. She was struck by the amount of Christmas decor peppering the space. She'd been too exhausted to take note of it last night, but Christmas was everywhere. Not in an in-your-face Rockwellian way, but with little subtle touches: a dish filled with delicate glass ornaments on the kitchen island, satin ribbon threaded through sprigs of balsam along a corner display shelf, little nutcracker soldiers standing sentry on either side of the fireplace.

Miranda intentionally avoided the six-foot

251

tree wedged into a corner in the dining room. Instead, she walked over to the display shelf to take a closer look at the pictures that occupied it.

In one there was a large group of at least twenty, with two older people whom she assumed were Kyle's parents sitting in the middle, surrounded by their brood of children and grandchildren. They were a diverse bunch. There was a blond-haired Caucasian man, with his arms around a petite woman with Kyle's cheekbones, and a South Asian woman standing next to Kyle's look-alike. A man and a woman, who Miranda could only guess were Kyle's siblings based on their strikingly similar features, held small babies in their arms, while another obvious sibling had a toddler fused against his leg.

Miranda looked up at another picture that had just the Daniels children and their parents. There were five of them total, three boys — including Kyle — and two girls.

How lucky to come from such a large family. How lucky to still have so many of them there.

She suddenly felt a pang of disappointment on Kyle's behalf. As much as she appreciated being here with him, she was sorry that he was spending Christmas here instead of in Chicago with his family. If she'd had the option, there was no doubt in Miranda's mind where she would be.

She noticed an indentation on the frosted-glass wall and realized it was the seam to a door. She gave it a light push and discovered that it was the former spare bedroom turned office. Miranda recognized that she should have felt at least some guilt about entering his private office, but she'd spent the night in his bed. The bedroom held more sanctity than the office, didn't it?

Besides, she was much too impressed with his workspace to even think about feeling guilty for invading it. Compared to the little work closet she had, with contracts and magazine spreads strewn about like a tornado had torn through it, Kyle's office was heaven. The walls in this room alternated between panels of glass and the shiny hardwood that made up the walls of his bathroom.

She surveyed the plethora of framed documents mounted on the wall behind his sleek stainless-steel desk. She blinked several times, unsure if what she saw was real. Phi Beta Kappa Honor Society, Phi Lambda Upsilon Honor Society, a doctorate in organic chemistry.

"Wait? What?"

Miranda spun on her heel and marched

back into the kitchen to find Kyle standing at the kitchen island. His carry-on bag lay open on the counter; the packets of different spices he'd purchased in Turkey were lined up next to it.

He looked at her over his shoulder, a huge smile on his face. "I can't wait to start experimenting with these," he said as he rearranged the spices.

"You have a Ph.D.?" Miranda asked. She knew she wasn't mistaken when she saw the hint of unease that traveled across his face.

"Yeah," he answered. "In chemistry."

"I read that." She shook her head. "I have way more questions than I even know what to do with right now," she said.

Kyle walked around the kitchen counter and reached out for her hands. Taking both in his, he led her to one of the bar stools.

"Let me answer a few for you," he started. "No, I wasn't a child genius, but I did skip a couple of grades in school and earned my Ph.D. at a younger age than most people. Yes, I actually used my science degrees for a while, some years ago when I worked for the EPA. No, I don't have any degrees in computers. That was all self-taught, but turned out to be much more lucrative. And, no, I don't think I wasted all that time in school studying chemistry."

"Of course you didn't," Miranda said. "There's chemistry that goes into concocting those beer recipes, right?"

"Yes, there is," he said. "I wish everyone could make the connection as quickly as you did."

"It's a no-brainer," Miranda said with a shrug. "However, none of that answers my question."

His brow arched.

"I want to know how someone as handsome, funny, accomplished — and with killer bedroom skills, might I add — is still single? Based on that picture over there, you're the only one among your siblings who isn't married."

"That's unfair," Kyle said. "You've spent the morning snooping around my house, learning about my family, and I still don't know anything about yours."

"Stop trying to dodge the question," Miranda said. "And I'm sorry for snooping."

He grinned. "I don't mind. I like that you want to know more about me."

"Well, answer my questions," she said.

"Fine." He released a highly exaggerated sigh, kissing her on the nose before continuing. "First of all, my older sister, Tammy, is no longer married. She got rid of her jerk of an ex-husband this summer, a few weeks after that picture was taken. It should have happened long ago. He's always been an asshole."

"What about you?" Miranda asked. "Have you gotten rid of a wife?"

He shook his head. "Never been married."

"Have you gotten close?"

He squinted, one side of his mouth twisting in a grimace. "About five years ago, my ex-girlfriend and I almost got to the point where we were almost talking about it."

"That's a lot of 'almost' there."

"Pretty much sums up the entire relationship."

"So?" Miranda asked.

He shrugged. "We recognized that we didn't want the same things out of life. She didn't want kids. She didn't want to settle down at all, really. It sounds cliché, but I like the thought of the two-point-five kids and the white picket fence."

"A white picket fence doesn't really go with this place," Miranda pointed out.

"I'd sacrifice it." Kyle looked over his shoulder at the vast landscape behind them. "Okay, maybe I'd keep it as a weekend home," he said. He grinned, but then his smile dimmed. "I want what my parents had. What they still have. They worked hard and were able to give their kids a good life. I didn't realize that we had what's considered a modest upbringing. We never wanted for anything. We were happy as kids — as an entire family."

Miranda figured the tidal wave of jealousy and resentment would crash into her any minute, but, surprisingly, it didn't. She wouldn't begrudge Kyle his carefree childhood, because she realized that she had one, too. Her childhood years were the very best years of her life.

Until everything changed fifteen years ago.

But before then, when she and her family piled into her mom's old minivan and set out on their yearly family vacation? Or when they'd make the drive to Pittsburgh to visit her grandma every Easter? Or on Christmas morning, when her dad would allow them to open one present before church? Nothing in the world could top the burst of joy she felt just remembering those memories.

"I know what you mean," Miranda said, unable to keep the wistfulness from her voice.

It was good to recall the happy times instead of focusing on that one tragic night. Why had she put so much emphasis on that for all these years? Why had she chosen to forget the good times?

Kyle continued to pull things out of his carry-on bag. He lifted a teardrop-shaped glass ornament, which Miranda instantly recognized as a *nazar* — the traditional blue amulet the Turks believed protected one from the evil eye. He headed straight for the area that she'd avoided up until this point.

Even after all these years, she still had a visceral reaction when she spotted a Christmas tree. But if she was finally going to move on, Miranda knew she needed to face it instead of avoiding it.

She followed Kyle to the tastefully decorated tree, which stood in the corner of the dining area.

"Your decorations are lovely," she said.

"Thanks," Kyle said, placing the amulet next to a silver-dusted pinecone. "Some people probably think it's silly to decorate for Christmas, seeing as I live here alone, but it's the holidays. I can't *not* decorate. It's tradition in my family."

Miranda nodded. It used to be a tradition in her family, too. The *best* tradition.

The emotions she'd tried to suppress welled up in her throat, threatening to spill forth. She managed to maintain her control.

Until she spotted it.

A tiny replica of Batman's Batmobile hung

innocently from a softly flocked branch.

The air rushed out of Miranda's lungs. Pain crushed her chest. Her heartbeat thudded in her ears, making her dizzy.

"Miranda?" Kyle reached for her, but she backed away, covering her mouth with both hands. "Miranda, what's wrong?"

She shook her head. "I'm sorry," she murmured. "I just need . . . I need a minute." She turned and raced up the stairs, locking herself in the bathroom.

Kyle stared at the bathroom door, unsure of what he should do. Unsure if he should do anything.

What in the heck could have freaked her out like this?

After about five minutes of vacillating back and forth, he finally decided to man up. Rapping lightly on the door with his knuckles, Kyle called, "Hey, Miranda, are you okay in there?"

His question was met with silence, and his anxiety tripled.

"Miranda?" Kyle called. He jiggled the door handle. A second later, the bathroom door opened, and Miranda emerged. Her deep brown eyes were luminous with unshed tears, though it was obvious that she'd shed some. She'd shed a lot if the tracks on her face were any indication. She'd tried to wipe them, but the evidence remained on her soft cheeks.

"Hey," Kyle said, smoothing a hand down her head and pulling her to him. "What happened down there?"

"I'm so sorry about that."

"Don't apologize, just talk to me."

She shook her head.

"Miranda, don't tell me it's nothing. Not to brag or anything, but you saw the degrees on the wall, I'm a pretty smart guy. I can tell when something's wrong."

"I forgot I was dealing with the world's sexiest mad scientist," she said with a chuckle that still sounded too much like a sob for Kyle's peace of mind. She swiped at her nose with a tissue, and said, "One of the ornaments on your tree brought back a memory that I wasn't ready to handle." She looked up at him, her eyes pleading. "Please don't press me on this. I'm okay now," she said. "Honest."

Kyle believed that in the same way he believed Santa would come down his chimney tonight to deliver presents, but if avoidance was what she needed right now, he'd roll with it.

She plastered on an overly bright smile and said, "It looks as if this storm isn't letting up anytime soon. I should text Erin to let her know that I'm probably going to miss Christmas at her place."

"If she's been following the news at all, she probably already knows," Kyle said. "However, I say we make this Christmas one for the record books."

She snaked her hands around his waist and pressed her body up against his. Kyle's hands automatically dropped to her backside. He palmed it, giving her a firm squeeze.

"And how do you propose we do that?" Miranda asked with a smile that was so damn naughty Kyle wanted to strip her naked this very instant.

But he knew a diversion technique when he saw one, and after what just happened with the Christmas ornament, he knew that anything that happened in that bed right now would be nothing more than a distraction for her. That wasn't necessarily a bad thing, but he didn't want her linking sex with him to whatever had sent her running up here.

He gave her ass a light pat. "I love knowing that's what's on your mind, but it's not what I meant. Back in Istanbul, you said that Christmas isn't a big deal to you, but as you can probably tell, it's a pretty big deal to me, especially Christmas Eve. There are a few traditions that I can't skip. You game?"

She hunched her shoulder. "When in Rome," she said. Then she pointed a finger at him. "Unless it involves singing Christmas carols. I stop when it comes to off-tune versions of 'Silent Night.' "

"No singing," Kyle said. "Unless it's 'Grandma Got Run Over by a Reindeer.' That's a classic that's loved by all."

That garnered him an eye roll, followed by a laugh. He was so relieved to hear that sound from her after what happened a few minutes ago. On the one hand, he wanted to know what had triggered her swift mood change, but when he thought about the plea he'd witnessed in her eyes when she'd asked him to drop the subject, Kyle just couldn't bring himself to press her on it.

Instead, he vowed to take her mind off whatever had troubled her, and make this Christmas Eve one she would never forget.

A few minutes later, they were settled on the sofa with a bowl of popcorn between them and two bottles of the Pecan-Honey beer he'd brewed before leaving for Istanbul.

"This is, by far, my favorite Christmas movie. I've watched it every Christmas Eve for the last twenty years. It's tradition."

Miranda expelled an overly dramatic sigh. "Please don't tell me I have to sit through *It's a Wonderful Life* or *Miracle on 34th Street.* I know people the world over love those, but I'd rather hold my hand over a hot fire."

"Yeah, right," Kyle said as he pressed a couple of buttons on the remote. "Do I look like the *Miracle on 34th Street* type?"

The television came to life and the opening credits of *National Lampoon's Christmas Vacation* began to roll.

"Now this is a classic," Kyle said. "Chevy Chase at his finest."

Miranda shook her head. "I should have known better."

It was obvious Miranda hadn't seen the movie nearly as many times as he had. Less than five minutes in and she was already wiping tears of mirth from her eyes. They'd just watched the scene where Cousin Eddie pulls up in his mobile trailer, when Miranda asked the question that made Kyle's entire Christmas Eve a thousand times better.

She held up her empty beer bottle and asked, "You mind if I have another? I don't even like beer, but this is fantastic."

Pride ballooned in his chest. He rushed over to the fridge and grabbed a couple of different brews, along with several of the double shot glasses he used for sampling.

"If you liked that one," Kyle said as he made his way down the steps of the sunken living room, "maybe you'll like one of these." He set a flight of three beers on the table in front of her.

Miranda peered over the various beers, which ranged in color from light amber to a rich, dark brown.

"What am I tasting here?" she asked.

"We have a Belgian-style witbier, an Irish-style red, and an English-style oatmeal stout."

"How very international of you," she quipped.

Kyle shrugged. "What can I say, the guys across the pond know how to brew a beer. I've been playing around with some traditional flavors, adding just one or two surprises to make them unique."

"Which one do I drink first?"

"One minute," he said, and pointed to the television. Once Clark Griswold finished his tirade about his Jelly-of-the-Month Club Christmas bonus, Kyle returned his attention to the beers.

"Sorry, but that's my favorite scene in the entire movie," he said. He gestured to the glasses. "The proper way to sample a flight of beers is to go from light to dark. The lighter beers have less hops and bitterness, so it's gentler on your palate." He handed her the witbier. "I call this one Tasty Tangerine Tango. Witbiers tend to have citrus notes, so the tangerine works."

Kyle looked up to find her staring at him with a curious smile.

"What?" he asked.

"You're really into this beer-making thing."

"I did just fly all the way to Istanbul because of this beer-making thing," he said with a laugh.

"You have to admit that it's not every day that you come across someone with a doctorate degree who brews beer for a living. How did it come about?"

His shoulders hunched in another shrug. "It started as a hobby. I have a couple of friends I met a few months after I moved here — I've been in Colorado about eight years now. We'd get together for a pickup basketball game at least once a week, then go out to have a beer. The micro-brewing craze had just started to get its legs around that time. It was nothing like it is today — everybody is brewing craft beers these days — but here in Denver, and especially over in Boulder, it was already pretty popular."

He picked up a couple of lingering popcorn kernels, then tossed them back in the bowl.

"One of the guys had just opened a bar. He talked about wanting to sell his own house brew, but he didn't know how to go about it. He'd been toying with some ideas, but his chemistry was off."

"Ah," Miranda said. "And that's where you come in."

"Hey, might as well use some of that fancy education, right?" He said it tongue in cheek, but Miranda noticed a bit of an edge to the words. "Anyway," Kyle continued, "once I started to play around with it, I discovered that I liked it. A lot. Things were really stressful with the tech company, and the beer making turned into somewhat of a stress reliever."

"How did it go from just a stress-relieving hobby to a potential business?"

"I sold my company," Kyle said. "Earlier this year. I'd been fending off buyers ever since the first big app went viral. One of them finally made me the offer I couldn't refuse. I'd become tired of the rat race. I'd made more than enough money to live on, so I didn't really need it anymore."

"That's the kind of story most people would kill for," Miranda said. "You're very lucky."

Another shrug. "Some people may think I'm crazy. A lot of people — my dad included — think that by abandoning my tech company, I threw away my chances to make even more money. But it isn't always about what's sitting in my bank account. I love what I'm doing right now."

She brought her hand up to his jaw and caressed his skin. "I think it's awesome that you're doing what you love. So many people spend years of their lives being unhappy because they cater to what others believe is best for them. You listened to your heart. Forget anyone who thinks it's crazy. I think it's an amazing show of strength and character."

Kyle considered responding, but knew nothing would get past the lump of emotion lodged in his throat. She couldn't possibly know how much he needed to hear those words.

"Thank you," he finally managed to get out.

She smiled. "You're welcome."

Miranda went through the rest of the beer flight, choosing the apple-cinnamon-flavored stout as her favorite. They shared a lunch of loaded-baked-potato soup, which he'd thankfully had in the freezer, then watched another of Kyle's favorites, *Christ-*

mas with the Kranks.

"You have way too many Christmas movies in your DVD collection," Miranda said as they returned to the sofa.

"I told you already that this is my favorite time of the year. I love Christmas. Always have." He settled back on the sofa and pulled Miranda to him, fitting her back against his chest. The soft roundness of her ass resting snug in his lap triggered an immediate case of lust, but Kyle managed to control himself.

He wrapped his arms around her and buried his chin against her neck, placing a light kiss on her jaw.

"What's the best thing you ever got for Christmas?" he asked.

She didn't even hesitate. "A camera."

Hearing the smile in her voice was like sweet music to his ears. Even though hours had passed, Kyle had been on edge ever since the debacle with the Christmas tree.

"I should have guessed that," he said.

"It was my very first digital camera," Miranda continued. "It was back when digital cameras were the new big thing, and you could only take about twelve shots before all of the memory was filled up. And the only way to get the pictures off the camera was to hook a cord to your computer. There was no uploading to the Internet. I don't even know if smart cards had been invented back then."

"Wow, back in the real Dark Ages," Kyle teased.

"Pretty much." She chuckled, then released a nostalgic sigh. "But — oh, my God — how I loved that camera. I spent that entire Christmas Day outside taking pictures of any- and everything. Every twenty minutes, I would run back into the house, upload the pictures to our old desktop computer, which was about the size of a Honda Civic, and then run back out and take another dozen. My dad had to come get me that night because, even in the snow, I just could not make myself stop snapping photos."

"Based on that monster camera you carried all around Istanbul, you've come a long way equipment-wise."

"Yeah, I have, but I still have that very first camera," she said. "It actually survived the —" She stopped short. Kyle didn't know what to make of the hitch in her voice. "It survived all these years," she finished. She expelled a deep breath and looked up at him over her shoulder. "What about you? What was your favorite Christmas gift of all time?"

"That's easy," Kyle said. "It was the year

my dad got us Chicago Bulls tickets."

"So you're a basketball fan."

He nodded. "Big-time. The same way your dad had to drag you inside from taking pictures, it's the same way my parents would drag me and my brothers inside at night. My mom always said that the day my dad first hung a basketball hoop over the garage was the day her sons forgot how to tell time." Kyle chuckled, remembering how his mom would come outside with her hand on her hips, demanding they come in for dinner. "We'd spend hours out there, shooting hoops. I was the youngest of us three boys, but do you think those two jerks took it easy on me?"

"I'm guessing they didn't," Miranda said.

"Heck no. Not even a little." He pulled her tighter to him, giving her a gentle squeeze. "That's okay, though. They've both gotten soft. If I were home right now, I would kick both their butts on the court."

That thought sapped up every bit of joy Kyle had been feeling, replacing it with a sense of melancholy.

He could picture his parents' house right now, bursting at the seams with his siblings and their families. Despite the ever-growing brood, no one dared to get a hotel room at Christmastime. The kids all slept in sleeping bags spread around the house. In the past few years, ever since Timothy had gotten married, Kyle had slept on the sofa so that Tim and his wife, Nimrata, could have the room he and his brother shared as kids.

Right now, his mom was probably sitting at the organ, with the rest of the family gathered around her, singing carols. Miranda had joked about singing "Silent Night," but that's exactly what Kyle would be doing if he was back in Chicago. His mother, who'd taught music for twenty-five years and had been the organist at their church long before Kyle had been born, had made sure all her children and grandchildren knew how to sing. There would be no off-key notes sung at the Daniels house. Their rendition of "Silent Night" would be soulful and wonderful.

Kyle mentally batted away thoughts of what he was missing back home. After the huge blow up between him and his dad on Thanksgiving, he'd convinced himself that he didn't need to celebrate Christmas with his family this year. He just didn't anticipate how much it would hurt to miss it.

"Hey, are you okay?" Miranda asked.

Kyle went for a carefree smile, but he knew he missed the mark. "Yeah," he said. "I'm good."

She pointed to the television, where the credits were scrolling. "I thought the first movie was funny, but this one was even better."

"I can't believe you'd never watched either of these before." Kyle shook his head.

"I can promise you that it won't be the last time. I plan to watch them both whenever I need a good laugh, whether it's Christmastime or not. So," she asked, "is there another must-watch on your list?"

Kyle shrugged. "Not really," he said.

"Good," she said, turning around in his lap and looking up at him. "Because what I really want to do —"

"Yes?" Kyle asked, cutting her off. He lifted his brows suggestively.

Her cheeks reddened in the sexiest, most adorable way imaginable.

"I do want to do that," she said. "But you promised to show me how you make beer. I want to see that even more."

"Even more than . . ." Kyle wiggled his brows again.

Miranda threw her head back with her laugh.

"The beer is winning by a narrow margin," she said. She pushed herself up off the sofa, grabbed both his hands and tugged.

Kyle refused to budge.

"What's wrong?" Miranda asked.

"You just told me you'd rather make beer instead of going upstairs and letting me rock your world. I've earned the right to sulk for a minute."

She pulled her bottom lip between her teeth, her grin 100 percent wicked. She leaned down, placing her lips a hairsbreadth from his.

"It's only because when I *do* get you in bed, I don't plan to let you leave it until the morning."

Desire shot straight to Kyle's groin.

He allowed her to pull him up, but when she started for the kitchen, he tugged her back to him, clasping his hands at the small of her back and pulling her flush against him.

"I'm going to hold you to that," he murmured against her lips.

Her brows arched with her suggestive smile. "You'd better." She slapped his ass. "Now let's make some beer."

CHAPTER FIVE

Miranda watched with spellbound fascination as the well-honed muscles in Kyle's
arms flexed underneath his golden brown
skin. She was thoroughly mesmerized, staring at the way they contracted and released,
moving in a subtle, seductive rhythm as he
crushed several spices into a fine powder
using a marble mortar and pestle.

"The trick," Kyle said, knocking her out
of her captivated trance, "is finding the right
balance of flavor for the type of beer you
want to make. Too much or too little of any
one ingredient can throw off the entire recipe."

"Umm-hmm," Miranda said. She stood
up straight and pretended to pay attention,
when, in fact, she'd lost all interest in her
lesson on beer making the minute Kyle
rolled up the sleeves on his gray cashmere
sweater and began combining ingredients.
There was just something about a sexy man

in the kitchen that made him even sexier.

He picked up a bowl with dark purple flower buds. "I'm not sure how this one will work out, but I thought up the recipe while browsing the Spice Market back in Istanbul. The Myosotis flower has a walnut taste. It should do well in this recipe." He handed her the crushed flower buds. "You do it," he said. "This is supposed to be a team effort."

With a wary glance, Miranda walked over to the pot of grain that had been boiling for the past half hour. "Should I be wearing protective goggles or something?"

"Goggles are for pansies. Take a risk," Kyle said. She looked back over her shoulder. "I'm only joking. You won't need goggles. You're fine."

"Where are all the tubes and kettles?" Miranda asked. "I once saw a show on the Cooking Channel about home breweries and there was a big setup that looked like a chemistry set on steroids."

"That comes later, just before the fermenting stage," Kyle said. "What we're doing right here is called mashing. By letting the barley steep in the hot water, it'll eventually convert the starches to sugar. It helps with the fermenting process. We have to cook the mash for another half hour before we can move to the next step."

Miranda let out an exaggerated sigh as she sprinkled the purple flowers into the simmering hops. Then she turned to him. "How long does this whole beer-making thing take?"

Amusement flickered in Kyle's eyes as he came upon her. He took the bowl from her hands and set it on the counter. He then took both of her hands and pressed a kiss to the backs of her fingers.

"Did I forget to mention that the number one ingredient is patience?" he asked.

"Yes, you did. Because if you *had* mentioned it, I would have told you that I have none."

"Really?" His brow arched as he took her hands and brought them around his waist. Then he clasped his at the small of her back and pulled her in, melding her body up against his. "We've been here nearly twenty-four hours and haven't made it to my bed yet. I'd say we're both kicking ass in the patience department."

Miranda felt the bulge that had grown behind his zipper. She ground her pelvis against him.

"I'm all out of patience," she said.

He reached over and turned the fire off under the boiling pot.

"I'm right there with you."

She brought her hands up and clasped the back of his head, bringing him into her for a deep, sensual kiss. She'd fought her body's demands, but it would no longer be denied. She needed him. All of him. And she wasn't stopping until Kyle gave her every delicious part of him.

Their kiss turned from mild to scorching in ten seconds flat — a ferocious clashing of lips, teeth, and tongue that shot a flood of mind-numbing sensations through her veins. With their lips still locked together, Kyle hoisted her up and Miranda wrapped her legs around his waist. His strength was as much a turn-on as his wickedly decadent kisses. He didn't break a sweat as he carried her from the kitchen and up the stairs to his bedroom.

Once there, Miranda slid down his body. Her own body hummed with want at the feel of his rock hard erection trailing down her abdomen. She tore the sweater over her head and peeled off her leggings. Her bra was the next to go. By the time Miranda fell back onto his bed, she wore nothing but her boy-cut cotton panties. She hooked her thumbs in the sides and pulled them off her hips, tossing them on the floor next to the bed.

Kyle had already rid himself of his clothes

and sheathed himself with a condom. Standing at the edge of the bed, he closed his palms around her calves and lifted her legs in the air, spreading them so that she was completely exposed to him.

Her center clenched with need. Just his gaze on her was enough to set every one of her nerve endings off like New Year's fireworks.

But she wanted more than his gaze on her. She wanted *him* on her.

"Please, Kyle," Miranda breathed with a gasp. "Please."

"No need to beg," Kyle said, tugging her down toward him and hooking her legs over his shoulders. "I'm about to give you all you can take, and more."

He lowered his head between her thighs and closed his mouth over her aching wet center. Miranda lifted off the bed, shoving her body against his mouth, gaining new life from the wicked way his tongue lashed at her. He plunged into her, his tongue dipping in and out. When his thumb joined in the erotic assault on her senses, Miranda was certain she would spontaneously combust from the sheer pleasure of it. It trailed up and down her soaking flesh, growing more insistent as he matched the rhythm of his tongue's continued licks. Then he switched tactics, rolling his thumb around her engorged clitoris, plucking at it, pinching it, flicking it, then finally sucking it into his mouth. Hard. So incredibly, shockingly hard.

Miranda's back bowed once again. She squeezed his head between her thighs, needing to keep him right where she had him.

Her entire body hummed with the pleasure driving through her at maximum speed. Just when she thought she couldn't take any more, Kyle sucked his middle and forefingers into his mouth, then shoved them inside her.

Her entire world exploded in a brilliant display of dazzling light. Her limbs trembled as the powerful orgasm tore through her.

That night in Istanbul had been one of the most satisfying of her life, but Miranda had the tantalizing feeling that it wouldn't be able to compare to what was about to happen. As her body continued to throb with the aftershocks of her orgasm, Kyle kissed his way up her body, pressing his lips against her stomach, then her ribs, then the undersides of her breasts. He gave special attention to her nipples. Licking and sucking and biting, driving her already overtaxed mind absolutely wild.

"God, Kyle. Don't stop," Miranda called

out, her voice hoarse with desire.

He continued his journey north, trailing his lips along her jawline, and up to her ear.

"Stop? Sweetheart, I'm just getting started."

Miranda shuddered at his warmly whispered promise, her body already anticipating what was yet to come.

Before she knew what he was doing, Kyle slid his hand underneath her and turned her over, maneuvering her limbs until she was on all fours.

Miranda shivered as she knelt on the mattress, her knees spread apart, her body open to him, presented like a decadent offering. She glanced back and was nearly singed by Kyle's scorching-hot glaze. Tingles cascaded across her skin, electrifying her entire body, sending her so close to the edge.

She tensed for the briefest second when Kyle nudged her opening, then released an indulgent moan as his rigid length pushed its way into her body. Standing at the edge of the bed, he grabbed her hips and guided her back and forth, rocking into her. Miranda whimpered with each delicious slide of his thick erection, the pleasure so intense, so potent, she could hardly wrap her head around it. Nothing had ever felt this good.

"Deeper," she groaned, arching her back

and driving her ass against his pelvis. Kyle shifted one hand to the small of her back, pressing down ever so slightly so that she bent a little lower.

The angle opened her up even more, letting him slide even deeper. He filled her completely. Luxuriously. It took everything within her not to scream again as hedonistic pleasure slammed into her body. Instead, Miranda bit her lip and concentrated on maintaining her composure. She was so close to another orgasm, but she didn't want it just yet. She wanted to relish in the unbelievable pleasure he'd released in her.

The hand at the small of her back traveled up her spine, until he reached her hair. When he wrapped a length of her hair around his hand and tugged with just enough force to garner a yelp from her, Miranda's entire body exploded with a mixture of pleasure-filled pain. A bounty of delectable sensations swirled inside her, all demanding her attention. Miranda didn't know which to concentrate on.

But that choice was taken out of her hands when Kyle's other hand snaked around her torso and trailed down her stomach, to her throbbing sex. As his thick erection continued to pummel her from behind, he swirled the pad of his thumb around her clit, over and over and over again, then he pressed it against her flesh.

The force of her climax sapped every drop of her energy.

Miranda collapsed onto the bed, her limbs no longer able to hold her up. Kyle followed her down, pumping into her — one, two, three times more — before finding his own release.

"Forget those Bulls tickets," he whispered against her temple. "You're the best Christmas present I've ever gotten."

As Kyle lay on his bed with Miranda draped across his chest, he realized that he'd never felt more replete in his life. Her soft snores brought a smile to his lips. It was probably the lingering effects of jet lag, but his ego was inclined to believe that he'd worn her out with their marathon lovemaking.

He stroked his fingers through her hair, imagining how things would have been if he'd never walked to the back of the plane yesterday — or was that two days ago?

Shit, maybe he needed to catch a few winks himself, but he was still too wired to sleep. Or maybe he was afraid that if he *did* go to sleep, he'd wake up only to discover that this was all a fantasy — some fatigue-induced defense mechanism to shield him from the pain of spending the holidays alone.

Kyle glanced down at the woman plastered against his chest and that satisfied smile traveled across his lips once more.

She was fantasy-worthy, but she was also 100 percent real. And, at least for this Christmas, she was his.

The thought caused his chest to swell with triumph, but just as quickly, a pang of sorrow quelled his excitement. To say he was overjoyed at the fact that she was here with him was an understatement. Even though the snowstorm that still raged outside had a hand in their current situation, she'd still made the choice to be with him. Despite his insistence that she come home with him, she could have just as easily insisted that she stay at a hotel. She was here because she wanted to be here.

But what if this was it?

What if, when she finally did get on a plane to Portland, she decided that this was all just a brief holiday liaison that shouldn't go any further? What if, after she got her fill of multiple orgasms, she announced that it would be better if they didn't keep up this new friendship, or relationship, or whatever this thing was between them?

Kyle's chest tightened with the fear of

hearing those words from her. He wasn't sure how the thought of losing someone he'd met just a few days ago could evoke such a visceral response from him, but it was there, clawing up his throat, its meaty fingers suddenly strangling him.

He felt Miranda stir. Her smooth, bare thigh brushed against his groin, and fears of her leaving were instantly usurped by more pleasurable thoughts.

"Are you finally awake?" he asked.

She sighed, lifting slightly from his chest so she could look up at him. "How long have I been asleep?"

"A couple of hours," he said. "There's some leftover soup. I can warm it up if you're hungry."

"I am," she said. "But I don't want to get up."

Kyle peered down at her. "Is that your subtle way of asking me to bring you dinner in bed?"

"No. I don't want you to get up, either. You're comfortable. Not as soft and squishy as my pillow, but I think soft and squishy may be overrated."

Kyle's shoulders shook with his laugh. He did that so easily around her. On this Christmas Eve, when he'd fully expected to be drowning himself in sorrow-filled thoughts about what he was missing in Chicago, he found himself not wanting to be anywhere else.

No, that was a lie. He still wanted to be back home with his family. But he wanted Miranda to be there with him.

Maybe he was jumping fifty thousand steps ahead — okay, he was *definitely* jumping fifty thousand steps ahead. They'd only met a few days ago, and other than a few cursory facts, he hardly knew anything about her.

But they meshed. That much he *did* know. It was undeniable. He'd never felt so at ease with another woman, not even the one he'd dated for over three years.

He kissed the top of her head and eased from underneath her. "I'll be back in a minute," he said.

Kyle pulled his favorite worn heather-gray T-shirt over his head, but didn't bother to pull pajama pants over his matching boxer briefs. The pants would just be an added barrier when the time came to do a repeat performance of what they'd done just a few hours ago.

He was in the middle of ladling soup into a bowl as Miranda came around the frosted-glass wall dressed in one of his white T-shirts that had been in the stack from the laundry service. The shirt's hem didn't quite reach mid thigh, and suddenly Kyle was hungry for something other than soup.

"God, that smells amazing," Miranda said, walking over to the stove in her bare feet. "You'll have to share the recipe."

Kyle knew he was jumping the gun again, but God, how amazing would it be to have her here like this every day? To spend lazy weekends together, making love, watching movies, making love, brewing beer, making love.

He wanted to capture this domestic moment in his mind and keep it there, a picture of what their future could be. Something beyond this little Christmas miracle.

"You'd have to ask the food delivery service I use," Kyle said.

"Okay, honest question here. Do you farm out everything?"

"Meaning?"

She ticked items off on her fingers. "You don't do your own laundry, or cook your own meals, or do your own grocery shopping. And, call me crazy, but I'm pretty certain you didn't decorate this place."

"What makes you say that?"

The look she tossed his way made Kyle bark out a laugh.

"Yeah, okay, I had an interior decorator

come in and decorate it," he admitted. "But I do have to cook the groceries that were delivered. However, I'm not going to go through the trouble of cooking this soup, when the caterer in town does such a good job of it."

He gestured for her to take a seat at the island, then placed a bowl in front of her.

"Give me a minute to grab the bread from the oven," Kyle said.

He did so, placing the warm baguette on a plate between their two bowls of soup.

Miranda motioned toward the pot of mash that had been cooking earlier during their beer-making session.

"Is that salvageable?" she asked him.

Kyle shook his head. "Nah." He leaned over and brushed a kiss against her lips. "But it was worth losing."

Once they'd eaten their soup, they made their way over to the sofa, parroting their earlier pose, with Miranda sitting between his legs, her back against his chest. Kyle pulled the moss-green chenille blanket he kept on the arm of the sofa over them, then tightened his hold on her. The Christmas lights twinkled on the tree, reflecting in the window.

He wanted this. He wanted what they had at this very moment — this comfortable silence, their twin heartbeats beating as one. He wanted it forever.

"Kyle, what happened between you and your dad?"

Her softly spoken words crashed into his peace like a three-ton boulder, rendering him momentarily speechless. When she twisted around in his arms, Kyle could tell by the look in her eyes that she wasn't backing down from her question.

He sucked in a deep breath and released it. Repeated it. Then repeated it again.

He didn't want to talk about this.

He experienced the familiar ache that squeezed his throat whenever he even thought about the fight he had with his dad — like something heavy and dull was pressing against either side of his neck, not hard enough to choke him, but with enough pressure to make him want to suffocate.

"Do you . . ." He stopped, then cleared his throat. "Do you remember what I said about selling my tech company?" Miranda nodded. "Well, my dad didn't think that was a good move. He thought I took the coward's way out."

"By making millions off a business you sold?"

"Did I say that it was millions?" Kyle asked. He usually didn't talk actual figures.

He didn't like anyone to think he was bragging.

"No, you didn't," Miranda said. "I just assumed it was."

He hunched his shoulders. "Yeah, well, it *was* millions," Kyle admitted. "But money, in my dad's opinion, and in mine, to be honest, isn't the only hallmark of success. Actually, it's not even in the top five. For him, success is more about finding one thing you do well and being the absolute best at it.

"When I left my job at the EPA, my dad wasn't happy. He thought it was a waste of all that education, but he saw how much I enjoyed working with computers, so he supported me. But when I sold my firm after only a few years, he saw it as me giving up — giving in to the pressure of the companies that had been trying to buy it. He called me a coward."

A sharp ache speared through Kyle's chest at the memory of them yelling at each other across the table during Thanksgiving dinner.

"But you didn't sell because you felt pressured, did you? You wanted to go into beer making."

"There were a number of factors," he said. "I'd taken my firm as far as I was willing to take it. The company that bought it already had enough things in place to grow it to its full potential, and at a much faster rate than I could. It was better for my employees. When I tried to explain this to my dad, he accused me of being a coward who can't make up my mind about what I want to do in life."

"And?"

Kyle jerked his head back. "And what?"

"What else did he say during the big fight?"

"You don't think that's enough?"

Her eyes went wide, and instead of the sympathy and understanding Kyle thought he'd get from her, she wore an expression of disgust. "Are you kidding me?" Miranda asked. "That's it? *That's* why you skipped Christmas with your family?"

She pushed up from the sofa and marched toward the television.

Kyle followed her, but he stopped when she turned and he saw tears forming at the corners of her eyes. He just stood there, stunned. When two slipped rapidly down her cheeks, he found the ability to move. He took her into his arms and brushed his lips against her temple.

"Miranda, what's wrong?" Kyle asked. "What is it?"

She stared up at him, her eyes two luminous pools filled with hurt and regret.

"Please," she pleaded. "Don't let this silly fight ruin your relationship with your family, Kyle. Especially at Christmas. Instead, be grateful that you have a family to share your Christmas holiday with. Some of us aren't so lucky, and haven't been for a long, long time."

Chapter Six

Miranda lifted the blanket from the sofa and wrapped it around her shoulders. Then, summoning more courage than she'd had to in years, climbed the couple of steps leading from the sunken living room and headed straight for the one place in the house that she'd most avoided. She walked up to the Christmas tree, her eyes zeroing in on the Batman ornament. It hung so innocently from the flocked branch. Miranda let the ornament rest in her palm, studying it for several moments before allowing it to fall back into place.

Kyle came up behind her, but he remained silent. When his hands came up and clasped her upper arms, she flinched just a bit.

"Miranda?" He spoke her name so softly, as if he thought anything louder would break her.

For a moment, Miranda thought the same. But she was stronger than she'd given herself credit for all these years. It wouldn't break her to talk about them.

She'd made her decision. In the moments as she listened to Kyle talk about the fight with his father, and told him how foolish it would be to let it ruin their relationship, Miranda recognized just what she'd allowed her own memories to do to her for the past decade and a half. She'd allowed the tragedy of one night to obliterate years of good memories.

"My little brother had one like this," she said, brushing her finger along the plastic Batmobile. "My brother and I used to collect the Hallmark ornaments. There was always a new one every year. I'm not sure if the company still does that or not, but it was a big deal in my family."

"I don't know," Kyle said. "My sister gave this one to me after finding it at a garage sale. She remembered how much I loved Batman as a kid." He paused for a moment, and then in a voice threaded with caution, he asked, "What happened to your brother's?"

Miranda swallowed, closing her eyes tightly before opening them again. She stared at their reflection in the window, grabbing hold of Kyle's gaze.

"It burned in the fire," she said. "Along

with my family."

She felt Kyle stiffen.

Moments passed. Long, heart-wrenching moments. Miranda braced herself for a tsunami of pain, but it didn't come. She didn't feel pain; all she felt was the overwhelming urge to talk. To finally give voice to the tragedy that had changed her life forever.

She turned to face Kyle.

"In my family, it was always the tradition to decorate the Christmas tree just after Thanksgiving, but we wouldn't turn the lights on until a few days before Christmas. It was some superstition my mom had. It's the way she and her family always did it when she was growing up."

Miranda took a moment to swallow past the lump that began to form in her throat. She could hear her mom chastising both Miranda and her little brother about plugging in the Christmas lights, claiming it was bad luck to light the tree too early.

"The year I turned fifteen, I missed the annual lighting of the tree," she continued. "My best friend, Rondalyn, invited me to a sleepover. I knew my mom was hurt that I wanted to skip the tree lighting, but she didn't say anything when I asked to spend the night at Rondalyn's."

She paused. *Breathe in. Breathe out.*

"I —" She cleared her throat. It had been years since she'd uttered a single word out loud about the incident, and while it wasn't as hard as she thought it would be, it was still undeniably difficult. "I didn't find out about the fire until the house had nearly burned to the ground," she continued. "My next-door-neighbor, Mrs. Caldwell, started screaming when she saw me running down the street in my bare feet and flannel Santa Claus pajama pants. She thought I was a ghost. Everyone assumed I'd been in the house, too."

"My God," Kyle said. He pulled her into his arms and squeezed her so tight Miranda couldn't breathe — or was that because she'd just talked about the tragic night that had forever scarred her?

"This happened when you were fifteen?" he asked.

She nodded.

"That's so young, Miranda. Who took care of you?"

She swiped at a wayward tear that had managed to escape the corner of her eye. "I went to live with my grandparents until I graduated high school, but they both died within a year of each other while I was studying at Ohio State. I've been on my own ever since."

Kyle pressed a kiss to the crown of her head. "I am so sorry. I knew something bad had happened. I could tell from the way you reacted when you saw the ornament this morning, but I never expected anything like this. This is more than anyone should ever have to deal with, and for you to go through it at fifteen?"

He choked up on the last word, and Miranda felt her own throat tighten with gratitude at his empathy.

She looked up at him. "I can't help but think that if I had never gone to Rondalyn's, maybe I could have saved them."

"More than likely, you would have died in the house, along with them," he pointed out.

She released a deep breath, then spoke the truth. "I'm not so sure that would have been a bad thing."

The pain that slashed across Kyle's face was raw and honest and brutal. "Never say that," he said, his voice rough with emotion.

"But that's how I've felt so many times over the years," she said.

"You can't blame yourself for what happened, and you can't feel guilty for living, Miranda."

"I've blamed everybody. I blamed myself for not being there. I blamed my parents for allowing me to go to Rondalyn's. I blamed her for inviting me over for a sleepover in the first place. I didn't talk to her at all after the fire. She was my best friend, and I completely cut her out of my life." Miranda shook her head. "A couple of years ago — the last time I told myself that it was time to finally move past this — I tried to contact her. I found out that she'd died from breast cancer the year before."

"My God," Kyle said, pulling her to him again.

"Yeah, my life is chock-full of regrets."

Kyle smoothed a hand down her hair, then brought it up to her cheek. He passed his thumb back and forth over her skin. "Did they ever figure out what started the fire?"

She nodded. "According to the fire investigators, a faulty light on the Christmas tree provided the first spark," she said.

He whispered a curse. "God, Miranda, I'm so sorry."

"It hasn't been easy," she admitted. "I've come to understand that this isn't the kind of thing you ever fully get over, but I no longer want it to consume me. I reached a crossroad this year. That day we spent together in Istanbul was the fifteenth anniversary of the fire. I've now been without my family for longer than I was with them."

"That's a pretty significant anniversary."

"Yes," she said with a nod. "I have to make a decision. I have to decide if I will let this tragedy dictate the rest of my life, the way it's dictated the last fifteen years, or if I'll finally allow myself to move on."

"And?" Kyle asked, his voice barely a whisper.

In the most earnest voice she could muster, she said, "I want to move on. I want to love Christmas again. It was always the best time, and I miss it."

"So, why haven't you celebrated it, Miranda?"

"For so long, it's felt wrong for me to feel happiness at Christmas. How can I, when it took my family away from me? I shouldn't feel joy when I look at this Christmas tree — I should feel rage." She looked up at him. "But I don't anymore. I look at this ornament, and I remember the way Kevin's eyes lit with excitement when my mom gave it to him to hang on the tree."

"Joy is what you *should* feel, Miranda. That's what this holiday is all about."

Kyle captured her upper arms in his hands and looked her directly in the eyes.

"What would your family want?" he asked. "Would they want you never to celebrate this holiday that meant so much to them, or would they want you to move on?"

Miranda couldn't speak. The collection of sorrow, hope, and cautious joy rioting through her was almost too much for her to handle.

"They would want me to move on," she finally managed to whisper.

"Yes, they would." Kyle kissed her forehead, then dipped his head again so that he could look her in the eyes. "It's not too late to make new memories. Christmas will never be what it was when you still had your family, but it can still be special. Let this be your new beginning. Let this year be the start of something new and wonderful." He captured her chin between his fingers and lifted her face. "And let me join you on this new journey."

Her heart was so full, it felt on the verge of bursting.

She wanted this. She wanted *him*. This man who'd caught her eye in the middle of a crowded market just a few short days ago. This man who was only supposed to be a passing fling. He'd come to mean so much more than she'd ever imagined.

Maybe it was fate that had brought them together. Maybe it was just coincidence. But it didn't matter how they got here, only that they *were* here now. She was exactly where she wanted to be in these hours before Christmas Day arrived. And, suddenly, all Miranda could think of was how much she wanted to be here with him for many more Christmases to come.

She captured Kyle's face between her palms and pulled him to her.

"Yes," Miranda softly whispered against his lips. "Please come with me on this journey. It would be the best Christmas present I could ever hope for."

Kyle stood in front of his huge computer screen, a smile drawing across his face as his niece panned the living room with her iPad. It was nearing midnight in Chicago, and everyone was in pajamas, waiting for the clock to strike twelve so they could open their gifts.

The look on his mother's face, like she wanted to both laugh and sob, caused a deep ache to settle in Kyle's chest. In that moment, he finally understood what his decision to skip Christmas had done to her.

Yet, Kyle couldn't regret it. If he'd gone to Chicago instead of Istanbul, he never would have met Miranda. And meeting her was, without a doubt, the best thing to have ever happened to him.

Kyle couldn't help but think that everything that had happened this past week was all part of a divine plan — a miraculous Christmas gift that was meant to be cherished for the rest of his life.

"I'm sorry I'm not there," Kyle said. It wasn't a total lie. He *was* sorry he wasn't at home with his family. They would all love Miranda. Hopefully, next year, they would both be there.

He swallowed deeply. "Um, Jayden, can you hand the iPad to Grandpa?" Kyle waited until his father's face came upon the screen. "Hi, Dad," he said. "Do you, uh, mind going somewhere a bit more private?"

Silence fell on both sides of the electronic devices. Kyle knew this wasn't the best time to do this, but he also knew that he would never be able to enjoy his Christmas Day if he didn't address this issue here and now. After hearing what Miranda had endured and seeing the courage in which she made the decision to let go of the demons of her past, Kyle knew that he could not allow this to fester any longer. She'd lost her entire family in one night. He still had his. He owed it to Miranda to do whatever he could to mend the riff between him and his father before it caused even more pain to his family.

The screen shook slightly as his father rose

from where he sat and carried the iPad into the formal dining room. Kyle heard the door click, then stared as his dad took a seat at the table and balanced the iPad at a slight angle.

"Yes, son?" his father said.

"I'm sorry," Kyle opened. He swallowed. "Back at Thanksgiving, I said some things that I shouldn't have. I'm sorry for being so disrespectful to you, especially in your own home. You didn't raise me to be that way."

His father nodded.

"I'm . . . um . . . I'm sorry for some of the things I said, too," his father said. "You're a grown man. You can do whatever you want to do with your life. Even if you want to make beer."

A smile tipped up the edge of Kyle's mouth.

"I don't just want to make beer," Kyle said. "I plan to do more. But I don't want you to think I'm a coward, Dad, because you didn't raise me to be that way, either. I didn't sell my company because I was scared. I sold it because it's what was best for the company and for my employees. I sold it, in part, because the people who bought it had the means to grow it into something bigger and better than what I could do on my own."

"Son, it doesn't matter what I think —"

"Yes, it does," Kyle said. "There are very few things in this world that matter more to me than what you think. It's always been that way. Making you proud has always been one of the most important things to me."

"Never doubt how proud I am of you, Kyle. No matter what gets said, you should never, ever doubt that you are the best part of your mother and me. Never forget that."

It was hard to swallow past the lump of emotion lodged in his throat.

"Thanks, Dad," Kyle finally managed to get out.

"Merry Christmas, son. We miss having you here."

"I miss being there," he said. "I'll try to make it out there for Mom's birthday in a few weeks. But don't tell her — I want it to be a surprise."

"Please come for her birthday. Maybe then she'll stop giving me those looks she's been sending my way all week. If there weren't so many people needing a place to sleep, I'm sure I would be on the couch."

Kyle laughed. "Make sure to tell her that everything is all right now."

"I will," he said. "I love you, son."

Kyle cleared his throat. "I love you, too, Dad. Give everyone a hug from me."

He disconnected the video call and released a sigh.

"Is that it?"

Kyle looked up to find Miranda standing just outside the door. She pushed it, coming inside.

"Was that really all it took?" she asked.

Kyle nodded. "That's all it took. We were both being stupid and stubborn to begin with."

"Just think, you could have been home with your family right now. I bet you regret being so stubborn."

Kyle shook his head. "Not even one bit," he said.

Her bewildered expression drew a smile out of him.

"If my dad and I hadn't had that fight, I never would have gone to Istanbul," Kyle explained. "And I never would have met you. There's nothing that could ever make me regret that."

Miranda's chest rose with the sharp breath she pulled in. She closed the distance between them and wrapped her arms around his waist. Laying her head against his chest, she softly whispered, "Kyle?"

"Yes?" he asked, his hand moving down her spine in a gentle caress.

"Would it freak you out if I told you I'm

falling in love with you?" She looked up at him, her eyes filled with trepidation and hope. "I know it sounds unbelievable that I could have fallen for you so quickly, but —"

He shut her up with a kiss. A long, leisurely kiss. The kind of kiss he never wanted to end. Miranda melted against him, a faint whimper escaping her lips.

"There's nothing unbelievable about it," Kyle said. "Not when I'm standing here feeling the same way about you." He captured her chin between his fingers and tipped her head up. "I love you, Miranda."

He kissed her again, pulling her to him as his tongue delved into her warm mouth.

"Just in case you were wondering, I have no problem doing that all day long," she said.

Kyle chuckled, giving her another peck on the lips before asking, "Did you talk to Erin?"

Miranda nodded. "She's upset that I'll miss Christmas, but I promised her that I'd make it up to her with a party for New Year's. Do you think you can spare a few days in Portland?"

"I can spare a lifetime in Portland if it means I get to be with you."

The smile that graced her lips was everything Kyle needed.

"There's no way I'm giving up this view," Miranda said. "I think we can go back and forth between our two homes, don't you?"

"Whatever the lady wants," Kyle said with a grin before dipping his head and taking her lips in a slow, sweet kiss.

EPILOGUE

Miranda snuggled closer to Kyle, fitting her back against his chest and pulling the blanket over both their legs. Together they stared outside his bedroom at the vast landscape. The moonlight glinted off the freshly fallen snow, twinkling within the trees.

Miranda brought the mug of warm apple cider to her lips and took a sip, relishing in the sheer perfection of this moment. She'd forgotten that this kind of contentment even existed; yet here she sat, basking in it with the man of her dreams.

"Only a few minutes left," Kyle whispered against her cheek. His fingers gently caressed her arm, gliding over her skin.

For the first time in fifteen years, Miranda experienced something other than pain as the clock ticked down the minutes to Christmas. She would even go so far as to call it happiness. She never imagined she could feel this way about the holiday again. But thanks to the man whose arms held her tight, she felt more than just happy. She felt loved and cherished.

She tilted her head to the side and turned slightly, giving him a kiss on the cheek.

Kyle looked at her with an incredulous frown.

"What?" Miranda asked.

"Is that what you call a Christmas kiss?"

He took the mug from her hand and placed it on the bedside table; then he urged her to turn. Miranda twisted in his lap. She brought her knees on either side of his thighs, straddling him. She wrapped her arms around his head, linking her fingers behind his neck.

"So, what's a proper Christmas kiss?" she whispered against his lips.

She caught sight of the numbers on Kyle's digital clock out of the corner of her eye when they switched from 11:59 to 12:00.

Kyle shoved a hand in her hair and lifted his mouth to hers. "Let me show you how it's done."

▪ ▪ ▪ ▪

FROM HERE TO SERENITY

K. M. JACKSON

▪ ▪ ▪ ▪

CHAPTER ONE

"A panic attack? You have got to be joking. Ross Montgomery doesn't panic." Ross ended his third-person statement by giving the young, pale-faced intern doing a spot-on Doogie Howser impersonation a withering look.

"I, well, I'm sorry, Mr. Montgomery. But it's what our data says," Doogie stammered out.

Ross turned to the nurse fiddling by his bedside, poking at him in a most uncomfortable way. She was brown-skinned and petite, with generous curves and alert brown eyes that seemed to miss nothing. Her bleached-blond, highly teased and sprayed bob was in sharp contrast to her deep skin tone. "Can't you get me someone else, honey?" Ross asked, adding extra molasses to his deep bass. "The kid here obviously doesn't know what he's talking about. As a matter of fact, I'm waiting for my private doctor, Dr. Nair, to come in. Can you go and check on her?" Ross gave the nurse a quick wink and his killer smile. It was the same one that usually had women either melting or jumping to do his bidding. But his smile stopped midstream when he caught blondie's brow raise and her sharp eyes go dead cold.

"Save it, handsome. Neither you nor doc over here is giving out any orders. I'm on a schedule," she said, sending a nod the young doctor's way and getting tight lips by way of a retort. "Now hold still while I get your temp and take your pressure."

Ross suppressed a retort, thinking it wise to clam up and let the woman do what she had to do and move on. Besides, he could respect schedules and taking care of business.

He opened his mouth for her to stick the thermometer under his tongue and dutifully gave over his arm. He knew when he was beat. He also knew going any further with the no-nonsense nurse would be a waste of energy. And he hated wasting energy. One of the things he prided himself on was being efficient. Efficient and a moneymaker. And right now, while lying in a hospital bed, being told that he indeed was *not* having what he could have sworn was a heart attack, when he was this close to closing a billion-dollar deal, he was being anything but efficient. Ross's jaw tightened at the thought.

"Hey there, Thor, you want to loosen up a bit so that I can get the thermometer back out." The nurse — Ross looked at her nametag now — Nurse Edwards was directing this at him.

"I don't see why I need this," Ross replied by way of mouth opening. "If it's just a panic attack, you might as well let me go now and stop wasting all our time."

Dr. Doogie and Nurse Edwards shared glances, and then Doogie finally spoke up. "Yes, according to our preliminaries, it was not a heart attack but a panic-induced episode triggered, most likely, by stress and other contributors. If we could just go over your diet for the week? With some changes, there are ways to nip this in the bud before it becomes a bigger problem."

Changes? Ross inwardly bristled at the word. His life was perfect as it was. He was a successful businessman, well on his way to making the *Forbes* magazine list within the next few years. Who knew, not long after that, maybe even surpassing his father's accomplishments, if not ever getting his esteem? He was rich, free, and single. There was nothing in his life that needed changing.

Except Serenity.

Ross frowned as thoughts of his four-year-old daughter came to his mind once again. He was thinking of her when the pain gripped at his chest as he was on the phone with his investors. And it was her he was thinking of when he was being hooked up to electrodes and beeping machines.

When was the last time he'd seen her? It must be going on eight months now. Which was a huge hunk of a lifetime for a four-year-old, and with his current schedule he didn't see a visit anytime on the horizon. Sure, he sent her extravagant gifts for her birthday, but he'd heard it in her voice during his last call that she was unimpressed. The gifts could have been from anyone. All she could do during their last conversation was go on about how much fun she'd had with her mom, Yasmine, and her new dad, Devon, during their recent trip to Disneyland.

Hell, what did his daughter need with expensive gifts when Devon could give her the magic of Disneyland? Ross's hands balled into fists.

"Okay, Thor, there you go again. Your pressure is going sky high. That's not gonna get you out of here any quicker, you know?"

Ross gave Nurse Quick Mouth a hard look, which she countered back with one of her own. He was actually starting to admire her. Maybe he could find a place for her in his corporation. Lord knew she could freeze balls with that look.

"She's right, Ross, you need to relax," his friend and primary doc, Misha Nair, came in saying as she pushed the blue privacy curtain aside.

"I don't need anything, but for you to tell Doogie over here to sign my discharge papers so that I can get out of here."

Doogie gave a cough and Misha pursed her darkly stained lips together, causing Ross to note her carefully applied makeup. He also took notice of the fact that she wore what looked like a black cocktail dress under her open lab coat and high stiletto heels. Though always polished, this was not the jeans-and-sweats Misha he'd been buddies with since college. She took his chart from Doogie and quickly gave it a flip through.

"Did I interrupt a date?" he asked.

Misha ignored him and continued reading his chart before finally meeting his gaze. "What do you think, Ross? I'm not having the hell pinched out of my toes for the fun of it. I should have ignored your messages, but that bulldog of an assistant you have never gives up. I was afraid he'd track me at the restaurant if I didn't come over. Not that you weren't in fine hands with Dr. Stein here."

"How would I know that? This guy says I had a panic attack, which I know is not true. I never panic."

Misha rolled her eyes as Nurse "No Chill," still not amused, shook her head and removed the pressure cuff, making her exit with a wry chuckle.

"Ross, the numbers don't lie." Misha held up his chart. "These, along with your last physical reports from my office, are telling me it's time to make some real changes, or the next time you won't be so lucky, and it won't be a panic attack."

Ross sat up straighter, while at the same time he tried dismissing Misha's words. "Stop being so dramatic."

Misha moved closer and put her finger to his wrist to take his pulse. "*Dramatic* is having me pulled out of a dinner date, not that it was going anywhere. Freaking Internet can suck it. But smart is listening to your body and coming in to get checked out when you think something is wrong. Even smarter will be taking my advice. It's time

316

for you to make changes." She looked him in the eye. "What exactly were you doing when this happened?"

"Nothing," Ross said as innocently as he could muster, which wasn't that innocent at all. "I was in the middle of a business call, negotiating the terms of a deal."

"And?"

"And what?"

Misha dropped his wrist and shook her head. "And you mean for me to believe that you weren't getting your pressure up as you were nailing some poor sap to a wall. What's the rest?"

Ross couldn't help his grin. She did know him well. "And I may have been having a bite while I was leaving the gym after a workout. You know how working out and making deals gives me an appetite."

For that, he got a punch in the arm, and Doogie gave Misha a look this time. "Dr. Nair?"

"It's okay, Stein. Mr. Montgomery and I go way back. I'll handle him."

Doogie shook his head, clearly annoyed at this dismissal. "Fine. He can go. Since you're his primary, I'll sign him over to you for the follow-ups with a consult to Dr. West in cardio." He made a few notes in the chart and handed it off to Misha before leaving.

Ross grinned and started to get up, but was stilled by Misha's firm hand on his chest.

"Not so fast. I didn't discharge you yet, Ross."

"Come on, Mish. What are you playing at? I can still get in some calls out to the Far East if I go now."

"This is serious, or at least it could have been. It's time to make a change. What did you have for lunch today?"

He frowned. "A pastrami from Sal's."

"And the day before?"

Ross gave her a look. She already knew it was the same, or a version of it. She knew his poor eating habits, but he balanced it out with tough physical workouts in the gym and twice-weekly boxing.

Seeming to know what he was thinking, Misha spoke. "Before you say it, sorry your workouts are not good enough to make up for the crap you put in your body. You're getting to the age where a workout can't make up for high-fat foods and chips. We're both not teens anymore."

"Fine, Mish, I'll clean up my act. You'll see."

"Bullshit those you can, Ross. Not me. And on top of it, you need to relax. You need a diet and a lifestyle cleanup. That's food and meditation. Less work, less stress, better food, and less caffeine."

Ross balked. "The devil you say, woman?"

Misha grinned. "Stop being such a big baby. It's the holidays coming up. Now's the perfect time. I want you to take a few weeks off and give the business a break."

Now it was Ross's turn to laugh. "Sorry. I've got a deal and clients I'm meeting over the holiday. I'm taking my new boat out to wine and dine them. You want to come?"

Misha glared. "Are you not hearing me? It's time to change. Your numbers are a mess. Your arteries are clogging as we speak. This is urgent, Ross."

"I hear you. But I have to make this deal happen. I can't let it go."

Misha shook her head, then looked at Ross dead-on. "What about Serenity?"

"That's not fair," Ross gritted out.

"I learned how to play from the best."

If it were anyone but his old friend, Ross would tell her off, or at least walk the hell out of there. But he couldn't with Misha.

"I'll tell you what," she said, reaching over to pull a small take-out box from her large tote, "though you interrupted my date, I did manage to snag dessert to go." She popped the top on a good-looking chocolate confection with cream on top and picked it up, holding it to Ross's lips. "Here, take a bite."

"What are you up to? First you want me to clean up my act and then you're trying to fatten me up with dessert?"

"Just shut up and listen for once. It's made by a friend of mine. She's a personal chef I met a few years back while on a yoga retreat. She specializes in low-fat, good-for-you food, and has really made a difference for quite a few of my patients."

Ross frowned at the mention of "low fat," and prepared himself for a mouthful of sawdust. But to quiet Misha, he leaned in and took a bite.

It was heaven. Soft and creamy, while rich and decadent. The flavors were sweet and sophisticated, calling him to reach for more.

Ross looked up at Misha. "What did you say this chef's name was?"

Misha grinned. "I didn't, but it's Essie Bradford. Her food is amazing and you'll never meet a sweeter, kinder, more Zen person. Let me call her. If she's free, I know she'll say yes. Essie just can't say no to a friend, and she is a friend, so don't mess it up," she warned.

He reached out and took the rest of the sweet from Misha's hand and snagged another delectable bite. "If she's half as sweet as this dessert, I'm sure we'll get along just fine."

CHAPTER TWO

"You have got to be freaking kidding me. She sent back my soufflés? As if she would know a whip from a flake. I should go over there and tell her where she can shove —" Essie stopped short there, closed her eyes and did a few quick, deep cleansing breaths before she opened them again to see Trevor, one of the waiters, waiting with an apology in his kind eyes. Normally, he was all party-on and a quick gossip, but it would seem the nightmare from table twenty-three had taken the wind out of his sails, too. Essie not only wanted to give her a good tell-off for herself, but for Trevor as well. Besides, after getting home last night and practically tripping over her boyfriend's packed bags, she was in the mood to lash out.

Trevor raised a hand. "No, hon. I don't think you going over there will do any good. You know, as well as I, that the dessert is

perfect. She's been complaining all night."
Trevor slipped a look to the woman at
twenty-three, who stared back at Essie in
the open-air kitchen with a smug now-get-
it-right look.

*Seriously, some folks should not be allowed
out in polite company without proper supervi-
sion.*

Who sent back perfectly good chocolate
soufflés? Not to mention the complaint she
had about Essie's coq au vin, which had
won awards. Heat rose in Essie's cheeks,
and it had nothing to do with the fact it was
sweltering in the prep line of her friend Julian's popular Westside bistro's kitchen. She
knew she had to tamp down on her emotions. One, because it went totally against
the Zen, no judgment, live-in-the-moment
lifestyle she prided herself on. And two,
because the kitchen was open and a focal
point, on display to all the diners. This was
normally a feature Essie enjoyed, but tonight, being as tired and emotionally raw as
she was, she'd rather be anywhere but here
on display for the New York IT crowd.

Essie had long told herself that if — *no,
when* — she'd saved up enough money,
coupled with the financial backing she
needed to open her own place, she'd have a
similar design. She was brought up to

believe that the food prep was all a part of the dining experience and should be shared. Now, considering the nightmare at table twenty-three, who did nothing but complain about anything and everything, maybe that interaction would have to be rethought.

Once again, Essie let out a calming breath. She really shouldn't get mad at the terror on twenty-three. Though Essie knew the soufflé was perfect, she grabbed a clean spoon to take a taste to be sure before throwing the rest away, with regret over the wasted food. Yes, the soufflé was fine. Actually, better than fine, but it lacked a bit of her usual spark, and she blamed herself for that. She should have told Julian no, that she couldn't fill in when he called, begging for her to cover for his usual head chef, who had an emergency. That's what she got for always saying yes.

Essie was exhausted and she knew it, having just come back home to New York from two months on the road as the private chef to an up-and-coming rock band. Six members, all with different tastes: one vegan, one veg, the rest true carnivores. It was quite the demanding gig. And no sooner was she back in her apartment, dropping her well-worn duffel on the floor, only to have them collide with the bags and boxes belonging to her ex-boyfriend, Cameron. She guessed if she hadn't gotten in a few hours early, she may have found out about his planned relationship departure via text, which was his usual passive-aggressive modus operandi.

No, she wasn't mad at the complainer over at twenty-three. She was mad at herself for being so gullible and not seeing Cameron for what he was, a cheater with a penchant for large-chested, petite women and continuing far too long in a relationship she knew was ultimately going nowhere. She should have known something was up when he was the one to encourage her to say yes and take the job on the road with the band. Telling her how great the money would be, and how he'd come out to meet her on the road, which he never did. *Damn that Cam. Always the user.* They had met while in culinary school when he asked her to tutor him with sauce reductions.

The thought pulled Essie up short. He was another "yes" that she should have said "no" to. *Him, and the hims before.* Always ready to use her up until a better option came along. So many yeses that started with hope, but then led to disappointment.

Just as she should have said no to Julian, and it would have spared her tonight's aggravation. Not to mention she could have been catching up on much-needed sleep. Yep, each time she put her own needs aside and gave in to the "yes" to satisfy others, it didn't turn out well. She was over being everyone's go-to "yes."

It was time she started living for herself.

Essie let out a breath before stepping forward, reaching for another just baked soufflé and topping it with powdered sugar, extra berries, and a drizzle of chocolate. She looked up and carefully handed it to Trevor with a weary smile. "Let's hope this time's the charm."

Trevor let out a sigh. "I doubt she'd know charm if it landed in her lap."

As she watched him walk over to table twenty-three, the woman made brief eye contact with Essie. Her clear blue eyes met Essie's own dark brown ones before she gave Essie a nod of triumph and took a bite. The woman smiled, a small, satisfied, smug grin, which made the hairs on the back of Essie's neck stand up a bit, and had her biting the inside of her lip. But Essie let it go as Trevor turned back her way and gave her his wide grin and a little thumbs-up.

People. Some just have to believe they're that extra-special snowflake or they'll melt away to nothing. She shrugged, trying to let the encounter roll off her back. Who knew? Maybe Ms. Twenty-three had a bad day, or a bad month, or her boyfriend of two years did a dump-and-dash. Shit happened.

Julian came and leaned over the counter, his piercing green eyes sparkling with both weariness at the late hour and excitement over the packed restaurant. "Essie, my love, thank you so much for filling in tonight and tomorrow. I know it's been a madhouse, but you saved my hide, like you will never know. I owe you big-time."

"Yes, you do. I'll add it to your list." She smiled, now feeling bad for thinking so harshly of him. He'd always been a good friend, and the money from tonight would be a help, now that she didn't have Cam's money coming in to share the rent. Not that he wasn't late, most of the time, anyway.

The thought of Cam and money made her wonder if her dream of having her own place would ever come true. Back when she was with him, they talked about opening up a place together. She couldn't help but wonder how she could do it alone now.

Essie fought to push the thought aside. It was almost too much to deal with, just one day back and one day into the breakup. As of now, she'd operate as she had. At least he picked a good time. She was solvent and would not need to work until after the holidays, when she had more private jobs lined up. For now she'd do what she so very much needed to do for herself: a blissful holiday to think things over and sort out her life. One where she would not have to serve others, but, instead, visit with her mother and enjoy being the one who was fed, nourished, and treated right for a change.

So when her phone rang as she was ending the night with Julian, and it was her friend Misha with a call about a job cooking for some rich bigwig over the Christmas vacation, Essie was only too happy to put her first "no" into practice.

CHAPTER THREE

Maybe it was the momentary hush that came over the restaurant, or maybe it was something else, but for some reason Essie looked up from where she was putting a final touch of sauce on a simple roasted chicken before it was to go out, and saw the hostess, Nikki, escorting a striking couple to table twenty-three.

Her unlucky table.

As she watched the gorgeous couple take their seats, Essie couldn't help but notice how compatible they seemed, in contrast to how she and Cam must have looked together. The woman was tall and statuesque, more legs than anything else, with glistening golden brown skin and a figure that was shown off well by the few artfully draped pieces of fabric that adorned her body, despite the biting winter chill outside. Essie's gaze wavered to the tall, dark figure in the expensively cut business suit. She involuntarily sucked in a breath, caught in her not-so-hidden perusal, as the male counterpart of this couple was, for some reason, looking directly at her, too.

His deep-set, dark eyes locked on Essie's, and across the expanse of the dining room and over the heads of the other diners, Essie could have sworn she felt something in that moment that was strangely like a touch. She reached up and ran her hand across the side of her neck as he gave her the slightest of nods. One side of his beautiful mouth quirked up in the most devilish way to let her know that yes, he was looking at her, and yes, she should take note of it. Essie's cheeks flushed hot, as if something dangerously like desire mixed with a twinge of anger flicked at her center.

What is up with that smile? Sit with your model, Mr. Rich, and leave the smiles for your date.

Essie nibbled at her bottom lip and turned away from the scene, quickly inspecting the chicken that was just put up for an order, then turning her attention to the sauce for her Bourguignon. One stipulation she didn't budge on when agreeing to help Julian out was the fact that she ran the kitchen her way. So for the nights she was filling in, Essie made sure to double check each dish after it was plated, be it savory or dessert. No matter the name on the restaurant's exterior, the food was still a representation of her reputation.

"Oh, my God, do you know who that is?" Trevor said as he came over to the window, practically bouncing out of his shoes.

She knew he was talking about the couple at table twenty-three, but Essie tried to appear cool and unconcerned. She had a reputation and beef to concentrate on. And not the kind Trevor was pushing, mind you.

"No, should I?" Essie let her gaze smoothly slide around Trevor, not at the man, but at the beautiful woman by his side. Now that she thought about it, she was sure she'd seen her on the cover of some magazine or another. And judging by the way some of the other patrons were gawking, she was probably right. The young woman may be famous, but she was clearly into the man. Leaning in, she was rubbing the back of his neck with one hand, while the other disappeared under the table, only to come up abruptly when he seemed to be, well, Essie could only guess by the girl's pretty pout, unmoved. She looked away from the couple back to Trevor. "She is pretty."

Trevor waved an impatient hand. "Oh, she's all right, but it's him I'm talking about. That's Ross Montgomery, the man of the millennium." Essie frowned. He was good-looking, but, come on, millennium? She didn't have time for this.

But Trevor continued. "And baby boy is paid with a capital *P*. He's been taking over real estate all up and down the East Coast, and with his taste in the latest beauty de jour, he's become a fixture on the gossip scene, too."

Essie was busy on her next dish when what Trevor said really hit her, and she suddenly stopped mid-glaze. *Wait. Ross Montgomery.* Wasn't the client Misha called her about last night named Ross Montsomething or other? She took another peek at table twenty-three, only to catch Mr. Millennium once again staring back at her.

"Holy hell," Essie hissed.

"That's what I'm saying," Trevor said, his voice now taking on a conspiratorial tone. "And he seems pretty interested in you. Asked that you be pointed out special."

"Crap." Oh, God. Mr. Tall, Dark, and Rich as All Get-Out was here, and he was checking her out. But as unexpected butterflies fluttered in her belly, Essie frowned. What was he doing here, checking her out? And checking her out at the tail end of a long dinner shift when she looked like who knew what? Not that it should matter. She'd turned Misha down last night, and she'd meant it. Her no meant *no.* It was high time her friends got to know the new, improved, more assertive Essie.

She would enjoy these few holiday weeks off, and then it was back to the grind with clients in January. She'd worked hard enough and would enjoy this well-deserved holiday. It didn't matter how rich — she peeked at table twenty-three again — or how good-looking the client was. She turned back to Trevor. "So, did Mr. Millennium even order anything?"

Trevor's eyes went wide. "Did he ever? Well, not that this has anything to do with you, but, of course, he ordered our most expensive champagne. But getting to your line of work, he and his" — Trevor paused dramatically — "date will be having caviar to start with, the foie gras, and the oyster tartar. From there, they will go on to the risotto and the sirloin. Then they are having the salmon and the cracked lobster."

Essie's jaw dropped. "Are you serious? There is no way two people are eating all of that."

"That's what I said," Trevor replied. "But the man wants what the man wants, so that's what you're making."

Essie let out a slow breath, long and slow through her nostrils, working to bring her equilibrium back, as she mentally went over the menu choices for table twenty-three. *I know what this is, mister,* she thought as her eyes once again slid over to where Mr. Montgomery was being touched and did- dled by his young lady companion. She watched as Teagan, the sommelier, uncorked champagne to the model's delight and Mr. Montgomery's look of indifference.

Essie shook her head and smiled, now more confident that she'd made the right decision turning down the job from Misha last night. He seemed like a total spoiled jerk. And it didn't matter that he'd turned up here tonight in Julian's restaurant to test her food firsthand, and possibly offer her the job once again. Her no was firm. She took the order to get it going with the rest of the crew. She'd wasted enough time and, at least for tonight, he and everyone else were paying customers. As such, they'd get her very best.

The meal was delicious, which was as Ross expected. The meat was tender, the fish was succulent, and everything was seasoned to perfection, leaving the most delicious linger- ing aftertaste in Ross's mouth. He already craved his next meal. Misha was right. He needed this chef in his life. Sneaky of Mish not to tell him what a pretty little thing the chef was. Pretty enough that, despite the fact his date for tonight was, Ross inwardly groaned now at the thought, this year's "Internet's Most Googled Body Under Thirty," his eyes kept wandering to the intriguing chef with the sweet smile.

There was something about her: smooth, rich umber toned skin, wispy bangs peeking out from under her bandana, which framed deep-set brown eyes, which somehow sparkled like diamonds in the dimly lit restaurant. She had a sharp, determined-looking nose, which led to luscious, full lips. When these opened into a wide smile, her lips seemed to take over her face and her smile brightened the entire restaurant with perfectly imperfect teeth that showed just a hint of the most endearing gap.

The owner, Julian, he remembered, now came by their table. "I hope you all enjoyed your meal. Can I interest you in anything else?"

Ross's "yes" came out at the same time as his date's "no," leaving the owner smiling with awkward confusion. Ross righted the situation. "Yes, we would like dessert. What specials is the chef offering tonight?"

"I don't want to stay for dessert," Lela whined. "I thought we were heading down to the Bowery for the sneaker launch party. Everybody is going to be there and DJ Extasy is spinning tonight. I don't want to miss that." Lela gave her hair a twist around her finger and let her hand trail toward her breast.

Normally, the blatant come-on would be just the thing to rev Ross's engines, but after last night, Ross was dog tired. All he really wanted to do was taste that pretty chef's dessert and then get the hell home to sleep, so he could get into the office early tomorrow. The last thing he wanted to do was go to some silly sneaker launch party and hear a DJ with a misspelled name.

Ross let out a sigh. This was his fault. He shouldn't have invited Lela out tonight and should have just come alone. Even if it was counter to his playboy image. That shit was getting tired anyway.

He reached into his pocket and peeled off a few hundred-dollar bills, then turned to his date and licked his lips before staring into her almond-shaped eyes. "I tell you what. You take my car and head over to the launch party and have a great time. Sorry, babe, but I'm not going to make it tonight."

He watched as Lela pulled her lips together in a pretty little pout.

"Come on, Ross. I thought we'd make a night of this. Have a little fun. See and be seen, and then end it back at your place."

She trailed her hand up his knee and higher along his thigh. When she got close to the point of no return, he stilled her eager fingers with his own.

"Like I said, it's not happening tonight, sweetheart." Ross gently put the money in her hands. His eyes stopped any further comment.

Lela shrugged, seeming to know the conversation was now over, as was the evening. "Okay, I guess I won't be seeing you in the morning then." She made a point to hide any disappointment from her face. Her eyes shined bright as she smiled wide and leaned over to kiss his cheek before gracefully exiting from their prime table, sashaying out of the restaurant with her trademark super-model walk.

Ross looked back to the owner. "Thank you. Everything was delicious. I'd like an assortment of the desserts, and please ask the chef, Essie, if she would kindly take a moment to join me."

Join him!

Essie fumed more steam than the

stainless-steel, industrial-grade pots surrounding her. Not that she didn't expect the special request, but still it rankled her nerves. Especially after seeing the way his date seemed to be dismissed. Still, Essie finished all the other orders and found herself taking special care with his. Why? It wasn't as if she had anything to prove.

As she followed behind Julian, who carried the desserts over, Essie fought not to pull down her smock or brush her hair behind her ear. Instead, she pushed her shoulders back, pulling herself up to her full five-seven height.

"Mr. Montgomery, here are your desserts, and may I introduce our chef for the evening, Essie Bradford," Julian said.

Essie was about to lean in and give him a quick handshake, when he surprised her by standing. His impressive height and broad shoulders made her feel fairly small as he reached out and took her hand gently in his own.

"It is my pleasure to make your acquaintance, Ms. Bradford."

His grip was warm and engulfing, his eyes dark and unnervingly unwavering, as he looked at her way too deeply for a person who wanted to talk about only her food. Essie fought to keep her chin up and not look down. She would not break contact. First to blink loses. And she knew losing to this man would not be good.

So she looked at him just as deeply, until something in him shifted and he let go of her hand, leaving her with a surprising chill. He stepped back to open space for her in the banquette. "Would you please sit with me for a moment? Join me for dessert?"

Essie looked at him with narrowed eyes as she walked around and purposefully went into the other end of the banquette and sat. "Sure, since you pretty much ordered everything on the menu."

He sat and Julian put down the desserts along with Trevor, who poured them each a glass of champagne before exiting.

"Well, after tasting the small bit from Misha last night, I had to have more. And seeing that you turned down my offer of employment flat, this seemed like the only way I'd get to sample all you had to offer."

Essie fought to ignore the instant rush of heat flaring through her body, and gave him a smile. "All? That's not nearly all." At his raised brow, the butterflies went swirling in Essie's belly again, and she shifted to tamp down on them. "And I'm sorry about turning down your offer, Mr. Montgomery, but I've been on the road for the past two months, and I really don't want to get on the road again. Especially not right now during the holidays."

"Please call me Ross. It's not like I'm your boss or anything. And I can totally respect you wanting to take a little time off after being on the road. But please understand, Ms. Bradford, I really do need your services. I don't know if Misha explained to you, but she called you from the ER. It's imperative that I get my diet and, as she tells it, my lifestyle in order, too. But I'm a busy man, and I can't afford to take the holidays off. This is a working one for me, like so many others, and I need to have a chef with me on this trip I'm taking."

Essie shook her head, partially to tell him no and partially to remind herself to stay strong in her new "NO" mode. "I really am so sorry, Mr. . . ." Essie paused, then said, "Ross. But I don't think I can do it. On the other hand, I can recommend to you some other quite capable chefs."

Ross reached over with his spoon and dipped into Essie's chocolate tart, taking a bite.

He closed his eyes, letting the flavor she knew so well permeate his senses. He smiled as he swallowed, looking like he was enjoying every moment before he opened his eyes and looked back. He reached for another spoon, this time bringing some of her mousse toward her lips. Essie's eyes went wide. "What are you doing?"

"You need to taste this."

Essie gave him a stern frown. "It's from tonight's specials and my own recipe so I have tasted it." For a moment she thought she saw something like a spark in his eyes.

"Yes, but when was the last time you *really* tasted it?"

Essie gave him a challenging stare to match his own. "Fine." She opened her mouth slightly, and before she could reach for the spoon, it was already to her lips. Rich and creamy. That's what it was, rich and creamy, with a hint of smokiness that exploded on her tongue in a perfect melody of notes. Essie closed her eyes and let the flavors hit her. *Damn, you did good, Essie,* she thought as it slid down her throat. *Real good.*

Essie opened her eyes and fought back a blush over the way Ross Montgomery stared with a smug smile that said he had her. *Oh, hell.* So what if he was right about her cooking? It didn't change anything. "Thank you so much for the flattery. I really do appreciate the offer, but my answer is still no."

He seemed somehow completely undisturbed by her answer, and Essie watched as he took a sip of his champagne and finished off the tart.

Then he looked up at her. "Aren't you going to have more of the mousse? I'm sorry I finished off the tart, but it's a testament to your artistry."

"No, I really should be getting back to the kitchen." She started to rise when he put his warm hand on top of hers, stilling her.

"If I could just have another moment of your time, please, Ms. Bradford?"

Essie sat back down as he seemed to assess her from top to bottom.

"How about this? Now, I know I can't make up for you not being home with your family on the holiday, but I can assure that you do get the rest, or at least some of it that you're craving. And I get our mutual friend, Misha, off my back, which, for this, you would be doing me the hugest favor."

Essie smiled. She knew how tough Misha could be when it came to her patients and friends.

Ross continued. "For this holiday I'm taking my new yacht, the *Serenity,* on a trip from New York to Miami to impress clients to invest in my new resort. This is a huge deal for me, so I can't put it off, as Misha so boldly suggested." He looked at her now and gave the corner of his lip a light lick, which was entirely too sexy. "Misha said your food was delicious, and she was absolutely right about that. She also said that you do a fine job of cooking healthy food in a new way, and you do wonders with changing your clients' lifestyles. I want you to do that for me."

Essie's whole body went on alert. In that moment there were way too many things she wanted to do for him. But she needed to focus. Get the "no" in gear. She forced herself to listen to his words and not just watch his sexy lips.

"Sadly, I usually eat on the run and I need to change that. And though I hate to admit it to Misha, I do my share of burning the candle at both ends. So if you would join me on my yacht, I'll give you great accommodations, and in exchange you'll take care of my dietary needs, take a fabulous trip, and I'll pay you handsomely."

"Mr. Montgomery, I don't think you're hearing me," Essie started, hoping she sounded more secure than she felt.

"Ms. Bradford, I don't think *you're* hearing *me*. I know your going rate, and I previously offered a five-thousand-dollar bonus, but I'm willing to make that ten thousand dollars if you take the job. And on top of that, my boat comes with another chef, so you won't be working alone to feed everyone on the trip. Your job will be mostly taking care of my dietary needs. The other chef will do all the heavy lifting. Now, will you please take the position?"

Essie was stunned. A ten-thousand-dollar signing bonus on top of her usual rate to luxuriate on a yacht and cook meals for one person? She would be crazy to say no. But how was it that he was coming to her now when she already decided her new motto was "NO"? And how could she leave her mother alone over the holiday? This would only be their second one without Dad. She should just keep to her original schedule and spend the holidays with her mother. But what would her mother say if she found out she turned this offer down? This would go so far toward her savings, and so far toward her dream of her own restaurant. Not to mention the fact that she now had to cover Cam's half of the rent. She looked back at Ross and saw a bit of a twinkle in those ridiculously gorgeous eyes.

Damn. He probably knew he had me the moment he walked in the door. "You don't have to look so smug, Mr. Montgomery. I didn't say yes, you know."

"Yet," he said. "You didn't say yes . . . yet.

And don't look so pitiful about it. I'm taking you on a yacht, Ms. Bradford, not the *Titanic.*"

Essie picked up her spoon and dug into the chocolate mousse at the same time Ross did. "So should we toast with chocolate mousse?"

Ross grinned and raised his spoon. "As long as I have you on my boat next week, and in my galley, I'll toast in any way, with anything you want, Ms. Bradford."

Essie got a tingle then, where there was no place for a tingle to be given. They were now boss and employee, so she gave him a sharp look. "I would tell you to call me Essie, but since I'm now working for you, I guess we'd better stay on a last-name basis, Mr. Montgomery."

CHAPTER FOUR

"I don't know about this, Mish," Essie said into her cell as the cab made its way down the highway in the early-morning hours. The air was crisp and still gray, the sun only being hinted at as it glinted off the mirrored chrome of the New York skyscrapers.

"What's not to know? You should be thanking me," Misha replied. "I know you didn't plan to work during the holiday, but with Cam hitting the wind and you needing extra money, this is perfect. Besides, it will be good for you."

Essie could feel Misha scheming through the phone and her eyes rolled skyward. "Good for me how? Cam and I have only been broken up for less than a week."

Misha let out an impatient snort. "Oh, please. You and Cam were broken up the moment he screwed his assistant, and I'd bet that was at least two months ago, if not more. The moment you hit the road to work with the band, you two were done."

"Ouch, leave it to you not to pull any punches."

"What good would it do? Life is too short. Now you remember that while you're sailing with Ross. He'll be a tough client, but I've known him a long time, and he's a good guy underneath."

It was Essie's turn to snort. "Underneath what? The latest supermodel? Let Google tell it. He's got a deli number-counter at the foot of his bed."

Now Misha laughed. "You, more than anyone, should know that outside appearances can be deceiving. I know you're not totally the 'Little Miss Zen' you want the world to see. Now go and whip my friend into shape. Tell him I want great numbers on his next visit. And from you, I want a report that you had a fabulous time. Doctor's orders."

"Yeah, whatever you say," Essie said before switching off.

The taxi began to slow as it turned by the piers, and the most beautiful boat Essie had ever seen came into her view.

"Oh, my freaking God," she whispered as she got out of the cab, pulling her carryall in one hand and her cooking supplies in the other. Essie knew the galley would more than likely be fully stocked, and she had sent over a list of what she wanted available. But she wouldn't assume it would be stocked with her favorite organic oils, not to mention her homemade spice blends and whenever possible, she never did a job without her old faithful set of stainless pans and, of course, her knives. She paused as two crewmembers in white pants and long-sleeved black shirts appeared, their hands behind their backs, sunglasses on, watching her as she made her way.

When she was finally in front of them, the one that looked a little older, but only because of the light graying at his temples, gave a little nod and a small smile. "And I'm guessing you are Ms. Bradford. Welcome to *Serenity*."

"Thank you, and please call me Essie." She looked up at the ship and its impressive height. "So, *Serenity*? A ship this size I expect to be called the *Enterprise*."

The man grinned and stepped forward. "I'm Jeff Grayson, the ship's captain, and this guy right here is Cooper Westport, our chief engineer."

Cooper smiled next to Captain Grayson, and though his sunglasses covered a good portion of his face, Essie could still tell from his thick blond hair, chiseled jaw, and his blindingly white smile that he was a good-looking man.

"Great to meet you, Essie," Cooper said with a cute Aussie accent.

More tall men in the same uniform came out and stood along the deck as Cooper made the introductions.

"That right there is my second, Ethan Chambers." Ethan gave a nod and smile. "And next to him is our deckhand Jayce Spencer." Jayce gave a slight bow and then came for ward to take Essie's bags from her. "And then we have Quincy Bell, our head steward. He'll help with any personal needs you may have."

"Very nice to meet you," Quincy said. Another man with a lovely accent, this time it was from the United Kingdom.

Essie smiled and shook hands.

"You all are being so kind. I'm sure I won't need anything. I'll try and not be too much of a bother."

"I'll be the judge of that," came another new, slightly gruffer voice.

"And finally," Cooper said, his own voice now slightly apologetic, "we have Chef Simon Scott. I guess you and he will be working pretty closely together."

Essie looked toward Chef Scott, who wore shades just as the rest of the crew was, but unlike the others, his were pushed up onto the top of his clean-shaven head to reveal his sharp, assessing eyes and stern brow. And though she bestowed on him her easy smile, he countered back with nothing but a slight nod.

Fine, that's how you want to play? Essie had been in the cooking game for a long time. Chef Scott was surely not the first, and he wouldn't be the last, temperamental chef she'd come across. She'd give it a day, and she was sure they'd be getting along just fine. If not, it didn't matter. This job was only temporary. "It's very nice to meet you, Chef. I'll be in and out of your hair in no time flat," she said.

"Is that a promise, little lady?" Chef Scott stated more than asked.

Essie looked at him dead-on and stepped onto *Serenity.* "It's a statement, nothing more. I've learned early on that promises are worth no more than the breath it takes to make them."

Quincy finished giving Essie a quick tour of the ship and she was officially in awe. *Serenity* was 130 feet, four levels, and no luxury spared. There was a formal and informal salon, a gym, two hot tubs, jet skis, a diving plank, a formal dining room, as well as an informal one. By the time she got to the galley, her mouth hung open. Hell, she was thinking she should be paying Ross for this trip, but she knew she could never afford it. Not in a million years.

Quincy showed her the crew's quarters and lead her to her own room. She turned a corner too quickly and walked into a solid wall that was Ross Montgomery's chest. "Oh, my goodness, um, I'm sorry, excuse me."

"Please don't apologize, Ms. Bradford," Ross said. His large warm hands righted her, steady in the most unsteady way. "Things can get a little tight on this ship."

At his words his and Essie's eyes met, and if she were still fourteen and believed in such a thing, she'd swear fireworks went off. Essie quickly lowered her eyes and stepped back, but not before catching the laughter in Ross's eyes. *Damn.*

"I was just giving Ms. Bradford a tour, sir, and leading her to her quarters," Quincy said, breaking the unspoken tension.

"I'll take over from here, thank you," Ross said, his voice low, but still definite and commanding.

Essie watched Quincy's retreating back and, for some reason, wanted to follow him down the narrow hallway, but she knew she couldn't, so she stood where she was. "I didn't know you were on board," she said.

"Yet here I am," Ross said matter-of-factly. "I was finishing a work call when you arrived. I'm sorry I couldn't greet you. But now that you are here, we may depart."

She felt a brow shoot up. "But I thought you said this was a business trip and you were taking clients down to Florida."

"This is a business trip, but no, we're picking up clients in Florida. I hope I didn't give you the wrong impression."

Essie, relax. This isn't a big deal. It's still business and still a trip.

Just with a lot less passengers on the way down than she anticipated. It didn't matter. She wasn't here for his clients anyway. She was here to get him on track to good food and a new lifestyle. Essie brought her shoulders up and looked him in the eye. "It's no matter who is here. It's you who's paying me, and you are my client."

Essie couldn't help but notice his jaw tighten at this statement. "This is true, I am paying you, but as we discussed, you're still my guest. So, how about you let me show you to your room?" He put his arm out in a gesture for her to follow him. They climbed a narrow flight of stairs, going from below deck up another level, to where the accommodations were more spacious and, if possible, more luxurious.

Ross took Essie past some of the most sumptuous staterooms she had ever seen, all done up in marble and wood. This was a world of luxury beyond her imagination. At one point he stood outside a room and waved his hand. "These are my quarters, and my office is right next door. Since this is a working trip, I will be in my office quite a bit. Though, per Misha's orders, I promise to go above deck and get some sun while I work, from time to time."

Essie smiled. "I'll hold you to it. Do you mind if I take a look?"

"Not at all."

Essie peeked in the door of his stateroom. It was decorated in the same modern way as the rest of the yacht, but here there was a classic twist that was a little bit dressed down so that it was more casual and, somehow, more sexy. The low-profile bed had a utilitarian feel to it, and the artwork that hung over the bed was done in tones of gray, with a splash of red. The gray lamps by the bed added to the coolness of the room. The thick gray carpeting made her want to take off her shoes and sink her toes into it. Everything about the room was sensual and inviting in an ultracool way. So very much like the man himself.

Essie swallowed and looked up at Ross. "It's a cool space." *Cool?* She wanted to bang herself in the head. Instead, she swallowed and gave a weak smile.

Ross's smile threatened to turn her legs to noodles. "Thanks."

He opened the door next to it to show his office. This was a continuation of his bedroom, sexy, sleek, and modern. With one wall made of all glass windows to take in the sea view.

"I hope I won't find you always in here. According to our agreement, you have to learn some things from me about food and perhaps cooking?" Essie challenged.

He frowned and closed the office door. "We'll have to see about that, Ms. Bradford."

"That we will, Mr. Montgomery."

Ross turned away from his office door and surprised her by turning to a door right across from his own. "And this will be your accommodations."

Essie stepped inside and this time she really couldn't stop her mouth from dropping open. "Oh, Ross, this is too much. I mean, Mr. Montgomery. Really, I can sleep down in the crew's quarters. They are more than generous."

She watched as his lip worked a little at

the corner in amusement. "You will sleep here, Ms. Bradford, and not insult me. According to our agreement, you're not one of the crew, and though you are not one of the official guests, you are my guest, and this is your holiday, though a working one it may be. So please enjoy this room with my compliments. I won't hear any arguments."

Essie frowned, looking at the ridiculously luxurious accommodations. She had never been in a room so beautiful. It was mahogany and marble like the rest of the ship, but this was designed with a woman in mind as the décor was accented in creams and natural stone. Not to mention the beautiful orchids she spied. And in the bathroom there was both a stand-up shower and a beautiful Jacuzzi tub. After this, how would she ever go back to her small one-bedroom apartment? She looked at Ross and shook her head. "You always make it this hard for a girl to turn you down?"

"I do my very best, Ms. Bradford."

Essie let out a sigh as she eyed the huge bed. "That's what I'm afraid of, Mr. Montgomery."

CHAPTER FIVE

Ross fought the urge to retreat to his office. Instead, he went up to join the captain on the bridge. Not that he wanted to retreat to his office, or that he wanted to join the captain. No, what he really wanted to do was stay with the pretty Ms. Bradford and kiss her on that deliciously large bed until that skeptical look she kept giving him gave way to one of glazed passion.

Shit. What is wrong with me? Number one, she was now an employee, at least for the next ten days, so she should technically be off limits if his normal code of ethics applied. And number two, which was the head-scratcher, she was not his type, so he didn't get the intense, almost uncontrollable, physical attraction.

It had been there as soon as he caught a glimpse of her in the restaurant, even before he knew who she was and their eyes locked for the first time. He didn't get it. This type of thing never happened to him. He didn't believe in happenstance or anomalies out of the realm. Ross lived in absolutes. And Essie Bradford was a wild card.

She was nothing like the usual strain of models. She was tall, sure. That fit his bill. But that's where it ended. His usual women had a certain — Ross paused in his thoughts, looking for the right description, and he grimaced when all he could come up with was "body shop shine and polish" to them. It was as if the women he usually went for stepped off the showroom runway, dyed, plucked and blown out, falling that way into his bed.

But not Essie Bradford. She was tall and slim, but he could tell by her well-fitting jeans and no-nonsense sweater, she had delicious curves in all the right places. And her skin, Ross sucked in a breath, there was something about her skin, with its rich, chocolate tone that seemed to glow from deep within, made him long to touch it, taste it, be a part of it. *Freaking hell!* Even to his own mind he was already sounding whipped.

But still, her eyes came to his mind. Deep and soulful, sparking like onyx jewels, only there to enhance the full lips he wanted to kiss so very much. Those plump lips that made him think of her delicious desserts and all the ways he wanted to devour her.

Damn it! This whole thing was a huge mistake. He knew that now. Just as he knew that Misha, wherever she was, must be laughing her ass off. Ross reached the bridge and Captain Grayson turned around. "I just want to check if we're on schedule and you have everything you need."

The older man smiled and looked around at all the shiny new equipment. "I have more than I need, sir. I can't wait to get her out in the open water. It will be an honor to sail her."

Ross grinned. "Well, I'm happy to have you in charge and on board. I'm going to go up to the fly deck and watch the launch."

"Enjoy, sir. The weather is optimum, so we should be good."

Ross exited while the captain made an announcement for all hands to be ready to leave. On his way up top, Ross thought for a moment about going to collect Essie and invite her to join him, but stopped. Setup or not, he wouldn't play into Misha's hands. His life, if not his numbers, was fine as it was. And he didn't need the complications of some goody-two-shoes, interfering chef.

Really he should have invited Lela on this trip, or a version of her. It wouldn't have been hard. But something stopped him from doing that. Yes, it was a business trip, but he knew his clients. Most were married and would be bringing their wives, and those without would bring girlfriends or expect some sort of female entertainment. They all expected him to show up with a beautiful woman on his arm, as he always did. And that night at the restaurant when he first saw Essie, he was so close to inviting Lela to come with him, but he stopped and he let her go on to that sneaker party. The question was why.

Just as Ross got topside, as if by some divine answering, there was the "why" at the railing. Her face was lifted up to catch the breeze; her hair was whipping playfully, fighting the wind and losing. But still she smiled to herself, saying a silent good-bye to cold New York while *Serenity* backed away from the city. Taking her away from home and family and him away from nothing but his newly remodeled three thousand square feet of . . . now that he thought about it, way too open apartment space.

The moment filled Ross with an unexpected sense of melancholy. In his mind he saw visions of skating with his little girl, hand in hand, under the colorful lights of the Rockefeller Center Christmas Tree. Ross shook the thought off with an inward snort. Not that it would be happening. She was in California and would be enjoying the holiday as she always did, with her mother and stepdad. She was happy, and that was enough.

"The view is beautiful, isn't it?" Ross said as he eased next to Essie and leaned against the railing.

She turned slowly and faced him, as if she knew he would walk up and stand next to her. "It really is. It's been so long since I've seen New York from the water. As a kid I used to love to take the Staten Island Ferry to get this view."

Ross smiled. "I used to do that as a kid, too. Best cheap view in the city. That, and the Roosevelt Island Tram."

Essie's eyes went wide. "You're so right. I love the tram. I used to go back and forth just for the fun of it. Now that I'm over the free kid height, no more back and forth for me. Not with the way metro fares keep going up. More and more it seems the joys of the city have been priced out for regular folks." Essie averted her eyes, as if remembering she was on a yacht with a real estate developer. "I'm sorry, I didn't mean, well, you know."

"No offense taken. You don't have to be

360

sorry for saying what you think. I agree. The city is way too expensive. And there should be simple luxuries and joys available to everyone. Now, I know that sounds crazy coming from me, with us standing on my yacht, but it's true."

Her eyes got that skeptical gleam once again. "Okay," she replied with a shrug, turning away.

Ross crossed his arms. "You don't take anything at face value, do you?"

She frowned and turned toward the city, staring a long time before turning back to him, her expression once again a mask of calm. "That's not true. As a matter of fact, I take everything at face value. I'm the type of woman who believes what I see. I believe people show you who they are, and, as Ms. Angelou's saying goes, when they do, believe them."

She smiled brightly; then those full lips went wide and once again she showed that quirky armor-shattering space in her front teeth, which he found so endearing. But her statement said a lot. This woman had a history, and she'd also been hurt. For some reason Ross wanted to know more. He frowned then, about to question her, but she cut him off flicking her wrist and checking her watch.

"Look at the time. Quincy sent me your usual schedule and I'd like to take a little time to get to know your galley before I start to prepare lunch. Do you have anything you absolutely don't like?"

Knowing this was the end of that particular conversation, Ross relented. "Never been a fan of asparagus or Brussels sprouts."

"I'll make note of that, sir."

Ross frowned.

"What is it? Is it something else?"

"I also don't appreciate you calling me 'sir.' "

"Why? I've noticed everyone else does aboard the ship."

"Well, you're not everyone else. You're working for me, but we've established we have a special situation, and since we share a mutual friend, can we, once and for all, get on a first-name basis and get a little less formal?" Ross didn't know why he made this little speech. Maybe it was the way she held her arms so tightly together, or maybe it was the rigidity of her spine, or the way she tilted her chin up at him. But all he wanted in that moment was for her to soften her stance at least a little bit. If all he could do was get it in a name, then so be it.

It was crazy, he knew. But somehow looking at her, and the way she looked at him,

Ross knew respect was not what he wanted from her. He wanted something different, something more. Something strangely close to admiration, approval, or maybe something even more dangerous. Something like affection.

Essie gave him that weary look once again, and then her eyes went soft at the same time something on him went dangerously hard. *Oh, hell.* She stuck out her hand and smiled. "I'm Essie. Nice to meet you."

Ross's lips quirked, feeling shy, an emotion he definitely didn't welcome. He took her hand in his, enjoying the feel of its powdery coolness. "I'm Ross. It's nice to meet you, too."

Essie's eyes narrowed as she pulled her hand from his, leaving him feeling slightly bereft. "Okay, I'm going to give you a warning. Now that we're officially friends, there will be no holding back from me. I'm going to be as tough on you as Misha would be. Today starts the rest of your life. So remember you asked for it."

Ross watched as Essie made her way from the deck and disappeared going toward the galley. "Don't worry, Essie. I'm sure I'll enjoy every moment."

CHAPTER SIX

Every moment? What the hell does he mean by every moment?

Essie made her way to the galley, wondering if Ross knew she'd heard his parting comment, and happily only getting turned around twice, which she attributed to the size of the boat and not her "Ross infatuation." Freaking Misha. Sure, he would be enjoying every moment. He had a silly chef who mooned over his broad shoulders and smooth handsomeness at every turn. What was there *not* to enjoy?

Get your crap together, girl. None of her usual emotion-filled, wear-your-heart-on-your-sleeve ways. She had to be strong. She'd been burned one too many times by smooth-talking men to take anything they said at more value than playing a game, or playing her. She'd gone on long enough listening to her heart. It was the head's turn to lead. And as for listening to regions farther south, which seemed to be blaring horns and trumpets when Ross Montgomery was in spitting distance, she was putting that area on mute, as it was not to be relied on for good advice.

When Essie got to the kitchen, Chef Scott was leaning against the counter, arms folded as if he was standing guard over his domain.

She smiled. "Hello, Chef. Once again, I hope you don't mind me butting in on your domain. I'll try my best to stay out of your way, but I may ask for a little help from you, as I'm new to finding out what Ross" — Essie paused — "I mean, Mr. Montgomery likes, and I've been charged to convert his diet to something a bit more heart healthy."

She watched as the already-rigid chef drew his body even tighter and stood taller, while plumping his chest out.

"Do you mean to tell me there is something wrong with my food? Are you trying to say there's something unhealthy about it?"

"Of course not," Essie soothed. "I'm sure your food is top-notch, or there is no way you would have been hired to be the head chef on such an exclusive boat. I was brought on as a nutritionist and a consultant. My expertise has nothing to do with your capability. Like I was saying, I'm sure there's plenty I can learn from you."

"Oh, what do I care about how he spends his money? You are just another in a long line of more of the same."

Essie bristled, but refused to bite, keeping her smile, but lowering her tone. "You're right. It is his money, and I suggest you do your job, and start by showing me around the kitchen and pantry properly. I want to be sure the items I listed to be supplied are all accounted for."

She and Chef Scott stared at each other, and once again Essie was up against a man she knew she could not back down from. But just when she thought he was about to break, a voice came from over her shoulder. "Why are you not moving, Simon? Like you said, it's my money. What? Are you afraid you may learn something?" Both Essie and the chef turned around at the sound of Ross's voice.

"I . . . I didn't mean anything by it, sir," Chef Scott stammered out.

Ross gave him a steely stare. "Let's be sure you didn't, because if you did, I can easily find other ways to spend my money than on your paycheck."

"Why, yes, sir, of course."

Essie saw the bloom of embarrassment take over the chef's face and a hint of anger as he clenched his jaw.

"Ross, really, it's all fine. Chef Scott and I were having a discussion about working arrangements. This is his kitchen, and he was showing me around."

Ross shot her a look that was at once caring, but somehow dismissive, and the smile he gave her didn't quite reach his eyes. "Now, in all actuality it's my kitchen." He turned to Chef Scott. "Am I right?"

The chef gave a nod of his head as his eyes went downcast. "That you are, and as you said, I'm sure there's plenty for me to learn."

Ross nodded then and smiled. It was that sexy and somehow dangerous smile that made Essie want to step away from him, when, at the same time, she wanted to step forward into his atmosphere.

He clasped his hands together, casually breaking the serious mood. "Well, then, I'll leave you both to it. Essie, I can't wait to taste what you have in store for me this afternoon."

As he left, Chef Scott lowered his hands and let out an audible sigh. Then he shot Essie a look that, while full of disdain, showed his defeat. "You heard the man. This is his boat, his home, and, as of now, it looks like you're the lady of the house." He made a wide gesture with his arms. "What's mine is now yours. So please tell me, how can I be of service to you?"

CHAPTER SEVEN

Though Ross was deep in conversation with his lawyer, he somehow felt Essie's presence outside his office door, even before she gave it a knock. "Hold on a minute, Barry. Come in," Ross said.

As Essie entered, Ross felt his body, his entire body, immediately spring to attention, like a trained Pavlovian dog. He couldn't help but notice the look of surprise she tried to hide at seeing the mess his office had become in the short time he'd been working. He was a bit of a manic worker and liked to spread things out, so just about every available surface was covered. There was no place for her to set the tray.

He watched as she did a little spin, which showed off her figure nicely, but as she came up empty, she turned back to him in frustration. "Barry, I'm going to have to get back to you. I'll call you in a half an hour or so." Ross cut off his call without waiting for a reply and got up from his seat.

Essie gave him a quick glare. "You didn't have to do that. I need a place to put the tray, and then I'll go so you can work."

"Who said I was hanging up for you? Presumptuous, aren't we, Ms. Bradford?" Ross gave Essie a grin. And he got back a hard stare.

"Not at all. I thought we agreed we were on a first-name basis, Ross. Now, do you care to let me know where to put the tray? It's getting pretty heavy."

Ross ran over and cleared space on the seating area's coffee table. He then took the tray out of Essie's hands, and fought to ignore the little spark of electricity that sizzled through him when their fingertips grazed. He had no time for shivers or sparks. He had a deal to get done, despite what Misha's plans for him were.

"Thank you. I hope you enjoy it."

Shit. Even her voice gave him shivers. All sweet and full of sass, but still with a hint of honey, even though she seemed mad as all get-out. "I'm sure I will. Now, tell me what it is. And while you're at it, you can tell me why you're ready to spit nails at me." Ross took a seat on the couch and lifted the cover on the plate, giving it a look over.

His eyes popped up when Essie cleared

her throat. "Lunch is a simple ratatouille. Eggplant, bell peppers, onions, zucchini, some tomatoes, all served over quinoa. And for dessert you've got a seasonal fruit plate with a vinaigrette dressing."

Ross looked over the tray and frowned.

"What's the matter?"

Ross gestured for Essie to take one of the chairs and watched as she seemed to do a double take before taking a seat, as if the chair would bite her or something.

"Okay. I'm sitting. What's wrong? I'm here to serve you."

Ross couldn't help his raised brow at that last comment, and still she was as taut as a fully loaded slingshot. "Are you going to tell me what has you so stiff-lipped and fired up?"

"I don't think I'm being stiff," she said. "But what is slightly bothersome to me is the fact that I didn't need you butting in when I was hashing things out with Chef Scott."

Ross was quiet. It wasn't as if she was wrong. He had been high-handed, but a guy like Simon needed to be pulled in, and pulled in quick, otherwise he could get out of hand. "I apologize for that. But as I said, this is my vessel, and I know Simon's reputation. He can be a bit of a bully, and

371

you are my guest. I wanted to make that clear, so he wouldn't think anything otherwise. I will apologize, though. I don't want to make you feel uncomfortable in any way. If it was any other situation, I would let you handle it yourself. But since you're my guest, I felt it was my duty to step in."

Essie's lips tightened. He could tell she didn't like his high-handedness, but, hopefully, she couldn't fault his logic. She looked over at Ross as he was eyeing the green smoothie.

"I see you are frowning. Is there something wrong with your lunch?"

Ross looked up, slightly bewildered. "There's no chocolate." He searched the tray again. "None of your chocolate puff pastry, chocolate tart, not even a hint of my favorite, your chocolate mousse."

Essie gave him a long look before speaking slowly, as if he were a child. "First of all, man cannot live on chocolate alone."

"So say you, but I beg to differ."

Essie let out a snort, but at least he got a hint of a smile. "As I was saying, man should not live by chocolate alone. And how was I to know that you wanted it at every meal? Is that why you hired me, for my chocolate?"

His brow shot up and she blushed. A

distinct rosiness radiated under her deep brown skin. She knew she walked right into that one, and it was cute as hell. Essie shook her head. "Really, Ross. Grow up. Besides, Misha would have my ass. There is no way she would sanction that sort of diet for you."

"Why? It's not like I need to lose weight. I'm in great physical shape."

Essie looked him over then, and with her dark, assessing gaze, his old jeans and sweater suddenly felt about two sizes too tight.

"Okay, I'll give you that," she finally said. "You can have a bit of chocolate, but you need to up your fruit, too."

He grinned at a small victory, then frowned again. "And I'm not really a fan of quinoa."

"Please don't tell me my newest client is a five-year-old. Misha warned me your taste in food was somewhat" — Essie paused — "shall I say, juvenile?"

"Hey, just because I like a burger now and again doesn't make my tastes juvenile."

"Fine. But if those burgers are from a fast-food restaurant that you've had your driver pull up to more than three times a week, I'd call that *juvenile.*"

Ross gave her a hard stare and she gave him one in return. He blinked and Essie grinned, no doubt enjoying her moment of victory.

"You know, nobody who works for me gives me so much grief."

"Why am I feeling that nobody gives you grief if they work for you or not? Now pick up your fork and eat your lunch like a good CEO."

Ross shook his head and did as he was told. Essie smiled, clearly enjoying the fact he was enjoying her food. She took pride in her work and he could respect that. For so long with him it always seemed to be about the bottom line, just numbers on a page. But when was the last time he really looked at the work he was doing? Took time to look and enjoy all he'd built?

"What is it now?" Essie asked.

He looked her in the eye, enjoying the moment of getting lost in their depths. "Nothing at all. This lunch is terrific, Chef."

She grinned a wholly satisfied grin, which was nothing short of glorious on her.

"Well done. You can stop gloating. You know you did great."

"You caught me. Later we'll talk breathing and maybe some meditation?"

At that, Ross let out a growl and Essie chuckled as she got up to make her exit. "Okay, I won't push my luck. At least not for today. I'll see you at dinner. Don't work too hard."

"Don't worry, I always do."

As Ross watched Essie's retreating back, and then headed back toward the phone, he was surprised by how much he enjoyed the banter with Essie. He couldn't remember the last time he had fun simply talking to a woman, or anyone for that matter, about a subject that wasn't business related. With her, talking came easy. And now as he picked up his phone and looked at the closed door, he found himself already looking forward to dinner and their next conversation.

CHAPTER EIGHT

Essie was laying out the dough for her puff pastries when Quincy came in with Ross's discarded tray. "Well, it would seem your first lunch was a hit, Ms. Bradford."

Essie grinned. "That's good to hear, and please call me Essie."

Quincy reached over and nabbed a strawberry from her bowl. "And you can call me Quince. So, what brings you here to sail away with our little crew?" Quincy made an exaggerated fanning motion. "You know, besides the fact that our fearless leader is the hottest eligible bachelor on the planet?"

Essie's head shot up from her work. "That is definitely not the reason I'm here. I'm here to cook, and that's about it. Just doing a favor for a friend."

"Oh, my dear. You must have some really good friends. I need to hang with a better class of people," Quincy said with a laugh.

Essie laughed along with him as Ethan,

the bosun, came in, followed by Jayce, the deckhand, who lifted his T-shirt to wipe at his sweaty brow, despite the chill of the sea air outside. Essie averted her gaze, but not before checking out his rippled abs. She bit back a giggle as she fought down a blush.

"Oh, darling, you have a lot to learn about us guys at sea. We are one big happy family on this boat," Quincy teased, catching her look.

Cooper came over and gave her shoulder a squeeze. His crystal blue eyes sparkled with sweet charm. "That's right, E."

She grinned, already liking her new nickname.

"We all get along like peas in a pod here. All for one, and one for all. Those are the rules." He dipped his pointer finger into her bowl of chocolate and took a long lick. "This is delicious!" He looked at his mates. "Guys, this woman's food is as sweet as she looks. We've got a winner here."

Essie gave him a smile along with a playful shove. "Watch those hands, Cooper. And definitely no double dipping."

"All right, boys, that's enough," came Ross's deep voice, stopping all conversation like a scratched record. "No dipping your fingers into my bowl without permission." At the double entendre no one knew whether to laugh or not, so it was Essie who broke the tension, refusing to let Ross once again come into the kitchen and ruin what she was trying to build.

"You'd better be talking about these stainless-steel bowls, because if not, you'll be meeting the hard end of one of my frying pans."

Ross stepped down from the stairs and fully into the galley. Everyone was silent as Ross and Essie stared at each other. He raked his eyes from her eyes to her lips, down to her breasts and on to her hands, back up to her lips, then her eyes again. Each point he hit seemed to flame along his route. "Now, what else could I possibly be referring to?" he finally growled out before walking over to the fridge and pulling out a beer, twisting the cap and taking a pull.

"Sir, I could have brought that to you," Quincy spoke up.

He gave Quincy an exasperated look. "I'm not helpless, Quince. But what you can do for me is prepare the small dining room." He then looked at Essie again. "If you wouldn't mind joining me there for dinner, Ms. Bradford?"

Oh, boy, so bowls licked and they were back to that. Essie gave him a cool smile.

"Sure, Mr. Montgomery. I'll see you at eight."

The smile she got in return before he walked off could have frozen the water they sailed on, but she ignored it and continued her work. She wouldn't let him get to her. No way was he ruining her mood or her food.

Essie finished her work, filled her pastries, and then handed Cooper the spoon.

He laughed at that. "Oh, E, you are a tough one."

"Of course I'm not. You said it yourself. I'm as sweet as my chocolate, and don't let anybody tell you different."

CHAPTER NINE

The petite dining salon might as well have been called the grand salon for all its opulence. The wood of the table was polished to a high shine as was the modern glass chandelier above with its golden accents. Not to mention the china was also gold edged and gleaming. Quincy had done a beautiful job with the settings. *Maybe a little too beautiful,* Essie thought as she caught the reflections of the candlelight in the large windows, which offered a beautiful view of the glistening moonlight bouncing off the dark sea.

Crap, this is looking a little too much like a date! It had Essie feeling uneasy. First, about how her meal would be received, which was ridiculous because she was always confident in her food. But after seeing this setup, she was really nervous over the fact she'd be sitting and sharing a meal with Ross.

Alone.

For the first time.

Butterflies started to flutter, threatening to swirl in an uncomfortably familiar way in her belly. This was silly; she had to get it together. It wasn't a "date" date; it was Essie and a client sharing a meal.

That was it. She'd consider it an assignment.

But as she was laying out her dishes in the center of the table, and removing her chef's smock to reveal the simple black cotton dress underneath, Ross walked in, looking like 110 percent of movable sex and money in his slacks, high-shined shoes, and expensive dress shirt. The butterflies went wild.

Essie brushed at her bangs and tugged on her casual dress, which now felt like an old painter's smock. "Sorry, I didn't have anything particularly dressy to wear. I really only came with more casual work clothes and these easy dresses." *Oh, God, why am I explaining myself to this man? Shut up, Essie.*

Ross smiled as he walked over to her. His closeness and clean freshly showered scent, with a hint of some expensive undertone, sent her senses into overdrive as he pulled out the chair for her. The urge to lean over and lick his neck was overwhelming.

"You look absolutely perfect."

Oh, hell, if that wasn't the worst thing he could have said. The butterflies went into a tailspin as her hormones followed behind.

In that moment Essie longed to be in the crew dining area, enjoying a casual laugh-it-up dinner with them. The safe kind, like she'd had with the band. Nothing felt casual or safe about tonight. With her out of her chef's smock, and him looking at her like he saw entirely too much, this dinner had her up front and out of the kitchen — very much on display as Essie. *Just as Essie.* She didn't like it one bit.

Thankfully, Quincy came in with the wine. "Sir, tonight we have a Pinot Noir, and I believe it will complement your meal beautifully."

Ross gave Quincy a nod as he continued his intense scrutiny of Essie. "And what is the meal for the evening?"

Essie let out a breath, which she realized she'd been holding way too long. Finally they were in her wheelhouse and she could be herself. Essie put on her best serene smile. "Well, we're starting with a pear, arugula, and warm goat-cheese salad. Then for the main dish we have sea scallops with light lemon reduction and spinach. And for dessert you'll be happy to know I've made your own mini chocolate mousse." When she spoke the word "mousse," she gave him a wink and was rewarded with a smile that was as sweet as a kid's at Christmas.

"It all looks wonderful. Can we start with the dessert?"

Essie laughed. "Oh, my goodness. I think I had it right. Deep down you are five years old."

She noticed Quincy smirk as he finished his pour and discreetly left the room.

Ross gave her that quirky brow of his. "You know you are going to ruin my reputation with my crew."

Essie reached over and began to plate the food for him. "Somehow I doubt that. No matter how much I tease, you'll find a way to wash away any bit of playfulness."

Ross took the plate and looked up at her. "Are you trying to imply that I'm no fun?"

Essie finished plating her own meal, sat down, and looked across at Ross. "I'm just saying that I call things as I see them, which I explained to you earlier, and so far all I'm seeing you do is work and be slightly scolding to your crew."

"And all I see you doing is being highly judgmental toward me. So by your logic, I can surmise that your whole world revolves around cooking and judging people." Ross took a bite of the salad and closed his eyes to let the dressing's flavors flood his senses. He gave her a smile. "One of which you're very good at" — but then he shrugged his shoulders — "the other, not so much."

Essie frowned and began to eat her meal in silence. *What does he know? Though he does have right the part about me cooking well.* The man had excellent taste when it came to food and chefs. But, hey, she was a pretty good judge of people. Essie paused in her thinking as Cam came to mind, and the waste of time and space. Roger before him. It's just she wasn't the best judge of boyfriends. So what if every time she thought she found Mr. Right, give or take a few months or few weeks, they always turned out to be Mr. Wrong. Oh, well, hell! Maybe Ross was right and she was too quick to judge, and judged in the wrong direction.

Which was why she was over trusting her "yes"; from now on, caution was the way to go.

Essie stared at Ross. He looked every bit like a bite of sweet, sexy chocolate heaven as he ate his meal. Maybe giving up her "yes" was hasty. But there was no way she was going all in and giving up her heart for a man, when all it would take was a little taste to satisfy her need.

Essie smiled to herself as she took a sip of her wine.

"You look quite content there. It's like you've had a full-on internal powwow without me. I'm starting to feel slighted. Penny for your thoughts?"

Essie stared at him for a few beats and then looked around the opulent dining room. It was lovely, but void of any personal touches. So very different from the way she lived. Thoughts of home and her mom came to her mind, and she wondered what her mother must be doing right now. Probably pulling out their old artificial Christmas tree. But would she really want to do it alone? Sadness swept through Essie in a sudden wave. "You know you can afford to pay way more than a penny for my thoughts."

Ross's lips quirked up. It was like a switch went off with that little quirk, the way her nipples hardened and the shiver sizzled down her spine.

"You're right I can pay more, but how about you share anyway. You were far away for a moment there."

She looked at him and took another sip of wine. "I was thinking about my mother for a moment and what she must be doing right now."

"And what might that be?" he asked, seeming genuinely interested.

Essie briefly considered the time. "I was thinking tonight she'd be putting up the Christmas tree, but I'm wondering if she would have wanted to do it without me. I should have made time to do it with her before I left. It's our favorite thing." Essie smiled, wanting to lighten the mood. "If she's not into tree trimming, I'm guessing, given the time, she's watching her favorite show on TV, with her feet up, having something warm to eat. Probably a leftover stew of some sort from Sunday. My mother always likes to make large pots so she doesn't have to cook during the week, since she still works full-time at the post office."

"And what does your father do?" Ross asked.

Essie's shoulders tensed as the usual ache settled in her chest. "He drove, boy did he drive." As she heard her voice start to fade off, Essie forced herself to snap back. "He passed away two years ago," she said quickly, and then tried to cover it with a smile she hoped was bright enough. "But my mom is up for retirement soon, and I'm looking forward to taking her away on a long-awaited and much-deserved vacation one of these Christmases."

"I'm really sorry. I didn't mean to bring up a subject that would cause you pain." His voice was low and deep, full of so much sincerity that it made her pause and swallow down a lump in her throat.

Essie waved a hand across her face in dismissal. "Oh, it's fine, really. It's been a couple of years. It's just that, well, my mother and I have never been apart during the holidays, so I do worry about her being alone. But she won't really be alone. My aunt Viv invited her to come and visit with her family, so as long as there are no big fights between her and Aunt Viv between now and Christmas" — Essie rolled her eyes — "all will be fine."

Essie wanted desperately to get the subject off her and on to anything else. She noticed Ross's plate was empty and laughed. "I see you hated tonight's meal. How about we get started on dessert?" She stood to move his plate to the side buffet, when he reached out a hand to still her, and the charge was instantaneous. She turned and stared.

"I'm sorry I took you away from your mom on Christmas. You sit, and I'll move these."

Essie sat, but only because she was more

stunned by this apology than anything else. She watched silently as he moved the plates to the buffet and then came back to top off her glass of wine. She looked up at him with a half smile. "I hope you aren't trying to get me drunk."

"You say that as if I would need to."

Part of Essie wanted to call him a "cocky asshole" for that comment, but his matter-of-fact way of stating it held no arrogance, and hell, it wasn't like he was lying. He was hot as sin and definitely wouldn't need to get her drunk to get her into bed. So Essie watched as he expertly served the mousse from the left and took his seat.

"You do this like you've had your fair share of practice. Have you ever worked in a restaurant?"

"As I said before, you, Essie, are quick to judge, and yes, I have."

Essie furrowed her brows. "But I looked you up. Your family is quite rich."

She saw his mouth harden a bit. "That's my family — though I did get a good amount of money when my mother passed away."

"I'm really sorry," she said, but he continued to talk, wanting to gloss over his lost parent in the same way she had.

"Don't worry. It's been even more years

for me than you. And my father has not always been that forthcoming with sharing his wealth. I will say he was right in wanting me to learn all facets of business, though. I worked a few summers in the kitchens of his resorts. I did kitchen, grounds, hospitality, as well as working construction. I've seen every aspect of the business while working through college. He made sure to let me know my education would not come free."

Essie studied Ross closely and was careful with her words. "He sounds like a tough man. Are you close?"

Ross picked up his wineglass and drained it before looking at her. "That we are not. I always seem to fall just short of Dad's expectations. No matter, though. I've ceased looking for my father's approval and now only seek to satisfy myself." Ross smiled, his eyes seemingly quite far away before he blinked and his gaze turned warm and approving. "And I will say, right now I am quite satisfied."

Part of her wanted to blush and possibly preen under his approving gaze, but something in her wanted to go back to what he was clearly trying to cover up. "You have me at a loss right now, Ross. For all the judging you say I do, I can't quite figure you out. What I know from Misha is pretty much stats. That you're a hard worker, maybe overly so, and you have poor eating habits, though not the worst I've ever seen. But you counter that with hard, grinding workouts that are just as hard as your work ethic. With you, it seems to be all or nothing. For some reason Misha speaks very highly of you. I've known her for quite a while and she doesn't speak so highly of that many people, so that makes me wonder why."

Ross shrugged. "Of course Misha likes me. What's there not to like? I have that kind of effect on women."

Essie narrowed her eyes. "Yeah, I don't think so. I've known Misha a long time. She would tell me if that was the case. Either way, I think there's a little something more to you, too. What's the real reason you're working so hard that you end up in the ER, having a panic attack that scares you enough to fear it's a heart attack? What are you running from, Ross Montgomery?"

With that question Ross got up and took her hand, pulling her into his arms. His embrace was swift, but not so fast that she couldn't push back if she wanted.

But she didn't want to.

She wanted to stay where she was, her

body flush against his solid hardness. Ross looked down, his dark eyes meeting her own in a challenge as old as time.

"Maybe I'm not running from anything, sweet Essie, but running toward something? Did you ever stop to think of that?"

The question took her breath away because she hadn't thought of it. She blinked in the wonderment of it all, yet at the same time she steeled herself against the emotional onslaught as his lips came down toward hers.

Quincy walked back into the dining room, breaking the sexually charged tension. "How are we doing here?" he said brightly, and stopped short when he realized what he'd walked in on.

"Oh, I'm sorry. I'll go and, uh, get you another bottle."

Essie attempted to back away, but Ross, unfazed by the interloper, kept his arm firmly around her waist and challenged her with his gaze.

"Yes, you can, Quincy," Ross said, cool as ice. "Thank you. I think we'll have it in the main deck's salon."

"Very good, sir," Quincy said as he quickly left the dining room.

"I think it would be nice to continue this conversation where we can enjoy a view of the sea."

"Why did you do that?" Essie asked, trying hard to keep a tight rein on her temper. "You may not care about what others think of you, but I sure care what they think of me."

He seemed to study her hard after that statement, making her increasingly uncomfortable under his critical eye.

"Maybe that's your problem."

Essie's gaze sharpened. "What are you talking about? I don't have a problem. Besides, it's you I'm here to fix. It's you with the problems."

He raised a brow. "If you say so, Essie."

Essie pulled back sharply, yanking herself from his embrace, then hating the decision as soon as the coolness of the broken contact hit her. "I say so."

"Methinks the lady protests just enough to try and convince herself," he said, smooth and easy. "What are you trying to do? Do you think if you play nice and be a good little girl the world will reward you? I've got news for you — it doesn't work that way. It's eat or be eaten. You're a chef. You should know that. Survival of the fittest, and all that. But Lord knows there are opportunities for a swift ass kicking around every corner."

Ross took a dangerous and altogether too-alluring step toward her as Essie fought to slow her rapidly beating heart. He was just above her, so close that she could feel his breath against her lips.

He spoke again. "But if you're smart, you'll also grab swiftly to any chance of pleasure you can get. I know I do."

Essie snorted, her mind going to him in the ER. "Yeah, and look where it's gotten you."

Ross got a dark smolder in his eye, his expression taking on a look of pure sex. "Yeah, look where it's gotten me. The question is, where will it take you?"

Essie swallowed as Ross stared at her, then gave his head a small shake as if he were dismissing her and the idea that she could be like him: a person who could swim with the big fish and hold her own. The type who could know herself and, really and truly, live in her own pleasure, come what may with the consequences.

Essie studied the idea for a moment. *Could I?* God, in that moment she really wanted to do so. All she wanted to do was to take Ross with both hands and taste all he had to offer. At least for this moment. But how could she? She barely knew him beyond two conversations, a Google search, and a friend's recommendation. Jumping into bed like that was definitely not her style. Not to mention, she was in a business relationship with him. Ten days later and maybe, yes, fine, they could go on a date and see where things went. But now? No, it couldn't be done. It shouldn't be done.

Still, Essie couldn't help the small twinge of satisfaction she got from seeing Ross's eyes widen when she surprised him by suddenly reaching up and fisting his shirt in her hands and, against all her better judgment and his presumptions, pulling him down into a kiss.

CHAPTER TEN

Holy hell, could this woman kiss!

Ross was instantly swept away by the sweet, decadent, and surprisingly addictive taste of Essie Bradford.

Where he thought she would be timid and demure, she proved him wrong by taking charge, pulling him down to her with two hands, and rising up to meet his lips forcefully with her own. And what a first meeting it was. Those full, ripe, pillowy lips were everything he dreamed they would be. Soft and luxurious, sweet to the taste, the first touch had the normally unflappable Ross just about going weak in the knees.

But he steeled himself. Telling himself to be strong and not to lose it too quickly. Giving himself a pep talk, not unlike he did when he was a teenage boy. Think baseball stats, cold showers, bespectacled librarians . . . okay, maybe not librarians. But still, how was it this almost-unassuming woman, a chef to cook his meals, could come in here and, with a mere brush of her lips, just about lay him flat? Ross closed his eyes and let the feeling take him away.

He felt Essie's excitement as she pushed her soft body against his and her rapid heartbeat vibrated against his chest, giving him a rock-hard hard-on. She tilted her head and leaned in, going further with her kiss, tentatively easing her tongue out, to run along the seam of his lips. He was only too happy to open his own lips to let her in to taste him fully for the first time.

But with a dangerous first taste, his own emotions went out of control and Ross wrapped his arms around her body and pulled her in tight. His hands traveled down to cup her curvy bottom and pull her up against his hard erection. His tongue snaked out hungrily to taste the sweet wine and chocolate as it clung to her very clever tongue.

He wanted to taste her everywhere, to see if the sweetness continued all the way down her body. As the kiss changed, Ross took control, moving down her neck, pausing to lick along her delicate collarbone. Ross couldn't help but smile when she sighed, and his erection jumped in response to the erotic sound as it escaped her lips and her head lulled back in unabashed pleasure. That's all he wanted to do. Give her pleasure from now until the sun came up, and then do it all over again and again and again. Getting her to sigh could easily turn into a life's mission for him.

Ross reached a hand up and cupped Essie's breast and she drew in a quick inhale. Something in the quick indrawn breath pulled his attention up to her face. Seeing her beautiful dark neck thrown back in submission, her lips swollen from their passionate kiss, her eyes fluttering in dark ecstasy, about did him in. He could have her right now if he wanted. Just like so many women before, he could have her.

And then what?

Ross frowned at the unwanted question. It was one he hadn't thought of in a long time, causing him to draw back ever so slightly, breaking contact only a minuscule bit. But that bit was long enough and Essie's eyes fluttered open, looking at him with the question he asked himself, unsaid but reflected there.

And then what?

"I think I should forgo the second bottle of wine and go up to bed. Or is it down to bed?"

When Essie stepped back, she left Ross

feeling more alone than he cared to admit.

"Besides, it's starting to get late and it's been a long day. How about we pick up again tomorrow? I'd like to prepare for the day and really get you started on your regime."

Letting her go anywhere, especially to bed tonight without him, was the last thing Ross wanted to do, but he wouldn't push her any further. Besides, she was right. It had been a long day. Maybe what they both needed was a little space and perspective. Also, Ross didn't want any woman to feel pressure to end up in his bed. That was a strictly-by-choice situation, always had been and always would be.

Ross cleared his throat and hoped his words came out even, and the turmoil he secretly felt was hidden. "You're right, it has been a long day. Thank you so much for dinner, it was wonderful. Misha was correct. You are a very talented chef, and I look forward to all you have in store for me during the rest of this trip."

After what they had just shared, he didn't quite know how to end the evening, which made him feel like a damn fool, since he usually knew what to do in just about every situation, especially when it came to women.

Thankfully, the surprising Essie once

again took matters into her own hands and gave him an easy smile. "I'm glad you enjoyed the meal, though you will be a challenge, and I have to think of ways to counteract all the chocolate you're going to demand."

At his raised brow they both laughed.

"Don't start, Ross, just say good night. I'm going to go make sure everything is fine in the kitchen, and then I'm heading to bed. You gave me enough to think about for one day and night," she said as she casually walked off toward the galley, leaving Ross with nothing better to do than take a chilly but welcome walk along the outer deck to hopefully cool his heated passion.

It took all of one point five seconds into the new day for the night before to come flooding back to Essie's mind.

Oh, God, did I really do what I know I did?

She wanted to cringe over the embarrassment of the shameless, brazen way she came on to Ross, but at the same time she couldn't fully regret kissing him. She so wanted to give herself a high five and the "atta, girl" she knew her girlfriends would.

Essie stretched, surprised at how comfortably she had slept when she finally did drift off. *Serenity* was just that: a sure ride that cut the ocean smoothly, its engines a low hum, combined with the sensual tingle she received from Ross, sent her to sleep way more contentedly than she'd expected.

Essie went to the large window and saw the sun just coming up over the horizon, beautiful soft shades of orange where it met the still-slumbering sea. Essie longed to be outside, to smell the sea air.

She changed into her workout clothes of leggings and a tank top and grabbed her yoga mat to take her morning practice above deck.

On the way out she purposely closed her stateroom door softly so as not to wake Ross as she slipped past his door. According to the schedule, she had an hour before she had to start to prepare breakfast and then she had all day to deal with Ross and what happened last night. Before Essie went to bed, she mulled it over in her mind numerous times, and still had yet to come up with how she would handle this new facet of their equally new relationship. All she had come up with was to take it slow and continue to be a professional.

Which, to her ears, sounded quite dull.

The only voice she could hear over her own was Misha's, and it was telling her to let loose and enjoy herself. She needed this.

Cam had left her, high and dry, and this was supposed to be her holiday — a working one that it was, but still her holiday. Not to mention it had been over two months since she'd had sex. Not a desert, but bordering on a parched spell for sure. Why not let go and see where these days with Ross could take her? Why not say yes, for once, to herself and to what she wanted?

But just as she was on her way out to head to the outer deck, sure of herself and her decision, Essie heard grunting and a constant *thwacking* sound as she passed the gym. There was Ross, looking like he had been working out for at least the past hour, glistening, rich brown and drenched in sweat. He pounded hard at the heavy bag. Essie instantly felt her body go on full alert as she took in his stance. Sure-footed and strong, his arms were muscular and powerful; his loose-fitting shorts were barely being held up by the tie at his trim waist. His wide back and broad shoulders were well accented by his wet tank. When he punched the bag again, and she watched those muscles contract and release, Essie couldn't help but let out a breathy sigh.

Ross stopped and turned around, meeting her, eye to eye. "Good morning." His voice was strong and raspy. Essie could tell he was fighting to catch his breath.

"You going a bit hard for so early in the morning, aren't you?"

Ross's eyes raked over her body, and in that moment Essie could practically feel his hands grazing over her skin. He stopped briefly at her yoga mat and then came up to her eyes with a playful smile. "And I see you like to take things slow and easy in the morning. Duly noted."

Essie's eyes narrowed. "Here it is, the sun is barely up, and you are spoiling for an argument."

"With you, Ms. Bradford, I'd hit the mat anytime, any way."

Essie smiled, then looked at the fairly large, cleared workout area in the exercise room. It could easily accommodate a yoga session for two. She looked back at Ross with a challenge in her eyes. "Okay, Mr. Montgomery. Just be sure you remember you said that. The session starts now."

Ross was only too happy to oblige. He loved to shake her up. Liked to see that little spark of fire she got when they sparred a bit and he called her Ms. Bradford. She really had no idea how hot she was. And time in a possible downward-dog position with the delectable Essie Bradford? He'd be a fool to hesitate.

Eagerly, he took off his sneakers and let her place him in position on the mat. Her strong but gentle fingers at his waist instantly put his body on alert, reminding him of the fact that thoughts of her put him through a tortured and restless night.

It wasn't so easy making it through this workout. Ross spent most of his time torn between wanting to look at her beautifully shaped form in her workout gear, and fighting looking at said form because of the effects on his body.

He took the edge off by going tried and true, thinking of sports, stocks, anything but her shapely figure. Thankfully, Essie wasn't easy on him. Starting out slow and easy, after a while picking up the pace, taking him through a series of moves that had him panting for air like he did with his cross-fit trainer back home. When she was down in a sort of modified plank and swooped into a cobra and quickly went from there — back to plank, then up into some mad one-armed twisted-pretzel thing — all Ross could do was lean back and marvel at her strength as his own muscles cried "uncle."

Essie gracefully came out of position and gave him a saucy wink. "You've had enough?"

"I may regret saying this, but yes. I give up. You got the best of me this morning, Essie." For his acquiescence, Ross was rewarded with a smile so sweet that he suddenly felt like he could do twenty laps around the deck and not break a sweat.

"Okay," she said, her voice going low, taking on a softer tone. "How about we relax and cool down for a minute. Just stretch and breathe before we really start the day?"

She took him through an easy series of floor stretches and some light breathing, only to test his willpower to the max when, in order to get his legs stretched wider apart, she used her own outstretched legs to open his. "Are you trying to be the death of me, woman?" he asked, giving her a look that left no question as to what he was really talking about.

But Essie played it cool, taking his hands in hers, and giving him a tug forward toward her most intimate of places. "I'm only trying to challenge you. Make sure you're getting all you paid for."

He leaned back, gently pulling her forward toward him. "There are some things I never pay for."

At that, she stilled, and there they were for the moment — both suspended, legs spread, hand in hand, eye to eye, both wanting the same thing, but pulling in opposite directions.

There was a noise from the gym door way, a discreet cough that had both their heads turning. Quincy.

"Once again, Quincy, your timing is perfect."

Quincy was impeccable, despite the early hour and the embarrassing moment of the night before. "That it is, sir. I'm sorry to disturb you, but you have a call that said it can't wait. Would you like it here or in your office?"

Ross reluctantly let go of Essie's hands and helped her up. "Thank you for an exuberant workout."

"Thanks for joining me. I'll go and get breakfast started. It shouldn't be long. I didn't expect you up this early."

"It's no problem. I never eat before working out. Please take your time." He then turned to Quincy. "Thank you. I'll take it in my office."

As Ross left Essie in the exercise room, he wanted both to curse and thank Quincy for his second, not-so-well-timed, interruption.

CHAPTER ELEVEN

Essie prepared breakfast for Ross and even got to score a few points with Chef Scott by asking him for advice on Ross's preferences, and by helping the chef with prepping the crew's breakfast. She was putting the finishing touches on Ross's tray as Simon gave her a gentle ribbing.

"He won't like it," Simon said, his tone light and teasing as he referred to the fruit kale smoothie she added to the tray.

"You wanna bet?"

Simon looked her up and down, then shook his head. "Nah. The money would be too easy. You do yourself a favor and heat one of your sweet pastries from last night. I know Ross, and no matter how much fruit you try and sweeten it with, he's not drinking that green smoothie."

Essie rolled her eyes and took the tray. "I'll just leave and take that as a compliment on my baking, Chef."

Simon laughed.

As Essie made her way toward Ross's office, she once again almost literally ran into him as he came down the stairs. "Hi. I was just bringing this to you," she said, keeping a tight hold on the tray and her unsteady emotions.

His sudden appearance towering on the stairs surprised her. He was clean and freshly showered in easy sweatpants, which hung low on his hips, and he wore a finely threaded cotton tee, which defined his muscles well. He was no less powerful from when she saw him at the heavy bag that morning, and his clean, freshly showered smell and close presence set her off-kilter. Thankfully, he reached out and took the tray from her hands.

"Come, have you eaten?" he asked.

"I have." She'd grazed from her homemade muesli while prepping, and she had her own shake before heading up, too. Their exuberant workout session made her more famished than normal.

"Well, please still join me while I eat. Chat awhile?"

She studied him for a moment. It wasn't like she really could say no. He'd paid for her time for the duration of this trip. And, honestly, it wasn't like she wanted to say no. "Of course. But don't you have work to do?"

He turned to head up the stairs, but instead of turning left and going toward his office, as she expected, he continued up and went to the large salon. "How about we sit outside? You'll find that it's warmed up. We've had to take a detour, and we'll be making a brief stop along the way at my resort in Bermuda."

Essie looked at him in surprise. "But isn't that way off our course? How long will it delay the trip?"

Ross put the tray on the table nearest the doors to the outer deck and then opened them wide, letting in the fresh air. The view of the open water was stunning. The sun had fully risen and the water glistened a gorgeous crystalline blue through the large windows. "Don't worry, it won't delay us long. And it will give me a chance to show you my resort. You'll get an idea of what I'm planning, with the partnership of these investors." He readied to take a seat, but pulled out a chair and gestured for her to sit first.

Essie came over and, instead of sitting, gave him a small shove into the chair. "I thought on the way to Miami you would get a little relaxation. Seems you found a

408

way to find some extra work."

Almost instinctively, Ross pulled her down onto his lap. The easy snug fit had them both looking at each other with a bit of shock. Ross reached up and brought his finger to her cheek. "I didn't go looking for this work. It came and found me."

Essie knew she should get up, push back, act affronted, something. But sitting on Ross's lap, doing exactly what she was doing in that moment, was the only thing she wanted to do, and right where she was, was the only place she wanted to be.

She took in his dark eyes as he looked at her with a raw, unrestrained desire, the type she had never experienced. "I swear, you make me do the most unprofessional and inappropriate things, Ross Montgomery. When I'm around you, I feel like I'm somehow not my usual self."

Those sexy as hell lips quirked a little at that, and she wanted to kiss him again.

"Is that so bad?" he asked.

Essie thought for a moment. "It sure isn't good. What must you think of me? What must the crew?"

He let out a low, husky growl as he pulled her in close and nuzzled at her neck, sending the most decadent thrill sizzling throughout her body.

"Why are you so worried about what the crew thinks, or what I think for that matter?" he asked as he leaned back a bit and looked up at her seriously, and maybe a little too deeply. "Why not think about yourself and what you want and feel — do you ever do that?"

Once again he read her and came back with a too-clear summary. She was always caring what others thought and putting their needs before her own. Wasn't it just what she was saying was her downfall and what she had to change most about herself? Essie looked at Ross now and came out with the truth. "No, I usually don't ever do that."

He ran a hand lazily up and down her side, the shivers turning into lazy waves that lulled her into some sort of Ross Montgomery spell.

"Is there any particular reason you don't?"

Suddenly he felt too close to home, and Essie wanted to dodge the subject. She shimmied around and reached for his tray, pulling it toward him while trying to get up. Essie pulled the cover off the plate, and once again Ross pulled a skeptical face. Essie laughed. "Really, again? What were you living on? Drive-through breakfast specials, too? You really have to change your palate." She hoisted herself up.

"*Aww*, come on now," Ross said as Essie went around to the other side of the table.

"Come on, yourself. Pouting isn't cute on a CEO. For lunch you'll join me in the kitchen. I think a lesson is in order."

Ross surprised her by grinning as he held up his smoothie. "Fine. I welcome joining you in the kitchen. I'll show you where the fryer is and we can dispose of whatever monstrosity made this."

Essie rolled her eyes. "That is incredibly healthy and delicious."

Ross laughed, shaking his head. "Well, I finally found the one thing you can't cook." He sipped at it again and grimaced. "You didn't really cook this, did you? You're pulling one over on me."

"Well, technically, it's not cooked."

Ross cocked his head to the side as he put the smoothie down and dug into his omelet and salmon. "Well, therein lies your problem. Food is meant to be cooked."

Now it was Essie's turn to frown. "Why is that a rule?"

"It's my rule."

"And what? Your rules are somehow law or something?"

He shrugged before taking a long pull of coffee. "Or something."

Essie leaned back, crossing her arms. "You

411

are annoyingly self-assured."

"It's not the first time I've heard that, and you have to know I can't say I take it as an insult."

"I'm not saying I meant it as one." Essie let her gaze wander from him as she looked out at the view. Jayce walked by with an easy wave. It was a glorious day and she suddenly longed to go out.

"I'm glad to hear it. Usually it is not said so kindly."

Essie looked at him once again, and there was a hint of something in his eyes. A certain longing. A hurt. For a moment she couldn't help but wonder if it was a woman bringing that look into his eyes. She wanted to ask, but she knew it wasn't her place. And then he blinked, and as she'd seen him do before, his expression quickly changed and he was cool. Not emotionless, but there was no sign of the brief hint of hurt she had seen. Just the smooth assurance he usually exuded.

"The sun is getting strong. Would you join me for a stroll around the deck? We never took that walk last night."

Essie looked at him and thought of Misha and her ever-so-obvious setup. She wondered if he was in on it, too, and felt her lips twist. What if he was? Would that be so bad? What was the harm in having some fun for a change? She'd earned it, working pretty much nonstop this past year. "Fine, but you'll join me in the kitchen after we go out."

"Of course," he said, getting up and heading for the deck's open doors, confident in the knowledge she'd follow. When she didn't immediately, Ross paused and turned back, putting out his hand. "Please walk with me awhile, Essie?"

Fighting not to overthink, Essie reached out and took Ross's hand in her own, ignoring the smooth, easy fit. "Okay, Ross, show me around. But after that, it's my turn and in my kitchen, and you're my student. So I'm in charge?"

He grinned. "Deal," he said with a mischievous look in his eyes. "How about we seal it with a kiss?"

Essie pushed at him playfully, but followed it by pulling him down until his lips met hers once again. She kissed him until she felt they both needed to jump into the water and cool off. Ross's low moan followed by his erection when she rubbed against him was her clear indication she'd gotten the best of him. She pulled back and looked up into his eyes. "I told you, Ross. You make me do the most improper things."

He smiled. "And once again, I'm so glad for it." But he pulled away from her and took her hand again. "Still, I don't want to rush you. At least not an hour into our first full day together. Besides," he said, taking a breath, "if I don't slow down, I may embarrass myself."

Essie couldn't help the inner smile that showed on the outside with that one. She knew she was good-looking enough and did fine with men. At least no one was kicking her out of bed or turning her down, but no one was openly expressing to her that she made them feel out of control. It was nice, if not surprising, and she couldn't help but wonder if it was some sort of line. She looked at Ross and tried to hide her skepticism.

"Sure. Let's walk. Tell me about your project."

As they walked, Ross told her about the resort he was building. It was an offshoot of his Bermuda resort. But closer to Miami. Essie was amazed at the size and scope of the project and the fact that it sounded like a mini utopia, sort of a *Fantasy Island* for the new set. If he could pull it off, it would be great. Not that she'd see the likes of it. It sounded like "if you have to ask the cost, you can't afford it." Single residences, with private chefs, twenty-four-hour maid and concierge service. All top-notch. No amenity spared and, he'd added, practically no wish, within reason, denied. Essie couldn't help the heat that rushed to her cheeks as her mind wandered to the types of hedonistic fantasies she could explore with Ross in a place like that.

They made their way back toward the main salon area, and Ross and Essie took lounge chairs on deck to relax in the sun awhile. Essie turned to him. "The island sounds fabulous, and like it's a huge undertaking. I can see why you've been under so much stress with that in the works, plus your other holdings in the city. What made you take it on? Your resort in Bermuda is already successful."

Ross's expression got serious for a moment before he spoke. "I don't know. Bermuda is wonderful, but I'm ready to expand. In New York I can always go up, and, believe me, I will. But my father made his mark in resorts, and I know he always wanted to do something like this. Could never do something like this. I'm going to be the Montgomery to make it happen."

Essie frowned. "Have you spoken with your father about it? Is he one of your investors?"

Ross's eyes grew cold. "No. He's given up on that part of the business. Told me I was a fool to do it. I plan to prove him wrong. Once and for all."

Something in Ross's voice let her know she'd gone far enough with the questions for one morning. She gave him a smile. "Well, you'll need your strength to do that. What about we hit the kitchen?" She stood and then reached out a hand to pull him up, but Ross pulled her back down on top of him. Her body hit his with a gentle thump.

"I'd much rather spend time learning more about you, Essie."

His lips were strong and self-assured. There was no tentative pretense in this kiss. Ross pulled her into him, his large hands roaming up her thighs and cupping her behind perfectly as if he had some sort of claim to stake as he rubbed her against his hard body. He coaxed her lips apart and his tongue expertly intertwined with hers, stroking against hers until her body was aflame from her toes on up.

Essie let out a moan when he moved a hand from her behind to the underside of her breast. His thumb teased over her nipple in a circular motion and her most intimate spot went instantly to liquid. "Hell, the things you won't do to get out of cooperating," she said, her voice a hoarse whisper as she pushed up against his chest.

Ross chuckled. "I didn't get this far by playing fair."

Essie came to her feet, taking gulps of air and smoothing down her hair. She looked down at him with narrowed eyes. "No, I don't think you did."

CHAPTER TWELVE

As they stood at the galley counter, side by side, Ross tried his best to concentrate on what Essie was saying and not just stare at her luscious lips, not to mention her curvy hips. He was ready to break out into a sweat. They had already gotten the shrimp stir fried for the spicy Thai salad they were having for lunch, and now he was chopping, or supposed to be chopping, cucumber. But Essie looked so cute at the stove, her hips giving a little wiggle, which he could almost swear she was unaware of, as she stirred the mixture of shrimp, lime, fish sauce, and onions. At first it seemed like a lot to put together, but he had to admit, she made it seem fun and easy. Essie turned and gave him a smile. Damn those lips. His knife slipped and he nicked his finger. "Ouch!"

"Watch it!" She came running over to check him out, pulling his hurt finger toward her for scrutiny. "You have to pay attention or you're going to get hurt. It's not as simple as it looks."

Ross kept staring at her. "Nothing ever is."

Essie pulled him toward the sink as she simultaneously turned off the stove. She rinsed his cut thumb, then dried it. She pulled the first-aid kit down with a quick, no-nonsense air and bandaged him. "It's nothing much, but you have to be careful." She started to plate their lunch then and, without fanfare, served him at the counter.

Her eyes now held a seriousness that Ross didn't want to accept. He leaned in to kiss her, but she backed up and waved a fork.

"Eat. And enjoy your work. But think about being more careful when you're in my kitchen."

He took a bite, then paused to smile. It was good. Essie gave him a nod of pleasure. "You did well for your first try. You can cook. I don't see why you rely on eating out so much. All I can tell from our short time together is that you go way too fast. You're reckless."

Ross gave her a frown. A look that normally would end most conversations, but still Essie continued.

"Save the look, Ross. I see it. It may have gotten you far in business, but if you're not careful, it could be your downfall."

"I doubt that." He said the words, but something about them still hit him hard.

"Really, then why am I here?" At this, Ross raised his brow and she dropped her fork. "That's bullshit, Ross. And it doesn't look good on you. Be serious with me for once. It was Misha who first called me from the ER. Something got you in there, scared as shit. You have a boat called *Serenity,* but it seems like your life is anything but. Why would you even name your boat *Serenity* if your life is full of chaos?"

Ross swallowed, trying hard to push down the truth he was sailing from as fast as his boat would take him. But he let it out. "It's named after my daughter."

Essie stared. Her eyes wide, her mouth shut. He wished more than anything she'd say something. Anything. Just fill the silence. Right now he didn't want it. The silence was worse than anything. Bringing her on board gave him something do to, something to think about besides the fact that he thought just the other day he might die and would be missing another holiday, maybe his final chance to be with his daughter.

Finally she spoke and said just the wrong thing. "I'm sorry."

"I don't need your pity. I'm fine," Ross

said in a low voice.

She laughed and somehow it made him feel better. "Yeah, I can see you are."

Ross laughed then, too. "You really are a ballbuster, you know that?"

Essie surprised him by chuckling. "You know, that's about the nicest thing you could have said to me."

Essie was glad to break the tension. She could see Ross's inner struggle, and though she wanted to be a little hard on him, she felt bad for causing him pain. It was clear that his emotions were erratic and raw. He warred with something in his mind and heart. Essie's own heart broke a little for him and she chided herself for it.

Shit. Now she remembered seeing behind his desk the photo of the little girl. She was so taken with him that she didn't look past the obvious and see deeper. Essie wanted to hang her head in shame. She was so focused on her own desires, she completely shut out what was happening with her client.

Essie could see Ross was uncomfortable, so she eased her way back to his daughter as they shared dessert, a simple brownie a la mode, which he helped make. "How old is your daughter?"

He swallowed before he answered on a low

whisper. "She's four."

The answer took her cracked heart and shattered it. One, because of her age, and two, because it seemed to put to rest any buried thought of a blossoming relationship with him.

"I can tell you miss her."

Ross shrugged. "You can't miss what you never had. I was only with Yasmine, Serenity's mother, for the first year of her life. A little less. I never even shared an actual birthday with her. I was on my grind, and I thought Yasmine was all for that, in the beginning. After Serenity, she changed. Said she wanted to settle down, and if it wasn't with me, then it would be with someone she could make a home with. I get it. For some women, they need that." He gave Essie a pointed look.

"Why are you looking at me like that?"

"I'm just looking," he said.

"Well, you're looking like you're sizing me up, which there is no need to, since I'm only here for ten days. Besides, we're talking about you and your daughter."

"Touché." Ross let out a sigh. "No matter, Yas and I were spending more time apart than together. Her modeling career was on a downturn and she was ready to settle down. I was not, and, besides, a kid needs stability. I get it. Her new husband has done well by her and Serenity. We talk and Skype. She knows I'm her father."

Essie wanted to say something, but the way he ended his speech, it made her wonder if he'd be receptive to anything she had to say. She took a gamble. "I'm sure she does and I'm sure, even if you don't think so, she misses you. Especially at Christmas. I know I miss my dad."

Ross's expression had her instantly regretting her words. "It's just he worked a lot. And it was only on his forced time off, Sundays and holidays like Christmas, when we got to spend time together as a family. I cherish that more than I think he ever knew." She smiled as the good times with her dad came back to her. The laughter and the good food they shared. "It was my father who first taught me how to cook."

Ross's eye widened. "Was he a chef, too?"

She shook her head. "Oh, no! Just a hungry man with a creative palate. Dad never made the same dish twice. It was always a little different, depending on what we had available. His only day off from driving the bus was Sunday, and he loved cooking for my mother. She worked so hard, so he'd make her these wonderful meals with whatever we had on hand. As I got a little bigger, I'd join him in the kitchen, and we'd laugh together and he'd tell me stories of his family, how one day it would be great to have a family restaurant where we could do this all the time. In the kitchen was the only place he wasn't stressed about bills, time, the next shift."

Ross glided the back of his hand softly and reassuringly along her arm. She gave him a smile as she continued speaking. "He always said we were blessed that God made a way so that we always had a little food on the table. My father died on a Sunday, going in to make a little overtime to get more for our holiday dinner. Christmas was our favorite time. Trimming the tree. Sharing a meal." Essie stopped talking when Ross reached out and wiped a tear from her cheek, which she hadn't known she'd shed. "Oh, hell. I'm sorry," she said.

"What are you sorry for? It's me who should be apologizing. Taking you away from your mother on Christmas. No job or amount of money is worth that."

She put her hand out to his lips to stop him. "No, this was my choice. You're bringing me closer to my dream of my own restaurant, and I thank you." She smiled wide, hoping to elevate the mood. "Now, enough talk. Let me clean this up, and you take care of whatever you planned for this afternoon, and I'll think up your next fabulous meal."

CHAPTER THIRTEEN

As *Serenity* docked in Bermuda, Essie didn't know what to expect. Ross told her his business for his resort wouldn't be more than a couple of hours. It was some trouble with the contractor who was doing renovations on his new state of the art golf course. But still, Ross planned on spending the day there. He wanted to take her out, to show her around, and then they could have dinner together before boarding and heading out to continue their trip to Miami.

She had to admit she was excited, but also hesitant. Ross wasn't the type of guy she was used to dating. And it wasn't as if they were even dating. As soon as they got off the boat, Essie spied the two drivers, with matching Mercedes sedans, waiting for them and knew this wouldn't be her usual roughing-it trek. *What? No mopeds available?*

Ross kissed her easily, as if they were a

couple in a comfortable, much longer relationship, when, in reality, they were anything but. She couldn't help but marvel at his outward show of confidence. Though when they were alone and talking, without the buffer of a sexual flame, she picked up on definite insecurities that waved off him. But Ross did an excellent job of not letting it show. Regarding the crew, he felt no need to make any explanations or excuses about their heating relationship; and, in turn, he encouraged her not to feel it necessary to do so, either. His strong confidence left no room for any second-guessing, and she found she barely got a second glance when she went in to make breakfast this morning.

Part of it bugged her. Made it feel like them hooking up was something the crew knew was inevitable from the moment she stepped on the ship. It also made her wonder how often he did such a thing.

As Ross pulled back from their kiss, he stared at Essie hard. "You're overthinking," he said.

She frowned. "You're right, I am. And it's a waste of time on such a beautiful day." Essie gave him a smile and rose up to kiss him, this time enjoying the thrill of his lips against hers. When would she get this opportunity again?

When she pulled away, he was smiling down at her. "I got you your own car for the afternoon. You take it into town, do some shopping." He reached into his pocket and pulled out some bills.

Essie shook her head. "I'll take the car, but I draw the line at taking your money."

Ross sighed. "There's my favorite judge. I was wondering where she went. How about doing your job? Do you mind buying some more fresh produce for the boat?"

Essie looked down, feeling bad for not giving him the benefit of the doubt. "Sorry," she said, her voice low as she took the bills.

"Never be." He kissed her as he moved around the driver and opened the door for her to get in the car. He kissed her once more. "You're too sweet to be sorry. Have the driver bring you by the resort around four. I'll show you around, and we'll have dinner."

As he closed the door and headed toward his own waiting car, Essie fought hard against her sudden feelings of missing him.

She had the driver drop her off at a spot in town, giving him no further direction except to make it as touristy as possible. She only had a few hours, so she might as well do it up. *Candy-colored houses and Bermuda shorts, bring it on!*

Essie explored the cobblestone lanes and colorful facades. She tried to get into the quaint cobblestone streets and the pretty shops, but the high number of couples — hand in hand, and arm in arm — kept bringing her thoughts annoyingly back to Ross. And she knew that thinking of him, or anyone for that matter, right now in the realm of couple's vacations, matching outfits, and long walks, was a total waste of mental energy.

Essie paused outside a pretty local art shop window, where there was a display of necklaces. It was funny how she didn't miss Cam at all. At least not in the way she thought she would. And here she was, just a week ago as he was walking out her door, thinking she'd miss him for a long time to come. Showed what a waste the past two years with him had been.

A lovely blue stone necklace caught her eye and made her think of her mom. No use mooning over any of this, but she'd get something for her mother. She'd already gotten her the pretty scarf she'd wanted, but this would be a bonus to make up for being away. That decided, Essie walked into the shop.

As Essie left the shop, her mom's gift in hand, she went in search of her car and driver, having decided she was set on having him take her to shop for fresh local food. Doing the tourist thing was a bore. She'd have more fun searching for ingredients.

Once they arrived at the roadside stalls, Essie was in heaven. So many fresh fruits and vegetables, not to mention fish. She knew that before going to the resort to meet Ross, they'd have to pick up a cooler or head back to the boat so the food wouldn't spoil.

At one stall Essie was so engrossed in conversing with a local woman about the tripe stew she was making, she didn't notice the tall man getting close to her until he was almost upon her.

"You like it spicy?" he asked, his leering tone letting her know he definitely wasn't asking about the stew.

Essie looked around for her driver, but saw he wasn't by the car. *Shit.* She pointedly ignored the man and paid the woman for two takeout bowls of her stew. As she tried to walk away and head across the road to the car, the man followed close. Too close.

"I asked you a question."

Essie kept walking until his hand came out and he made a move to turn her back in his direction.

"What? You too fancy to answer me, miss —"

Almost simultaneously a dark figure came into Essie's field of vision, and she saw Mr. Handsy crumble to the ground. He howled as his hands clutched his bleeding nose.

"I'm sorry it took me so long to get here." Essie looked up, her wide eyes meeting Ross's own. "But I was supposed to be meeting you."

He shrugged, unfazed by the man now on the ground, clutching his bleeding nose, and the gathering crowd. "And I'm here to meet you. I'm still sorry I took so long. You shouldn't have had to deal with the likes of him."

"What the hell, man?" Mr. Spicy said while attempting to right himself.

Ross looked down at the man. He had such a hard glint in his eyes, it almost made Essie back up. He stepped on the man's outstretched fingers, causing him to writhe in pain. "Get up. I dare you. You need to watch who and whose you make a move on next time." He reached into his pocket and pulled out a bill and dropped it on the man's chest. "Consider yourself lucky I'm feeling so good right now. Go get yourself cleaned up and something to eat." He took Essie by the hand and led her to the waiting

431

car. It was then that she noticed the cars had been switched. Her driver was gone and it was his car and driver.

"Where has my driver gone?" Essie asked as she got inside.

"Back to the dock. He's taken your other packages back to *Serenity*. Take us to the resort, please," Ross said. The last bit was meant for their driver before Ross hit a switch and the partition between them and the driver rose.

The look Ross gave Essie was one of pure primal sex and energy; it had the next question dying on her lips, forgotten instantly. He reached for her, and instead of putting her hand in his, she was on him. On top and straddling and kissing him, hard and fast and wet. She wore an easy sundress, which let her thighs go wide, and left her deliciously exposed and open to him. She rubbed urgently against his hard erection, her feminine center feeling like it was on fire. And for the first time in her life, Essie wanted to strip off her clothes and see what it felt like to be taken hard and fast by a man she barely knew.

The feeling made her not recognize herself, and she felt slightly afraid of the person Ross was unleashing. She moved from his lips to lick at the side of his neck. Wanting to go further, with shaky hands, she undid the buttons on his shirt and was rewarded by the sight of his hard chest and dark nipples. Essie leaned down and nipped at the beautiful tight nubs.

Ross groaned and grabbed her thighs, pushing forward. His hardness and the zipper of his pants were roughly rubbing against her. One of his large hands moved to her breasts, and Essie moved back, pulling the straps of her dress down, along with her bra. It wasn't elegant, and it wasn't beautiful, but she didn't care. He was elegant, and he was beautiful, and slightly rough, and aggressive, and she wanted him on her, in her, wherever, however, she could have him.

Thankfully, he obliged, drawing one of her nipples almost reverently into his mouth and licking it as if it were the most delicate of desserts. She felt him pulse beneath her, and breathed in deep as his hand went up her thigh and almost shakily reached under her dress to clutch at her behind. She could tell he was doing his best to hold on to his hairsbreadth of control.

"Why are you holding back, Ross?" she choked out, almost wanting to shake him as she saw his Adam's apple bob.

He looked up, a bead of sweat popping

out on his forehead as he put his head back. "Because I don't want to let go with you. I don't want to just take you in the back of one of my cars."

Essie swallowed, torn between telling him taking her in the back of one of his cars was just what she wanted, and knowing it definitely wasn't. She leaned down and kissed him gently. "Then take me to your bed, Ross Montgomery."

Ross set Essie to rights as they pulled onto his resort's grounds. She rolled down the window to catch her breath and take in the scenery — lush green and well-manicured grounds. They drove past a beautiful yellow main house that looked like it had maybe a hundred rooms, and off to the side of the main house were smaller villas. Around them were private balconies, and little golf carts sprinkled here and there.

Their car kept going, and when Ross caught her questioning look, he gave her a small smile. "We're going right to my private villa. I thought it best we dine alone. I hope that's all right."

Essie blushed. "It's fine, but maybe we should eat and then head back to the boat. I don't want you to get off schedule."

Ross leaned in close. "We can do whatever

you want. I will work around you. If you want to stay here tonight, we stay here. If you want to go, we go."

Essie looked at him as the car stopped. "I'd like to see your place here."

Ross's villa was so very him: minimalist, elegant, and sexy. Open concept with a large sitting area for entertaining and two bedrooms off to the side. The back of the villa was all floor-to-ceiling windows, which opened to a spectacular view of the fabled pink sand beach and had Essie gasping for breath. Out on the veranda, dinner was set with fresh seafood, sweets, champagne, and desserts.

"Ross, it's gorgeous. I don't think I've ever seen a beach so beautiful and all this food. We didn't need my stew after all." He came up behind her at the window and kissed the back of her neck, giving her a thrill that vibrated throughout her entire body.

"I think so, too. When I'm here, I can relax. Or, at least, my version of relaxing."

Essie laughed at that.

"That part of the beach is mine and private. When we have more time, I'd love to bring you back here to swim with me."

At his declaration she couldn't help but feel a little sad.

"What is it?" he asked.

"That. You don't have to make any sort of promise of anything beyond this trip. I know you can't. That's okay. Let's enjoy *now*."

Ross's lips twisted, but he didn't argue with her. "Don't look so sad. CEOs don't do sad." She moved forward to kiss him. "Now I think there are more parts of this villa you can show me. I'd love to see the master suite. That is, if dinner will wait?"

At that, Ross picked her up and threw her over his shoulder. He gave her a light smack on her behind. "Oh, hell yeah, dinner will wait. If I have my way, it will wait until breakfast."

"Hey, I don't think this is the standard tour!" Essie kicked and giggled.

He laughed, low and deep in his throat. "It's the way I do a tour. We're not in the backseat anymore, Ms. Bradford."

CHAPTER FOURTEEN

Despite the rough way he picked her up, Ross gently placed her down crossways on his large bed. He then pulled back, going to his knees to take off her slip-on shoes. He came up and kissed her long and hard, leaving her almost gasping for breath, before he eased up, to start a sweet, almost torturous, trail down her body.

Essie thought he'd linger on her collarbone, her breasts maybe, which he teased with his thumb through her dress, but no. He skimmed those spots, going lower, down to her ankles, spending time kissing them, making an anklet of feathery kisses, then working his way until he was behind her knee. When he got a desired response from her, he'd lick and nibble some more. As he was licking behind her knee, and she was distracted by the newfound glory of that particular erogenous zone, Ross's hand worked its way up to her most private spot, and he pulled her panties down as he brought his head higher.

With his first lick Essie thought she'd break apart. She was biting her lip and balling her fists tight so as not to come completely undone.

Ross was masterful. He licked and she rocked. He sucked and she rode. She was clenching and unclenching her hands until she grasped at his shoulders, letting go as she never had before. And when she finally reached her peak, with his name echoing as breathy gasps on her lips, Ross pulled back, tugging her dress over her head, taking her bra off, and giving her breast a last, long, gentle kiss.

"God, Essie, you are gorgeous," he rasped out.

Her instinct was to cover up, as gooseflesh suddenly tickled over her body. But something in his hot, admiring gaze made her feel so incredibly beautiful, she could do no more but reach for him. Essie kissed Ross hard and passionately. Undoing his shirt and pulling it out of his pants.

"You have on way too many clothes, Mr. Montgomery."

"You are so right there," he said, breathing heavy.

As she freed him, Ross handed her a

condom. Essie sucked in an anxious breath. He was glorious. But her awkwardness came out in her ineptitude with slipping on the condom, and she was thankful for Ross's help. His hand steadied hers as he guided her in easing it down over his hardness.

His first thrust stole her breath away with its power; and when she came once again, looking into the depths of his midnight eyes, he kissed her, sealing their moment with an unspoken promise of the next week of more glorious lovemaking to come.

They spent the next few hours making love in every way and every place in his villa, the bed, the Jacuzzi, his large shower. Somewhere in between, dinner got eaten, and Ross even convinced Essie to take a mad naked dash from his villa to the beach and into the water. Or maybe it was the other way around. Essie laughed so much she couldn't remember when she'd last enjoyed such a night. In fact, she knew she hadn't.

Just before dawn she woke with Ross kissing her shoulder. "I'm sorry to wake you so early, but do you mind if we get going to the boat? The captain may have to push it to make it to Miami in time with the delay."

Essie could feel his tension and didn't want him to stress. She turned and kissed him lightly. "It's fine. Just give me a minute to get ready." She stroked at his hardness playfully. "And stop being so serious. Just because we're back on the boat and I'll have you back to your routine, you'll still have me in your bed. There's no way I'm giving this up before New York."

Ross grinned and nipped at her shoulder again. "Whew. That's a relief."

When they arrived back on *Serenity,* Essie was shocked.

The boat, which had been decorated luxuriously, was now decked out for Christmas with lovely twinkling lights and sprigs of holly and evergreen. And there in the main parlor was a large undecorated Christmas tree. She turned to Ross with shimmering tears she wasn't capable of hiding. "Ross, it's beautiful, but why? How?"

"I couldn't let you not have Christmas," he said in a matter-of-fact way. "I thought while I was handling the contractor, I'd have the boys pick up a tree, festive the old girl up a bit. I had them save the tree decorating for you though."

Essie grinned then looked at him with barely restrained hope. "Will you do it with me?"

Ross made a face. "It's not my thing."

Essie's smile widened. "Well, let's make it your thing. We'll do it together. After dinner. Please. Decorating a Christmas tree is always better with friends. We'll invite the crew."

Ross shook his head, but something in his eyes lit. "Sure. Anything for that smile."

Dinner was casual and shared with the crew, once they got under way again. Essie and Chef Scott collaborated on the meal. She was glad they had come to a mutual working relationship, though he was still a bit gruff around the edges. They casually dined on shrimp rolls, haddock, and spicy noodles, since Essie had quickly learned that Ross loved all things with either a touch of sweet or plenty of spice. Plus, a lovely blend of mixed vegetables. There was wine for everyone, and the captain joined them while Ethan took over his duties for a while on the bridge.

When Essie came in with dessert, homemade ice cream with dark chocolate mulled wine sauce, the captain stood and raised his glass in a toast. "To Ms. Bradford. Thank you for gracing us with your beauty and your talent. You are making this maiden voyage a sweet excursion."

Ross grinned and stood, coming over to

kiss Essie lightly on her cheek. But the crew would not be satisfied with that, and they cheerfully started to clink on their wineglasses with their tableware. "Kiss! Kiss!"

Essie gave them a wave of her hand. "You all are incorrigible! Thank you so much. You almost make me not miss New York and the holiday snow. Almost."

But they would not be mollified. When Ross clinked his glass, too, she relented, taking Ross's cheeks in both hands. For a moment she enjoyed the feel of his scruff and pulled him in for a big, sloppy kiss. The guys all cheered as she pulled back.

"Okay, enough with you all. Bring your desserts around the tree. Let's get Christmas started!"

They all took turns adding the pretty gold and silver ornaments. The captain left early, letting Ethan come to take his place. When it was done and the rest of the crew left, Essie sat on the low couch as Ross turned down the lights and flipped the switch on the tree.

"It's lovely," she said as he put his arm around her and nuzzled her in close, kissing her behind her ear.

"Why is it I feel there's a 'but' in there?" Ross asked.

"There is no 'but.' It is lovely. It's just so

elegant — more elegant than any tree I've ever had. Ours at home is jam-packed with mismatched ornaments. My mom made a point of buying or we made a new one every year. Maybe it's something you could do with your daughter?"

But at the mention of the child, she saw Ross's eyes go dark and cloud over. She knew instantly she'd made a mistake. Trying hard to bring the moment back, Essie spoke rapidly to cover the awkward moment. "My mom still buys me one, and I'm no spring chicken."

Ross pulled back then quickly leaned for ward, nipping at her lips teasingly. "Get out! You can't be a day past twenty-two."

Essie laughed as she rolled her eyes, glad to be back on sure footing. It was fun to sit with him and be playful for a while. "I won't tell you how many years to add to that. But thanks again. I really do appreciate it. I know you weren't into the holiday. I just think it should be shared with family and those you love. But this" — Essie paused — "this is really nice. But I didn't mean to force it on you."

He looked at her and ran a hand up and down her thigh. "You didn't. No one forces anything on me."

Essie snorted. "Now, that I believe!"

"I wanted to make you happy. With you missing your holiday with your mom," he laughed then, "and the cold New York snow and all. You can't really be missing that."

She looked at him seriously. "I sure am. Who doesn't dream of a white Christmas? You can't be hardened to that. What's Christmas without snow?"

Ross shook his head. "You really are a sweet traditionalist, Essie Bradford. I don't know what you're doing here in my arms. A man like me would ruin you."

His last words were low and serious, and something about them made Essie's heart stop for a moment with a deep fear of loss she knew she had no right to have.

"What are you talking about?"

"Nothing," he said too quickly. "I guess I'm not used to any downtime. See what you did to me? Went and got me thinking." He pulled her tighter to him. "And you got me thinking about things with my daughter, too. I don't know." He looked down then and let out a sigh. "I guess things need to change."

She leaned in and kissed him. She didn't want to see him sad, and she didn't want to make this moment heavy. Soon enough they'd make it to Miami and before too long her assignment would be over.

Their kiss changed quickly from sweet to deep and passionate; and before long, Essie was breaking apart again, beside herself and feeling out of herself, all at the same time. She took a deep breath and then pushed up from Ross and the couch. She looked into his passion-darkened eyes and took him by the hand. "Your stateroom or mine?"

He stood. Tall and powerful, towering over her. "I'll let you choose. I always want this to be your choice. Your terms, Essie."

She smiled. "Yours, then. I want to try out all the beds you can offer me while on the trip, Mr. Montgomery."

He grinned and gave a quick nod. "Then let's go. What's mine is yours, Ms. Bradford."

When *Serenity* pulled into Miami's Biscayne Bay, Essie steeled herself against her heavy heart. She and Ross had spent a blissful three days together on board, both in bed and out. Their days were unstructured and carefree, and their nights were spent making love in ways she'd only fantasized about.

She cooked for him, and he surprised her by spending quite a bit of time with her in the kitchen, learning what she hoped were lasting lessons about food choices and the benefits of cooking for himself. They also had a lot of fun in the gym, with her giving him the benefits of yoga and meditation, and him giving her the basics of kickboxing. More times than not, their sparring ending up with either Essie or Ross flat on their back, one pinned under the other.

This time spent with him would go down as some of the best days of her life — at least the most fun and carefree. And reluctantly, when she felt him standing strong by her side, his arm draped easily over her shoulder, rubbing her arm in that endearing, absentminded way he'd taken to doing, she had to admit she was going to miss this. No, she was going to miss *him,* when all was said and done. A knot twisted in Essie's belly as the butterflies seemed to bunch up in one corner.

Shit. I'm falling for him.

But as Essie saw the stretch limo waiting for them as they departed, flanked by a female driver and two other beautiful women in short skirts and tight blazers, she couldn't help but stiffen. Normally, she was more confident. Seeing these women, who looked like versions of every woman she'd seen pictured with him, something in her deflated. It brought to mind the fact that it would all be over in days. But Essie forced herself to shake it off as a tall, slim young man stepped forward and came up to them.

"Good to see you, sir," he said before sparing Essie a glance. "And good to see you, too, Ms. Bradford."

Though Essie didn't know him, he did know her, and he seemed unsurprised by the intimacy of her and Ross's entwined hands. It raked at her and she stiffened.

"Essie, this is my assistant, Andrew Vaughn."

Essie gave the younger man a nod. "Nice to meet you, Mr. Vaughn." She let go of Ross and stuck out her hand.

"You too. I hope your trip went well. Please let me know of any supplies you need for the return, and I'll be sure to have them brought on board."

"Thank you. I think I'm pretty good. I do prefer to do my own shopping, but I'd appreciate it if you know Miami or have someone else who does, that could point me in the direction of the freshest markets."

Andrew nodded.

"Is everything all set and ready?" Ross asked.

"Yes, sir. You'll see these are the types of cars and drivers with the ladies as concierge that we sent to pick up the clients. They should be arriving at *Serenity* within the next two hours."

Essie was intently following along. It was a good thing Andrew was explaining because he wasn't giving out any introductions to the ladies. Essie thought of introducing herself but the women gave off a sort of aloofness that could tag the part of a gorgeous female spy ring or darned good exclusive club bouncers. A small bus pulled up and two more beautiful women got out, along with two men who were just as model gorgeous. They lined up next to Andrew. "These are Lacey, Ana, Marco, and Louis. Additional staff for guest-stew services."

Essie didn't miss the hot look Lacey gave Ross. It was an invite, an openness, as Andrew continued his introductions.

"They will be available for the clients for any and all entertainment while on board. Marco and Louis will help with deckhand services and anything else that is needed."

Essie couldn't help but bristle. *Serenity* was about to become quite the party ship, and she couldn't help but wonder at what type of services and or entertainment Andrew was referring to. But Essie pushed the thoughts back. She and Chef Scott would have plenty of mouths to feed. Playtime, at least for her, was definitely over. Though Chef Scott was a jerk, she would pitch in and help him with so many passengers coming aboard.

"Well," she said, looking up at Ross, "I guess I'd better get going with supplies so I can get back to help out Simon. We're about to get really busy."

Ross bent and gave her a kiss. "Fine, but Simon can handle the bulk of the cooking. You take this car and get what you want him to prepare. I want you by my side tonight. I'll stay here with Andrew, making a few calls if you don't mind."

Ross's words about being by his side pulled her up short, but Essie tried not to make too much of them. "Not at all."

But as Ross pulled away, he gave her a long stare. "Don't worry, I'll watch out. No buying stew in dodgy neighborhoods. And I won't be long. I want to be back" — she looked over the leggy woman eyeing Ross like the last crab leg at the all-you-can-eat buffet — "before things get too wild."

CHAPTER FIFTEEN

Essie made it back on board *Serenity* at the same time as the clients — a ruckus crew of three couples. Two married — the Cruzes and the Johnsons — and the other, an owner of a basketball team, Jimmy Paul, and his girlfriend, a model named Lola.

Essie tugged on her top and smoothed her disheveled hair as she was introduced to the bejeweled women. She didn't mean to be late, but while out shopping for supplies, she ran across the sweetest little Christmas shop. Though rushed, she couldn't help but go in. Once there she picked up an ornament for her mom. Though this one would be late, her mom would still love it. And when she saw they personalized ornaments, Essie couldn't resist getting a beautiful one with snowmen and palm trees, which she had personalized with the name Serenity. She hoped Ross would use it to both remember her, and to start a new tradition with his daughter when he was ready.

After the awkward introductions, Essie left the gift on her dresser and quickly changed for dinner, which as it turned out would be off board at a Miami hot spot.

Later, sitting on the deck with Mrs. Cruz, who refused an individual tart, as well, Essie noticed, as most of her dinner, Essie made attempts at small talk. There had to be a reason Ross wanted her here. Maybe playing hostess was it. "Though I'm sure you enjoy Miami, tell me, are you looking forward to traveling back to New York?" Essie asked. The woman was silent and had been for the past ten minutes. It was like pulling teeth, getting a word out of her.

"Surprising," Mrs. Cruz said as she turned and examined her with a critical eye.

"Excuse me?"

"It's you. You're surprising." She looked over at one of the new stews, the pretty Ana, who was serving a drink to Mr. Cruz in the Jacuzzi while showing off her cleavage to its best advantage. "Now that's more his usual."

The cutting comment from the woman hit Essie at her core and she felt heat rise in her cheeks. Her instincts were to argue. She had her talents and it was a waste to let insecurities over legs and boobs fill sacred space in her spirit. She was the one that Ross asked to be here. Well, technically, paid to be here. Just like every other female on this ship. Essie let out a low breath as she spotted Ana handing Ross a drink and adding an extra touch to his bared bicep with it. Her argument died in her throat.

Essie tried to shake off her sudden unwelcome uneasiness when Ross turned and gave her a smile that was more head than heart. The tranquil peace of The Serenity was gone. And as Essie lay down that night cradled in Ross's arms, spent from making love, the waves gently rocking the boat, she didn't sleep soundly.

It was morning and they were now under way to head to Ross's private island, where the resort would be built. It was a short boat ride away, just four hours. Near enough to Miami for party shuttles to go, and far enough for him to create his own secluded oasis.

The butterflies that had befriended her started up again, but this time their fluttering brought the most unwelcome feeling. She was not looking forward to her time with this bunch. And though she'd tried her best to straddle the line of help and hostess, Essie had not received a kind look or gesture since she met any of them. She feared the time back to New York with them would not go well.

As if feeling Essie's unease, Ross turned her way and gave her a warm smile. The butterflies eased down and she smiled back. She was probably being nutty and should just chill. Essie relaxed and decided to ignore the pinched faced women and enjoy herself, as she had been.

But things didn't get better on the island. Though the tour was fascinating, and Essie could totally see Ross's exciting vision, she was once again pulled up short by their arrival to the fanfare of scantily clad women and a few men scattered within. Drinks flowed like water and the promise of all the hedonism imaginable was thick in the air. Essie's unease grew as she watched Ross seem to swell bigger, louder, and bolder, until he somehow was wearing a mask of himself that no longer fit. But maybe this was him and the Ross she got to know when it was just the two of them was a mask he was wearing to woo her into his bed? The thought stopped her short.

By the time the tour was over, and their party on board *Serenity* readying to head back to Miami, the party had swelled to one with a band and dancing girls, two to each man, in Ross's case three, as the women seemed to want to be sure their check writer knew exactly who they were. And Ross played it up, sharing cigars all around while being loud and boisterous.

When Ross, at the encouragement of the crowd, took a shot from between the breasts of a curvy brunette in a barely there bikini and turned to Essie suggesting she do the same, she was done. She had a splitting headache and wanted to retreat and go to bed, away from this version of Ross.

"Come on, babe, go for it! This is a party. Why don't you act like it?"

Essie eyed the way Ross's hands were grasping the hips of the brunette and wanted to step out of the whole scene. She looked into his slightly unfocused eyes and felt both anger and sadness. Anger for being put in this situation and sadness over what she'd hoped it would be. "This is not my type of party Ross. And I'm tired."

Ross frowned and looked ready to argue, but Essie got her opening when Mrs. Johnson dropped her makeshift toga and shimmied naked to get under the limbo pole more easily. The crowd cheered and Essie got up and started heading across the room. But Ross saw her heading toward the stairs, and before she knew it, he was there at her side.

"Where you going?"

"Like I said, I'm tired, Ross. I think I'll leave you to your clients. It's late and the band is getting to me. I have a headache."

He leaned in to kiss her and his rum-and-cigar breath had her recoiling.

Ross frowned, his darkening eyes surprising her, but not more than the possessive hand on her arm. "But I want you here with me. Besides, I didn't say you were off the clock yet."

Essie heated so fast she felt like she may cause the whole ship to burst into flames. "Screw you, Ross Montgomery. I'm freelance, so I work for myself. You may own everything and everyone else on this boat, but you don't own me."

Ross looked down at his empty hand and closed it into a tight fist. It was all he could do, since all he felt was alone. His first instinct was to go after her. Go after her and pull her back into his arms. Kiss her long and hard with everything he had and let her know how much she meant to him. How he shouldn't have said what he said.

Ross took a step, then stopped short. But what did she mean to him? Did he even know? They'd made no promises to each other, which was probably a good thing. Sure, they had a good time aboard the ship. Secure in the world of just the two of them, but with just this simple test he could see they were no match for the outside world. He thought he had known with Yasmine. Thought he could play the role of happy-home husband and father, but what did he do? He went and fucked that up in less than a year. And now his ex was married to someone else and, worse, his daughter was being raised by another man. He didn't want to relive that all over again with Essie. It had already been proven he was his father's son, and the business was his first and one true love.

But still Essie called to him. If only so he could at least apologize for speaking to her and treating her so harshly. Ross took a step for ward and a hand grazed him lightly on his shoulder. He turned to look into the smiling eyes and glossy lips of — what was her name? Lacey?

"Mr. Montgomery, Mr. Paul sent me to retrieve you for a game of Twister. We're all playing and he said I'm not to take no for an answer."

As she said those words, the new steward slipped her polo over her head to reveal a white bikini top. Ross frowned and shook his head. "Please tell Mr. Paul I won't be playing, but to enjoy the game with my compliments."

She put on what Ross thought was a well-practiced pout. "I'm afraid he won't be happy, sir."

Ross suddenly wanted to be anywhere but there. Here he was with everything he thought he wanted: money, women, prestige, and the one thing he really needed was just out of reach. "Tell Mr. Paul to have an enjoyable evening on me," he said before he turned and headed for the stairs.

As Essie slammed the door, hot tears burned at her eyes. *Shit. Why did I ever get so close?* If she hadn't gotten close, he wouldn't have affected her. And what was with that Lacey? She didn't miss her lurking as she waited for her moment — all hair, lips, and boobs at the ready.

Still, Essie took a few deep breaths to calm her nerves. She really was tired, and then she thought for a moment of how tired he must be. He'd been tap-dancing for these people all day, trying to get their backing and support, and still he had more dancing to do. Essie's heart broke a moment for him, and then she saw her bag from the

Christmas shop earlier in the day.

She took the ornament out and crossed the hall to leave it on Ross's pillow. A peace offering of sorts to let him know though she was angry, she still cared. Besides, no matter what happened, his daughter should still have the ornament.

Essie woke feeling refreshed and hopeful that she and Ross could get back on track. She dressed to go to the galley, and found Chef Scott was up, already preparing a big breakfast. They were docked in Miami and would be there for a few hours before sailing back to New York with the clients to conclude the deal.

She thought of Ross and their argument the night before and how tired he must be today. But today was a new day and she was ready to start over again. Essie reached into the fridge and took out the last tiny chocolate mousse. "I'm going to take this to Ross. I'll be back in a moment to help you finish up," she said to Simon.

"He's not here."

Essie stilled. "What do you mean?"

"He's gone. Said he had urgent business and left instructions with the captain about returning the passengers to New York without him."

Without him? Essie was so confused. Where did he go, and why did he say nothing to her? She went back to her room in a daze and saw a gift bag on her bureau. One she didn't see before. Essie picked it up and numbly went to her bed to open it. Pulling out the mass of tissue paper, she was surprised to find a snow globe inside with a scene of Miami Beach that when shaken would be covered with snow. Attached was a plane ticket dated today with a Post-it and just the words:

Go home, Ms. Bradford, and get your New York snow. Thank you for a job well done.

Stay Sweet,
R.M.

Taped to the bottom was Essie's check with her full fee, plus her agreed-upon ten-thousand-dollar bonus. As Essie packed, she silently cursed her stupid tears. This was only supposed to be a little bit of fun, she told herself. Something to get over the hump so to speak. It was her own fault, opening her heart to a man who was only hiring her for a quick fix, nothing more. She'd done her job and now it was over. That should be enough. But as Essie walked the gangplank and left The Serenity behind, she couldn't help feeling somehow undone.

It was indeed snowing, and had been since Essie returned home. She'd received one text from Ross asking if she made it home safely. She guessed that as far as employers went, he didn't have to do that much. She replied to him with just two words I did.

They had no further communication.

It was now New Year's Eve and she was with her mom at her apartment. They were sharing a meal of good-luck peas and rice, waiting for the ball to drop on TV. She was sure by 12:15 a.m. it would be lights out. Way to start the New Year. *Woo to the freaking hoo.*

So when the doorbell rang at 11:30 p.m., they both looked at each other, wide-eyed, New York instincts going on full alert.

Essie went to the door. "Who is it?" she yelled with extra bass in her voice before looking out the peephole.

"It's me, Essie."

She knew the voice, but didn't believe her ears, so she took a look through the peephole. *Damn.* It was him. Tall, magnetic, his dark eyes seemed to connect with hers through the peephole, and then he had the nerve to have that smile. How did he even know she'd be here tonight? This had Misha written all over it. She'd kill her.

"What are you doing here?" Essie yelled.

"I'm here to see you. You going to open the door, or does the whole floor have to know your business? I'm fine either way."

Hesitantly, Essie opened the door a crack before finally gesturing for him to come in. No use letting the neighbors know her business. Her mom stood and looked at him with a strong and well-deserved side eye. "This is my mother."

Ross reached out a hand. "It's nice to meet you, Mrs. Bradford. I've heard wonderful things about you."

Her mom gave him a hard eye. "Can't say the same about you."

Ross looked confused as Essie crossed her arms. "If you're here to hire me for another job, the answer is no."

"What are you talking about?"

"What do you mean, what am I talking about? You leave without a word? Just a ticket? You turned out to be the rich jerk I pegged you for in the beginning. Judgy? Me? Hell yeah!"

"You didn't get my letter with the ticket?"

"What, your Post-it? Classy rich boy."

"Post-it?" He furrowed his brow; then recognition dawned in his eyes. "No. My letter. I enclosed a letter and told you I was so sorry for the night before. I didn't want to deal with those clients anymore, and I didn't want you to, either. I told you that you were right. That the holidays should be spent with the people you love the most. With family. So I went to see my daughter. I wanted to give her the ornament you gave me. And I wanted you to be with your mom at Christmas."

There was a sharp "oh" as Essie's mom took in Ross's speech. Ross grinned as Essie's mother made a polite exit to the other room. His smile widened when he turned and took in Essie's stunned expression and slack jaw.

Ross walked over to her and cautiously wrapped her in his arms. The chill of the outside still on his coat gave her a delicious shiver as he opened it and she eased into the warmth of his chest.

She looked up at him. "I can't believe you did that for me."

"Woman, neither can I. But I'm coming to find out there's not much I wouldn't do for you. So here I am. I'm so sorry for what I put you through. For how I treated you and spoke to you. It was uncalled for and will *never* happen again. I was showing off, drinking too much, and being all around just too much. Just like I wrote in the letter, which you obviously didn't get, I was an ass that night and I apologize. In my short time with you, you opened my eyes so much. You let me know what is truly important in life, and spending the holiday on a boat, named after the person I love dearly, with people I don't care about, well, there was just something wrong with that. And when you walked away from me that night, I knew I had to make it right."

His words stunned Essie. She was stunned by his openness and trust in her with sharing so much of himself.

Ross kissed her softly on her temple and continued. "I hope I can make it right with you. Because here I am taking off work on another holiday in order to spend it with the only other woman besides my daughter that I can say I love."

Essie froze.

Now it was her turn to gasp out a shocked "oh!"

But when Ross's lips came down on hers, and New York exploded as the crystal ball dropped and midnight struck, New Year's Day began for the both of them with the promise of a lifetime of sweet serenity.